Praise f

...ious Grace

"A chilling novel. . . . I couldn't put it down. . . . The best of the series so far."

—Fantasy Literature

"Darkly creepy plus brimming with raw emotions. . . . *Vicious Grace* takes urban fantasy to a new level."

—Single Titles

Darker Angels

"An urban fantasy packed with intense emotions, cleverly original escapades, and an engaging group of characters."

—Single Titles

"Written with such tension that the book nearly vibrates in your hand. I read it in less than twenty-four hours, barely pausing to work, eat, or sleep."

—Reading the Leaves

"A fascinating and entertaining thriller."

—Genre Go Round Reviews

"A wild tale in a s
with elements we

"A dark urban far
come addictive."

Unclean Spirits

"Smooth prose and zippy action sequences."

—*Publishers Weekly*

"I absolutely loved *Unclean Spirits*. The world that M. L. N. Hanover has created is fascinating without being overbearing, and it is unique enough that it stands out from the rest of the urban fantasy genre. . . . A must-read for any urban fantasy lover."

—Fallen Angel Reviews

"Hanover's debut blends various aspects of urban fantasy and her unique touches to create a series opener that should appeal to genre fans."

—*Library Journal*

"Tight, well-developed action and interesting characters—particularly the heroine, dropped bewildered into a fight against the tattooed wizards of the Invisible College. . . . This is a series to watch."

—*New York Times* bestselling author S. M. Stirling

"Jayné is a fresh, likable heroine who grows from being a directionless college student into a vigorous, confident leader as she discovers and accepts her mission in life. . . . With a solid concept and eclectic cast of characters established, I have high expectations for Book 2 of the Black Sun's Daughter."

—The Sci Fi Guy

"Between the novel's energetic pacing, Jayné's undeniable charm, and the intriguing concept behind the riders, *Unclean Spirits* is a solid entry in the urban fantasy genre."

—Fantasy Book Critic

killing rites

BOOK FOUR OF

THE BLACK SUN'S DAUGHTER

M. L. N. HANOVER

POCKET BOOKS

New York   London   Toronto   Sydney   New Delhi

Pocket Books
A Division of Simon & Schuster, Inc.
1230 Avenue of the Americas
New York, NY 10020

This book is a work of fiction. Names, characters, places, and
incidents either are products of the author's imagination or
are used fictitiously. Any resemblance to actual events or locales
or persons, living or dead, is entirely coincidental.

First Pocket Books paperback edition December 2011

POCKET and colophon are registered trademarks of Simon & Schuster, Inc.

For information about special discounts for bulk purchases,
please contact Simon & Schuster Special Sales at 1-866-506-1949
or business@simonandschuster.com.

The Simon & Schuster Speakers Bureau can bring authors
to your live event. For more information or to book an event,
contact the Simon & Schuster Speakers Bureau at
1-866-248-3049 or visit our website at www.simonspeakers.com.

Cover design by John Vairo, Jr.
Cover art by Cliff Nielsen

Manufactured in the United States of America

10 9 8 7 6 5 4 3 2 1

ISBN 978-1-4391-7634-4
ISBN 978-1-4391-7636-8 (ebook)

To Lankester Merrin and Damien Karras

acknowledgments

AS ALWAYS, my first gratitude belongs to Jayné Franck for the loan of her name. Also, to my editor, Jennifer Heddle, and my agents, Shawna McCarthy and Danny Baror, without whom I would never have come this far. This book in particular exists because of the kindness and understanding of my family, and Ty Franck and Carrie Vaughn, who have made this series better than it would have been.

killing rites

PROLOGUE

Now that she was alone with him, Marisol wished she'd paid more attention the first time Carl scared her.

The winter stars of northern New Mexico spilled out across the sky. There wasn't any moon, and this far out of town, there weren't any lights except the distant ant-trail of white and red on the highway. The patches of snow on the ground didn't have more than starlight to reflect. There were supposed to be meteors, but there weren't, and the codeine in the cough syrup Carl stole from the hospital didn't feel right. She lay in the scarred steel bed of the truck, shivering and watching the darkness. Carl wasn't even pretending anymore. He was sitting up, smoking one of those fucked-up filterless cigarettes he bought down in Española, and poking at her with his feet. The cherry kept going bright and then dim and then bright again. In the starlight, she couldn't tell where he was looking, but she figured it was at her. Not that she could see. She just felt like his eyes were on her.

He'd seemed all right when they were back at the bar. A little rough around the edges, but shit, who wasn't, right? A little angry, maybe. One time, when he got really drunk, he'd said some things that scared her, calling the other girls names and talking about how much he wanted to punch them out. But he was drunk then, and he was okay all the other times. She'd told herself that was her being stupid. When he asked if she wanted to go out, watch the stars fall, it had sounded kind of fun.

She hadn't known it was just going to be the two of them. Or that he wasn't going to look up.

"I'm cold," she said. "There's nothing going on."

"Just wait," he said. "You've gotta be fucking patient. Shit."

His toe poked her in the ribs again. Instinct told her not to react. He wanted her to, and she didn't know why. If her head wasn't all fucked-up from that codeine, she thought she'd be able to figure a way out of here. A way to laugh it all off and get him to drive her back into Taos, back to the bar. No hard feelings, laugh about it, be friends like before. If she could just think better.

She had her cell phone, but it was in her purse, in the cab of the truck. And out here, who knew if she'd even get reception. She could walk back to the highway. They'd been driving for maybe twenty minutes after he pulled off onto the side road. The roads were bad. They probably never broke twenty miles an hour. She could walk back to the road in maybe an hour, maybe more than that. Was that right?

He poked her again. She tried to move away from him without seeming like she was.

"You know what I hate? You know what I really fucking hate?" he asked. The cherry flared, and for a second, she could see his face by the light: dark eyes, bent nose, the lines etched into his cheeks. "I hate all those cock-teasing bitches at the bar. Don't you?"

The shift from not being sure to knowing was like someone reaching into her chest and turning a light switch. Up until then, she'd been able to tell herself that she was wrong, maybe. That Carl was just a little weird. That she was stoned and para-noid. That she could talk herself out of this one. But now she knew it.

He was going to rape her.

"I said don't you hate all those cock-teasing bitches at the bar?" Carl said. He poked her again. Hard this time.

"Yeah," she said. The word came out soft and small, like she couldn't catch her breath. "Hate 'em."

"Thought you would," he said. "'Cause you don't think you're like them, do you?"

"I'm on my period," she said.

The pause told her she shouldn't have.

"Why the fuck would you say something like that?" Carl said. There was a buzz in his voice, angry and deep. "What are you . . . I mean, *fuck*."

In the dark bowl of stars, a light streaked and was gone again. *Look, a falling star,* she wanted to say. *Just like you said there would be.* The truck shifted. His hand was around her arm, squeezing hard.

"Stop it!" she said, knowing that he wouldn't. That this bad night was just getting started.

And then he was gone. Something muffled and violent happened in the gravel by the side of the truck. Someone—maybe Carl—grunted. Something snapped, a deep, sudden sound, like a wet two-by-four giving way. Carl screamed once, and Marisol screamed too. The world went quiet. Carl was out of the truck, on the ground. She heard him panting. Her heart was like a canary beating itself to death against its birdcage. Carl moaned. Footsteps came to the edge of the pickup. They weren't Carl's. In the starlight, it was only a deeper darkness by the side of the truck. Her back was pressed against the side of the truck bed hard enough to hurt. Somewhere, Carl moaned and started to weep. Marisol heard herself squeak.

"*Cálmate, cálmate, hija. Estás bien,*" the shadow said. His voice was like a gravel road. "*No te preocupes . . .*"

"Who the fuck are you?" she said. She was crying. She hated that she was crying.

The shadow chuckled. The driver's-side door opened. From where she was, she couldn't see well, but she had the impression of dark skin, a white shirt with wide suspenders like her grandpa used to have. The stranger leaned into the cab, then stood back up. The door shut, and after the light, the dark was worse. She couldn't see anything.

"I'm guessing you've never had a colonoscopy, right?" the shadow said. When he spoke English, he sounded like something was funny. An object landed on the steel beside her with a clank. After a moment, she put out her hand. It was the rounded plastic bottle of cough syrup. "I haven't either, matter of fact. Doesn't apply to my situation. But that shit? That's what they give you before they snake a Roto-Rooter up your ass."

"Codeine?" she said.

His laughter was wet, and it clicked unpleasantly.

"That's not codeine," he said.

She touched the bottle. Carl was still on the ground, somewhere behind the shadow. She could hear his breath, his little gasps of pain.

"It's roofies, isn't it?" she said.

"No. Midazolam. Same class of drugs, but this one keeps you awake. Just dopey. You can still put up a fight, just not a good one, which is the way Carl here likes it. And it screws up your memory, so come tomorrow, you won't know what happened except for the bruises. This rat fucker's been using it on girls for the past six months. There was one of them even called him to apologize afterward. Thought she'd gotten drunk and tried to beat *him* up."

"Are you a cop?"

"Kiddo, I'm not even the good guys."

She heard a soft clinking of metal on metal. She was starting to make the shape out again, her eyes readjusting to the darkness.

"I know this is a pain in the ass, but I'm taking the keys. If I don't, you're gonna try and drive this, and really, you're more messed up than it seems like. Better if you don't have the option."

"But—"

"You can sleep it off here. Inside the cab'll be warm enough. There's a blanket in there. Walk to the highway come morning, you'll be all right. Cops find that bottle, ask a few questions around Taos and Arroyo Seco, and they'll connect the dots pretty quick. They'll look for him but no one's going to give you any shit about this. You won't take the blame."

"The blame?"

"Well, if there's any blame to be taken. That's the good thing about guys like Carl. No one misses 'em."

Carl said something obscene, spitting the words out. Gravel crunched, and the impact drove the shadow forward, slamming it up against the truck. Marisol heard Carl grunting, straining. She'd been around enough fights to recognize the sound of violence. She moved forward, the plastic cough syrup bottle in her hand as if she could use it as a weapon.

The roar was deep, ragged, and inhuman. It rose up like something out of the earth, the sound towering over the desert night. Marisol had heard mountain lions call before. She'd heard the howling of a wolf pack. This was worse. It wasn't even animal. And it was huge.

The shadow moved once, twice. Carl screamed, his voice almost lost in the overwhelming demonic wail. Marisol dropped to her knees. Even when she'd been alone in the truck with Carl, knowing what was going to happen, even when the shadow man had ripped Carl away, she hadn't thought to pray. It was that sound. That sound had her hands in front of her, clasped to her chest, and the Our Father pouring from her lips before she knew she was doing it. *Santificado sea su nombre. Venga su reino. Hágase to voluntad en la tierra como en el cielo . . .*

It seemed to go on forever. The thunderous voice rose and deepened, washed away the world. When it was gone, all that was left was a wet sound, like someone sucking something, and deep ripping. She'd heard that sound every night when they served ribs: meat coming away from bone. The cold air smelled thick with blood and something else. Shit, maybe. Or death. Or brimstone.

The shadow rose up again. He wiped the back of a hand across his mouth and let out a small, satisfied sigh. Then he bent down again, paused for a second, and reappeared. When he lit the cigarette, the lighter's flame showed his face for the first time. Ruined lips, yellowed eyes, shrunken, gaunt cheeks with the flesh tight across the bone. The front and cuffs of the white button-down shirt were soaked in fresh blood. It was a corpse, walking. It was a vampire. It was the devil.

The flame died. The cherry glowed, just the way it had for Carl. She realized she didn't hear Carl breathing anymore. That she hadn't expected to.

"All right, kid. I think we're about done here. A

little messier than I'd hoped, but you know. Fallen world, right?"

Marisol didn't speak. The thing bent down a third time, grunted, and stood. He had something in his arms. Carl's body. It was smaller than it should have been, like bits of it were missing. The shadow began to walk off into the desert night. Another star fell overhead.

"Hey!" Marisol said.

The shadow stopped, turned to look back. The cigarette was pointing toward her. She swallowed, loosening the knot in her throat.

"I'm not going to remember any of this? Really?"

"You're already forgetting, kid."

"I won't know I saw you."

"Nope."

She nodded. The red of taillights on the horizon. The stars overhead like snowfall.

"Thank you," she said. "I owe you one, okay?"

The shadow was still for a long moment. A pang of fear touched Marisol. When he spoke, he sounded tired.

"I know you're not going to remember I said this, but just in case it gets through, lodges somewhere in the back of your head, I'll give it a shot. You've got a bad fucking habit. And if you don't stop it, it's going to get you killed. So listen close, okay?"

"Okay," Marisol said.

The shadow shifted his burden, took a drag on his cigarette. She felt a chill that was only half about the cold of the night. She waited.

"Next time you see someone like him or like me, walk away. You can't make friends with predators, *mi hija*. That's just not how it works."

chapter one

"So, Miss Jayné," Father Chapin said, pronouncing my name correctly: Zha-*nay*. Either he knew a little French or he'd been coached. "You believe you are . . . *possessed*?"

"Yes," I said.

He wasn't what I'd expected. I only knew a few things about him—that he'd been my buddy Ex's mentor back when Ex had still been studying for the priesthood, that he ran some kind of Jesuit exorcism squad, that he was presently working just south of the Colorado border in the Sangre de Cristo Mountains of northern New Mexico. It had left room for me to imagine some kind of Old West demon hunter. If he'd walked into the ranch house wearing a black duster with a Sergio Leone movie soundtrack playing in the background, it would have been closer. Instead, he looked like someone's pharmacist or grocery manager. Close-cropped, wiry white hair, a beard that was more a collection of individual whiskers each doing their own thing, and watery blue eyes that were a little red about the rims. He was a small man too, hardly bigger than me. His shirt was dark to match his slacks, and he didn't even have the Roman collar.

I felt cheated.

He took a sip of the coffee I'd made while we waited for him. It was a little after six at night, and already an hour past sundown. If he was anything like me, the caffeine would keep him awake until bedtime. The pine log burning in the fireplace popped, scattering embers like fireflies inside the black metal grate. Above us, shadows danced between the vigas.

"What leads you to suspect this?" he asked.

"All right," I said, took a breath, blew it out. "This goes back a little way. About a year and a half ago, my uncle died. Got killed. Murdered. It turned out he'd left me everything he had, and he had a lot. Like more than some small nations a lot."

"I understand," Father Chapin said.

"It also turns out that he was involved with

riders. Demons, or whatever. We call them riders. Spirits that cross over from Next Door and take people over. Like that. I didn't know anything about it, so I was flying blind for a while."

"How did you discover your uncle's involvement with the occult?"

"There was a guy staying in one of his apartments. He turned out to be a vampire."

"The *varkolâk*," Ex said. "Midian Clark. I mentioned him before."

"So there was that," I said. "But then I started getting these weird powers, you know? Wait. That sounds wrong. I don't mean like I can fly or turn invisible or anything. It was just that when someone attacked me, I'd win. Even if I really shouldn't have. That, and everyone tells me I'm sort of invisible to magic. Hard to locate. We figured that Eric—that's my uncle— had put some kind of protection on me."

"What did it feel like?"

"What did what feel like?"

"When you felt you should have lost in some conflict, but didn't."

"Oh. It's like my body just takes over. Like I'm watching myself do things, but I'm not really driving that car."

"I see. Thank you. Go on."

I looked over at Ex. He was sitting at the breakfast bar, looking down at the couch and overstuffed chairs like a bird on a perch. His white-blond hair was tied back in a ponytail and he wore his usual basic black pseudo-priestwear. Looking at Father Chapin, I could see where his fashion sense came from.

I wished the others were there too—Chogyi Jake and my now ex-boyfriend Aubrey. Kim. The ones who'd been there from the beginning. I wasn't sure what to say that I hadn't already told Father Chapin. I felt like I was at the doctor's office trying to explain symptoms of something without knowing quite what information mattered.

"It isn't fading," Ex prompted.

"Yeah. That's right. It's not," I said. "The guys always told me that magic fades, you know? That when someone does some sort of mojo, it takes upkeep, or it starts to lose power. We were looking through my uncle's things for months, and we never found anything about putting protections on me. We never used any kind of magic to keep them up. But instead of getting weaker, it seems like I'm getting stronger."

"Have you found yourself taking actions without intending to?"

"Like what?"

He took another sip of coffee, his thick white eyebrows knotting like pale caterpillars.

"Walking places without knowing that you meant to go there," he said. "Picking up things or putting them down. Saying words you didn't expect to say."

"No," I said. And then, "I don't know. Maybe. I mean, everyone does things like that sometimes, right?"

"Have you been sexually active?"

"Excuse me?"

"Have you been sexually active?" he asked again with exactly the same inflection.

I shifted on the couch. The blush felt like someone had turned a sunlamp on me. When I glanced over at Ex, he wasn't looking at me. I didn't want to go into any of this, but I especially didn't want to talk about my love life with Ex in the room. We'd both been pretty good about ignoring that he wanted to be part of it. Hauling out the fact that he wasn't seemed rude.

Still, in for a penny, in for a pound.

"A couple of times in college. And since last year, I had a boyfriend for a while, yes," I said. "Aubrey. But we're not seeing each other anymore."

"Why not?"

"It turned out that my uncle—the one I inherited everything from?—wasn't exactly a good person. He used magic to break up Aubrey and his wife. To make her have an affair with my uncle. The phrase *rape spell* came up. When we figured that out, Aubrey kind of needed to go resolve that with her." I paused. "It's not really as *Days of Our Lives* as it sounds."

"No other sexual activity?"

"None," I said.

"Are you Catholic?"

"No."

"What is your relationship with God?"

I shrugged. "Well, we used to be really close, but then I went away to college. The whole long-distance thing was really a drag, so we're kind of seeing other deities."

No one laughed. I felt my own smile go brittle. I shook my head and tried again.

"So, look, my parents are evangelical. We went to church all through my childhood, but the older I got . . . it just didn't work for me. I decided to go to a secular college. Took a while to save up the money, but . . . Anyway, I haven't been to church since then. Haven't talked to my parents either."

Father Chapin's smile was a relief, if only because it meant he was skating over the "seeing other deities" comment. I was a little bit annoyed with myself for wanting him to like me as much as I did.

"What did you study?"

"I majored in prerequisites," I said. When he looked quizzical, I said, "I dropped out after a couple semesters. Then Uncle Eric died. Since then, I've been kind of busy."

The old priest sighed, wove his fingers together on one knee, and leaned forward. I had the feeling we'd just been making small talk and he was ready to get into the real business. I didn't know what he was going to talk about if my messed-up family, my faith breakdown, Eric's death, and my sexual history were just the warm-up.

"Xavier tells me that you have recently killed a man."

"Who's Xavier?" I asked. "You mean *Ex*?"

"He tells me the man was an innocent and willing sacrifice, and that you—"

"All this stuff started a long time before that," I said. "It's not related."

"Still, to take such an action could have—"

"It's not related," I said again, and my voice shook a little. My heart was racing. I felt a pang of anger at my body for reacting so obviously. Wasn't I supposed to be the cool-as-a-cucumber demon hunter?

"I'm not here to judge you, young miss," he said. "I know something of the circumstances."

"Then you know I've been seeing this freaky shit a long time before Chicago," I said. "If I've got a rider, I've had it since at least last year. Maybe longer."

"Yes," Father Chapin said. "Yes, I understand. Thank you for your candor."

The pine log popped again. The quiet got awkward.

"So, what do we do?" I said. "Is there someplace we should go and get our exorcism on? Some kind of rite to keep things together until we're full power? What?"

Father Chapin looked pained. He scratched at an eyebrow with the nail of his right pinky, smiling down toward the coffee table as he spoke.

"There are many things we will need to do. Little steps. Little steps to be sure that our action is right, yes? Move forward with our eyes open."

"Great," I said, clapping my hands on my knees. "Where do we start?"

"I would consult with Xavier, please. For a moment."

When I didn't hop up immediately, Father Chapin looked embarrassed, and I had the sense it was more for me than himself. *This is* my *problem* hunched at the back of my throat. *Anything you can say to Ex, you can say to me.*

"Just for a minute, Jayné," Ex said.

"Sure," I said. "No problem."

I walked out of the den, heading for the kitchen. But at the last minute, I turned right instead. Down the hall, and out into the December night. After the warmth of the ranch house, the air was like a sharp slap. To the southwest, the lights of Santa Fe were glowing against a sparse covering of cloud. The stars overhead were brilliant and crowded in the sky. A meteor passed over, a thin silver-white light, gone as soon as I saw it. I stepped out to a stretch of rough wooden fence that divided the scrub and stones near the house from the scrub and stones slightly farther away from it, sat on the top plank, crossed my arms, and waited.

It had been a little over two months since I'd killed an innocent man. I'd had a good reason— saving-the-world-from-madness-and-war-level good—and he'd known what we were going to do. He'd gone into darkness of his own free will. But I was the one who'd put him in the box, driven in the nails, and buried him and the thing living in his body while they screamed and begged. Me. Little old Jayné Heller. My palms were almost healed. There wouldn't even be much of a scar. According to my lawyer, the police weren't investigating. It was a missing persons case, and it probably would be forever. Once upon a time, there was a man named David, and then one day, for no particular reason, there wasn't.

I hugged myself closer, the cold pressing into my skin. I'd bought an overcoat when we were in London—soft black wool that went down to my ankles—and I thought about going in to get it.

The days since then hadn't been the best of my life. I wasn't sleeping enough. I had weird spikes of anxiety and fear that felt like I'd accidentally gunned the gas with the car in neutral. I didn't know if it was the aftermath of my very bad day in Chicago or more evidence for my new theory of why I kept winning fights I should have lost.

From the moment I'd told Ex my suspicion that I had a rider in me, I felt like I'd fallen into a wheelchair that he was pushing. He'd arranged for the ritual tests in Hamburg that we'd tried with spectacularly inconclusive results. He'd orchestrated the trip back to the States—plane tickets, car, hotels. He even drove on the way up from Albuquerque International Sunport to Santa Fe.

He'd brokered the meeting with Father Chapin and his cabal of Vatican-approved exorcists. He'd made them sound like the ninja SWAT team of God. And maybe they were, but right now, sitting on my fence, I felt more alone than I had since I'd left college. I heard the front door open and close on the other side of the ranch house, then a car door. An engine came to life. Tires punished the gravel. I watched the headlights curve over the landscape of piñons and cactus without ever seeing the car itself. I figured it was safe to go in, but I didn't. A few minutes later, the door behind me opened. I heard Ex's footsteps coming out toward me, and I smelled the hot chocolate before I saw it. He had a cup for each of us, complete with half-melted marshmallows.

The news was going to be bad, then.

He leaned against the fence, looking out toward the smudge of light that was Santa Fe.

"He's in the middle of something right now," Ex said. "There's an Akkadian wind demon that's been possessing people all through the northern part of the state and up into Colorado. They've tracked it through almost three dozen cases. Father Chapin says they've got a rite coming up that's going to stop it for good."

"Okay," I said.

"They've been chasing this thing for months."

He sounded defensive. I waited. I'd known Ex long enough to tell when he was working himself up to something. I let the silence push for me while I sipped the hot chocolate. It was good, but he always put a little too much cinnamon in it.

"There's some work we can do, though," Ex said. "So that we're ready when he's done with that. Hit the ground running."

"This is the part I'm not going to like, right?"

"Yeah," Ex said. "It is."

I popped what was left of the marshmallow into my mouth and talked around it.

"Lay it on me, Preacher Man."

"There's someone in Taos he'd like you to talk with."

"Another priest?"

"A psychiatrist."

I laughed. The amusement didn't reach down as far as my gut.

"It's not about you," Ex said. "It's standard. It didn't used to be, but . . . well, it is now. People come to him and say that they're hearing voices or that demons are trying to control them or . . .

anything really. What he does won't help people who are mentally ill, so it makes sense to have someone do that kind of triage. And he doesn't know you. All he sees is your history."

"And what does my history look like?"

Ex's sigh plumed out white in the freezing air.

"It looks like someone with a very controlled, fairly sheltered childhood who's been through a lot of changes in a very short time. Just falling into that kind of money can put lottery winners into therapy. Then there's everything else. It wouldn't be strange for someone who has been through all the things you have to be . . ."

"Mentally ill?"

"Shell-shocked."

"Great."

We were quiet for what felt like a long time. The moon was new, a starless spot in the star-strewn sky. The breeze was no more than a breath, cold and dry. For as long as I could remember, I'd had dreams of being in a desert not entirely unlike this one. I wondered now if they'd really been my dreams. Maybe they belonged to something else that was living in my skin. Or maybe that was really mine, and everything else in my life was the falsehood. I thought I was a woman, but maybe that was a mistake.

I bit my lip, pulling myself back from that train of thought.

"You know I'm not going to do it, right?" I said.

"Yeah, I figured."

"So do we have a Plan B?"

"Sort of," Ex said.

"What's it look like?"

"Step one: Make a Plan B."

"Let's get inside," I said. "I'm freezing."

He took my hand, steadying me as I got down. He kept hold of my fingers for a few seconds longer than he needed to, and I let him. My plan to tour all the properties Uncle Eric had left in my name and catalog everything I could find had gone off the rails when I'd been called to Chicago. In the aftermath, we hadn't gotten back to it. But of places I'd actually seen, the New Mexico ranch house was one of my favorites. It sat alone on fifty acres of undeveloped wilderness, a single gravel road the only way in or out. It had power from the grid and utilities from the city, but there was also a generator and a well. The walls were white stucco that caught the desert sunlight, glowing yellow at dawn, pink and red and gold in the five o'clock winter dusk. And there was a patio that looked out to the west, catching the gaudy, improbable sunsets that had been different every day I'd remembered to look. I couldn't imagine myself living there. It was too isolated. But I could see curling up there to lick my wounds for a few weeks. A few months. Years, maybe.

I went to the kitchen and poured out the hot chocolate now well on its way to tepid. Ex went to the front room and stirred the fire with a black iron poker. The floors were red brick with thick Navajo rugs over them. My cell phone rested on the couch next to the leather backpack I used as a purse. It said I had one new message. The number was Chogyi Jake's, and I told myself I'd call him back later. After dinner, maybe. A demon-ridden mob had beaten him a good three-quarters of the way to death in Chicago. All his news would be about recuperating, which I didn't want to know. All mine would be about my quest for a first-class exorcist, which I didn't want to tell him. It didn't leave a lot in the middle.

"I could be wrong, you know," I said, sitting on the couch. "Maybe there's another explanation. The whole thing about having a rider on board could be crap I made up, and I'm scaring myself for no reason."

"I'm not willing to take that chance," Ex said. "It fits the data too well. If we can't figure out what's going on and Father Chapin won't help us, then I'll find someone else. I'm not giving up on him yet, though. He'll be in a better position after he's done with this thing with the wind demon. If I can just get him to look at you himself, try a few cantrips and pulls to see what's there to see, he'll change his mind."

"You're sure of that?"

"I'm not."

"I thought this guy was your Yoda."

Ex smiled toward the fire. In the flickering shadows, he might have looked sad. It was hard to tell.

"He taught me most of what I know about riders. The occult. I trained with most of the men he's working with now. I was going to be one of them."

"So what happened?"

Ex shrugged. The fire muttered to itself. When it was clear he wasn't going to say anything more, I stopped waiting.

chapter Two

My bedroom was lavish. King-size bed, wide picture window looking out toward the mountains on the horizon. The master bathroom had a Jacuzzi tub with a separate walk-in shower big enough for two. On the other hand, the pillows smelled like dust, and the water was rusty for the first couple of minutes. And there were other things. The television set up for watching movies from bed dated from before the switch to digital. The only input that worked was a black VCR with a half dozen cassettes dating from the late eighties. I'd watched about the first half of *The Big Blue* while we waited for Father

Chapin's arrival, and while Jean Reno had been pretty cute before he got old, I couldn't quite bring myself to start it back up.

The only Internet access was a cellular card I'd bought for the laptop, and the signal kept fading in and out with no discernible pattern. Streaming was impossible, and even web stuff was problematic. I felt like I'd been cut off from the world. I propped my laptop on the bedside table, cranked up Pink Martini, and let China Forbes sing to me about losing her head on the Rue St.-Honoré. The music was so relentlessly cheerful that by the time she shifted over to telling Lorenzo that he wasn't welcome anymore, I was feeling almost human again.

I wondered how much time Uncle Eric had spent in this room, lying on this bed and staring out at the vast emptiness of New Mexico. The wind-paved desert didn't seem like his kind of joint. As little as I knew him, that might have been accurate or I could have just been making it up. Certainly, with all the places he'd owned, he couldn't have spent much time in any one of them. The more I looked at it, the more it seemed like anytime he'd needed to go somewhere, he'd bought himself a house or condo—sometimes a couple of them—fitted them out for whatever he needed, then left them in place. If there was a pattern behind it all, a great and secret plan that all these locations fit into, I couldn't see it. The more I found out about my uncle, the less he seemed like the guy I'd thought he was.

I lay as still as I could, my palms toward the ceiling, and my heels pointing at the bathroom door. I waited for my body to do something—twitch, speak in tongues, leap up in a killing rampage. Say something I hadn't meant to say or walk someplace I hadn't meant to walk or pick something up I hadn't meant to carry. Anything to show me that I wasn't the only one in my flesh. But if there was a rider there, living with and within me, it was onto the game. Apart from the vague Pavlovian impulse to curl a pillow around my head and sleep, I didn't feel or do anything.

"Hey. Are you there?" I said to the empty room.

In another lifetime, I would have pushed the words out toward God. Now they were aimed inward at my maybe-rider. Either way, there wasn't an answer.

In the kitchen, a radio came on announcing the news from Washington. I heard Ex open the refrigerator, then the clank of pots, the clatter of the blue ceramic dishes that we'd bought the last time we were out here. Dinner on its way. I sighed and sat up just as my cell phone rang. Once upon a time, the ringtone had been my uncle's voice. Now it was the first twenty seconds of Tempo Perdido. I took a deep breath, let it out, and answered the call.

"Hey," I said, forcing my voice to a brightness I didn't feel. "How's the Windy City?"

"Cold," Chogyi Jake said. "Unpleasantly cold. Damp too."

"Bummer," I said. "Sounds like you're recuperating pretty well, though."

The pause on the line told me that I'd said something a little weird. I bit my lip.

"I am recuperated," Chogyi Jake said. "They released me from the hospital five weeks ago. The stitches dissolved three weeks ago. I am as whole, I think, as I will ever be."

"Didn't let you keep the spleen, though," I said. "Could have had it infused with plastic or something. Made a great paperweight."

"How are you, Jayné?"

"It'd be a little Gothic, maybe, but how many people can hold down their taxes with a spleen? Auditor comes in, you can wave it at her and say, 'Stand back, I'm not afraid to vent this thing.'"

I got a chuckle. I pressed on before I lost the tempo.

"How are Kim and Aubrey settling in? Everything going all right?"

It was a noble effort on my part. I gave myself full marks. It didn't work.

"I'm worried about you," Chogyi Jake said. "Since you left, I've had the feeling that you didn't want me to rejoin you."

"Oh, gimme a break," I said. "You got hurt. You've been healing up. Of course I'm looking forward to getting the gang together again. It's just . . ."

The lies backed up in my throat. I had the sudden powerful memory of telling my mother that I didn't know who'd poured all the milk on my older brother's bed. The hot, choking feeling of standing by something that we both knew wasn't true was just as humiliating now as it had been when I was a kid.

"It's just?" Chogyi Jake said. When he wanted it to, his voice could be like warm flannel. My eyes were tearing up.

"Just not right now," I said. "I think Ex and I are probably about done here, and I'm not sure where we're heading next. But as soon as I've got a game plan, buddy, we'll coordinate flights. No problem."

"Ex isn't returning my calls either."

"Isn't he? There may be a service issue. The connections out here are pretty spotty. I'll ask him about it, okay?"

The sound wasn't quite a sigh. It was just an exhalation with a comment at the back. I lost control of one of the tears, and it dripped down my cheek. I felt annoyed by it. They were my eyes. I'd decide when they leaked.

"If you need me, you know I'm here," Chogyi Jake said. I could picture him just from the way he said the words. Leaning forward a little. The light playing off the stubble of his scalp. He had laugh lines all around his eyes, and when he was being gentle, they almost vanished into his skin.

"I know," I said.

"All right, then," he said.

"I'll call you later. When I know more."

I dropped the call and sat on the edge of the bed for a while. The voices on the radio chattered and slid around in an increasing and angry sizzle. The smells of garlic and tomato and onion and the dust that the heater kicked up. I wondered if crying without intending to counted as a symptom. Was I crying, or was it someone else? I hated the thought.

Ex knocked gently on the bedroom door and then let it swing open. I looked up at him through my hair. I probably looked like the bad guy from a Japanese horror film, but Ex just leaned against the frame, arms crossed. The light from the kitchen silhouetted him, making his loose white-blond hair look a little more like a halo.

"Chogyi?" he asked.

"Yeah."

"Did you tell him yet?"

"No."

"Jayné—"

"I don't want to," I said. "If we're right, there's nothing he can do we aren't already doing. If we're wrong, it'd just freak him out for no reason. Besides which, he'd tell Aubrey and Kim, and they have enough on their plates right now without worrying about me, right?"

Besides, I thought, I don't want him to see me like this. I don't want anyone to see me like this. Not even you.

"Dinner's almost ready," he said. "Fifteen minutes?"

"I'll be there."

He closed the door, and I went from feeling intruded on to wanting him to come back, like I was flipping a switch.

The best cook I'd ever known was a vampire. Chogyi Jake and Aubrey were about even for second. If there had been a pizza delivery that reached this far outside the city, Ex and I would have been smart to put them on speed dial. The evening meal that night consisted of slightly overcooked spaghetti noodles with store-bought marinara and frozen broccoli steamed to within an inch of its life. Ex closed his eyes and folded his hands, saying a silent grace. I just picked up my fork and started in. When he opened his eyes, he poured us both glasses of cheap red wine. Over the past weeks, it had become our ritual, and I couldn't have said if it was a mutual acceptance—his faith and my doubt making room at the table for each other—or a constant low-level challenge.

When it had been the four of us, there had been a pattern. But now it was down to just two, and my life with Ex was built around the things we didn't say. Things like *I know you think you're in love with me* and *You don't have to be so patronizing* and *I need you*. That's what I wasn't saying, anyway. I didn't know what his silences meant.

I cleared away the dishes, starch and tomatoes sitting high in my stomach. Ex went back to the front room and stoked the fire, throwing on logs of dried cottonwood that burned bright and fast. He sat on the couch reading Thomas Merton. The clock claimed it was eight o'clock, but it was dark enough to be midnight. The single-glazed windows let the cold press in against me. I made myself a couple of slices of cinnamon toast and a cup of decaf tea as dessert. I ate and drank standing in the kitchen, washing the plate as soon as I was done. Then I went to bed.

When I was in middle school, I had a run of pretty spectacular nightmares. In the summer after my one and only year of college, while my love life and circle of friends dissolved around me, my brain had tried insomnia for a while. They were about the worst sleep disturbances I'd had until now.

I lay in the bedroom, wrapped in the dusty sheets. As soon as my head hit the pillow, all signs of fatigue vanished. My mind was more than awake; it was bouncing off the inside of my skull like a rhesus monkey in a caffeine overdose study. My thoughts flickered from the insurance we'd gotten on the

new rental car, to whether I needed to fill out any
tax paperwork, to my older brother's impending
marriage, to the way the lantern had hissed while
I'd buried an innocent man alive, to the sound of
Aubrey laughing when he'd just realized something.
No thought connected to the one before it. There
was no predicting where my mind would leap next.
It was like someone had gotten my remote control
and was channel surfing my head.

I tried the meditation and breathing exercises
that Chogyi Jake had taught me to help focus my
qi, the vital energy of life and magic. I couldn't do
it. Every time I started to focus on my breath, I got
distracted with how my toe felt or whether my hand
had moved on its own or what was going to happen next in Jennifer Aniston's love life. An animal
howled out beyond my window. If might have been
a coyote, or it could have been a stray dog. From
where I was, I couldn't tell the difference.

I didn't know I was falling asleep at all until I
felt the shovel in my hand. The lantern hissed like
a snake beside me, and something just under my
skin shifted like a wave on the surface of a lake. A
black coffin was in a hole in front of me. In a grave.
Please, a voice shouted. *I'm not dead. I'm not dead.*
I felt myself lifting the shovel, heard the dirt on the
coffin. The dread was overwhelming.

I woke up screaming. My heart was racing, and I
fumbled for the lights. The bedroom flooded white

as daylight and the door burst open. Ex in a pair of dark green sweatpants and black T-shirt, and with a panicked expression. The light turned the windows into mirrors, and I caught a glimpse of myself huddled against the headboard. I was shaking, and I hated that I was shaking. Ex looked around the room, searching for danger.

There wasn't any. There was nothing there but me. My phone showed 4:30 a.m. I said something obscene, and then, liking the way the words felt, I let loose a slow, steady stream of profanity, like air slowly leaking out of a balloon. The tension left Ex's shoulders.

"Another nightmare?" Ex asked.

"Yeah," I said. "I'm fine. Go back to bed."

"Are you going to be able to sleep?"

"I'm fine," I said. "I'll be fine."

He lifted an eyebrow and walked out of the room. I went to the bathroom, and I was still standing over the sink, washing my face and waiting for my hands to get steady again, when I heard him come back in. The squeak of the bed as his weight pressed it down. The soft, unmistakable zip of playing cards being shuffled. He was sitting cross-legged at the foot of the bed, a legal pad and ballpoint pen beside him. The cards were a standard red-backed poker deck.

"Gin rummy?" he asked.

I pushed the hair back from my eyes. The

prospect of trying to force myself back to sleep or else make it through the long hours until dawn with no company apart from my thoughts had been charmless anyway. The sense of relief left me smiling.

"Sure," I said. "You deal first."

We didn't talk about it. Not about the secret thing living in my skin, not about the bad night in Chicago. Not about Eric or the nightmares or the shame that kept me from wanting anyone to know that I was struggling to make it through the day. Everything we said was about the cards or movies we'd seen when we were kids or the relative strengths of Wonder Woman and Superman. We were innocuous together. The anxiety faded slowly over the span of hours, but it faded.

It only occurred to me when the sky outside the window started shifting from black to charcoal and the distant mountains started to be a visible horizon that, with my dark hair and white T-shirt, I looked like I was trying to be a photo negative of Ex. I was up 620 points to 570 when Ex put down his cards, stretched, and yawned wide enough that I could see his back teeth.

"Coffee?" he asked.

"Sure," I said.

He touched my shoulder before he went out. Nothing more. Just a little contact, and then gone. While he banged around in the kitchen, I laid my head down on the pillow. I closed my eyes just for a minute to rest them. When I opened them again, it was almost noon. I heard the front door of the ranch house close, but then nothing, so I figured Ex had been heading outside. I got up, switched out my pajama bottoms for some blue jeans, pulled a thick gray wool sweater over my T-shirt, tugged on my boots, and headed out.

The kitchen and living room were shut down. Cleaned and everything put away the way it'd been when we'd arrived. The ashes were all gone from the fireplace. Ex's suitcase and laptop carrier were by the door, ready to be packed out. I snagged a rubber band out of my pocket, pulled back my hair, and tied it into a rough ponytail before I walked outside.

The cold felt like being slapped. Sunlight that intense and total didn't have a right to go with air that frigid. And it was dry enough I could feel my eyes getting gritty just walking across the wide gravel driveway.

Most of the places we'd gone, we'd rented minivans. But most of the places we'd been, there had been four of us and Aubrey had been driving. When I'd first met Ex, he'd had a little black sports car, a very pretty motorcycle, and a cot in a barely converted garage. Now he was leaning into a black and silver Mercedes two-seater with a roof that hardly seemed higher than my hips. Some tastes don't change.

"Hey," I said.

"Good morning, sleepyhead," Ex said. "I'm just trying to figure out how we fit all the luggage in here last time."

"With difficulty."

"Yeah, that sounds right. Well, there's still some coffee in the thermos there. I cleaned out the fridge, but we can stop in Española for some lunch if you're hungry."

"I take it we're going somewhere?"

"We are," he said. "Taos."

I crossed my arms. "Taos?"

"Well, not in the city proper," he said. "We'll be going through it, though. There's a little town about twenty minutes northwest of there called San Esteban."

"I'm not going to see Chapin's pet shrink," I said.

"No. You're not. The Catholic sanctuary in San Esteban is where Father Chapin and the others are. Their base of operations. We're going to see them."

"I don't mean to be dim," I said. "But why are we doing that?"

"While you were asleep, I figured out my Plan B. Father Chapin is . . . He's the best at what he does. Better than I am. Better than those idiots in Hamburg. He and I have a history, but I thought that if I told him everything about your situation, we could ask him for help. That was Plan A, right? Ask for help."

"That's what I thought. So Plan B is . . . what? Ask again?"

Ex closed the car door. I expected it to have a deep, satisfying clump, but some hidden hydraulics kicked in at the last second, slowing the door down and settling it into place with a barely audible click.

"Plan B is insist."

chapter Three

Since Uncle Eric died, it felt like I'd spent more time traveling than being anywhere. I tried to count up the hours I'd spent in airplanes and airports, and came to the rough conclusion that I could have gone around the world five times. Marco Polo and Magellan were homebodies compared to me. I expected the drive north to Taos to be just another trip: a couple of hours in a vibrating metal box, ending someplace I didn't know. Instead, going down the two-lane highway pointed out something I hadn't realized. Pretty nearly all the places I'd been to in my long, slow survey of my domain had been cities with airports. With big hotels filled with smartly dressed people lining up to give me whatever I asked for because I'd bodysurfed in on a wave of money.

Now we drove through a handful of towns that were barely more than a few hundred yards where the speed limit went down. In a couple, I could have counted the buildings on my fingers. Twice, we passed little houses set back from the highway like some kind of suburban dimensional warp. I imagined some anonymous subdivision, thousands of identical houses with one inexplicable lot of mountain and grassland. It wouldn't have seemed any stranger than this.

The cottonwoods by the roadside were black barked and dead looking. The names on the signs were places I'd never heard of, some of which seemed like jokes. I had a hard time believing there was a Rat, New Mexico, even if they were saying it in Spanish. Ex pointed out that there was Boca Raton in Florida, and Rat's Mouth wasn't particularly more dignified.

After we passed through Española, I let Ex change the road music from Pink Martini to the jazz piano that he preferred. There was more snow on the ground. At first, it only clung to the shadows where the sunlight couldn't reach it, but every northward mile gave it more courage. By the time we were threading our way along with a frozen river to the left and sheer and towering cliffs to the right, there was as much white snow as brown earth or green pine.

I wondered what it would be like to live out here, away from the world. I had a reflexive longing for it, as powerful as hunger. To fill up the heating oil, haul in a stack of books as high as my head and enough food to get through the winter sounded like a little slice of heaven. If I'd tried it, I'd probably have been walking the fifty miles to Starbucks within the week. It was a nice fantasy. That was all.

I'd also thought that we'd stick out on the road, a gleaming back sports car twisting through the back roads of rural New Mexico. We spent about half the time from Española to Taos between a silver Lexus and a Cadillac Escalade with a ski rack mounted to its roof. The closer we got to the city, the more the traffic seemed divided. Beater pickup trucks and fifteen-year-old Saturn sedans grudgingly made way for hundred-thousand-dollar SUVs.

The car had a GPS, but Ex didn't use it. We went straight through town and out the other side before we took an obscure fork from the main road. The road angled north and west, winding along the contours of the land. The asphalt didn't look like it had ever been adulterated by paint. The roadside was mottled with snow and ice, but the pavement was clear. A chain-link fence rusted in the middle of a field for no discernible reason. The traffic signs we passed were crusted with old snow, the top half of the speed-limit numbers fading to gray. I didn't realize we were getting close until Ex pulled the car to the right, eased down a short road, and killed the engine.

San Esteban spread out before us. Three streets with a few buildings on each one, like a giant had scattered a handful of gravel. About half were clapboard with pitched roofs. The others were flat-topped adobe with brown stucco and windows so deep that birds had built nests on the sills. A couple of metal Quonset huts crouched together at the north end. Once, they'd been painted in psychedelic swirls that still hung on as paint flakes. One had a gas pump out front so old it wouldn't read credit cards.

Ex had stopped by one of the adobe buildings with the deep-set windows. At a guess the sanctuary might have been a school once. Or a nunnery. There were no signs on the building to say what it was used for now. There were no street signs. When I looked at my cell phone it was wavering between digital roam with one bar and no service. The whole town was well on its way to not existing at all. Ex put the keys in his coat pocket, took a deep breath, and nodded to himself.

"Stay here," he said.

"Yeah, like *that's* gonna happen."

I thought he smiled a little as we got out of the

car. I trailed him down the walk to the blue-painted double doors. They were wood, and so worn by the years it looked like the paint was holding them together. The air bit at my earlobes and made my nose run a little. I kept my hands stuffed deep in my pockets and reminded myself to buy gloves next time the occasion arose. And maybe a scarf. A motorcycle blatted past, the only traffic sound there was. Ex knocked on the door.

We waited. I looked around. Across the street and about twenty yards farther along, a small house hunkered down in the snow. The windows had sheet plastic over the screens and a television flickered inside, blurred to mere light and movement. On the street, a beat-up gray Yukon and a sedan that had first hit the road when I was getting out of grade school.

Thirty or forty crows perched in the bare cottonwood across the street, calling to one another and shifting uncomfortably like old men at a bus station.

There was something wrong. It wasn't the stillness, exactly. Or the cold. Or the quiet. The world felt thin here, the spiritual world just outside ours—the place that we called the Pleroma or Next Door—close enough to touch. The sanctuary at San Esteban felt like magic, and it made my flesh crawl. Ex knocked on the door again.

"Maybe they're out doing the thing," I said. "Wind demon busting."

"They're here," he said, nodding toward the car and Yukon.

The crows clacked at one another accusingly. There was a term, I thought, for a group of crows the same way there was for a school of fish or a pride of lions. It was right on the tip of my tongue, but I couldn't quite remember it. With my black coat and hair, I felt like I should be able to spread my arms and fly up to the winter-killed tree, squat on the branches, and look down at the world.

As if alarmed that I'd even think it, the crows took to the air, cawing and beating their wings. They circled up into the hazy white sky, turned south, and departed. I watched them go, and behind me, the blue doors opened. The man who stood in the shadows beyond was maybe thirty. His skin was the brown of eggshells, and his black hair was combed straight back. A sense of weariness weighted down the air around him; I kept expecting him to sway on his feet. He wore the Roman collar under a thick wool sweater. When he spoke, it was with an accent that made me think of being eight years old with a crush on Ricky Ricardo. Old Havana, as romantic and unreal as Middle-earth.

"I'm sorry. You've come at a very bad time. You'll have to go away. Come back later."

"You don't recognize me, do you?" Ex said.

The man in the doorway looked up, shocked. His eyes were so brown they were black, and his expression changed from a shock that was almost fear to disbelief to an incandescent joy in the course of a single breath.

"Chewy? Is that you?"

Chewy? I thought, and Ex grinned and held his hands out at his sides as if to say, *Here I am.* Old Havana stepped out into the light. In the sun, the few gray hairs at his temples shone in the light, but they didn't make him look old so much as prematurely gray. He took Ex in a bear hug, and I stepped back in case his enthusiasm spilled over onto me.

"What are you doing here?" Old Havana said as he returned Ex to the ground. "I haven't heard from you in years. Not since Isabel—"

"It's been a long time," Ex said. "Chapin didn't mention me, then."

"No. Except . . . Were you the mysterious errand down in Santa Fe?"

"If it was yesterday, then I probably was."

Old Havana nodded more to himself than to Ex. Looking at him more closely now, I saw he was less Desi Arnaz and more Benicio Del Toro. He had the same distance in the eyes and the same well-worn masculine pretty. He looked at me as if noticing that I was there.

"This is Jayné," Ex said. "Janyé, this is Miguel Contreras. Father Contreras, I guess."

Old Havana—Miguel—nodded to me, smiling. I pulled a hand out of my pocket and waved.

"Hey," I said.

"She's why we came," Ex said. "We need to talk to him."

"We're in the middle of a ceremony."

"Akkadian wind demon," Ex said.

Miguel nodded, paused, then nodded again.

"We've been going for three days. The girl's in the back, and the devil wants her bad. Won't give her up. We've been pulling shifts."

Ex frowned.

"You mean he came down to see me in the middle of a rite?"

"We thought it was strange too," Miguel said. "Maybe a little less strange, seeing it's you. Are you here to help?"

Ex laughed softly. When he sighed, his breath was a plume of white.

"No," he said. "I came to make demands, actually. But I'll help if I can. If he'll let me."

"Come in," Miguel said, gesturing toward the still-open doors. "Both of you, please."

As if he'd said the magic word, about half of my anxiety faded. The sense that the town was malefic and aware of me didn't vanish, but it faded. The crows—gone now, anyway— seemed less like they'd been talking about me. I followed Ex through the doorway and into the warm darkness. The interior was all brick floors with thick Navajo rugs. The white stucco walls were wavy and uneven in a way that spoke of handcraft, and the dark wooden doorways were set so low that even I had to duck a little when I went from room to room. Religious paintings and sculptures hung in every room. Christ hung from His cross of wood or ceramic or worked iron. Mary wept or looked on serenely while her son died. A few of the paintings were bleak images of hell, heavy with threat and misery. I wondered who had painted them. Men's voices rumbled in the distance, talking low among themselves. The air smelled of wood smoke and old incense.

There were no corridors or hallways, just one room following on another like a maze. They were all lit, but the wiring was stuck on the exterior of the walls and painted white; the building was older than electricity. We passed a window that looked out into bare courtyard, and I could feel the cold pressing in from the glass. Miguel led us through four or five doorways, Ex sometimes going ahead of me, sometimes behind. At one door, we passed through almost together.

"Xavier, I get. Ex, I get. But *Chewy*?" I said softly.

He actually blushed a little.

"Long story," he said. "Tell you later."

"Promises, promises."

The kitchen was as small as any of the rooms we'd been through. An enameled gas stove sat in the corner like a refugee from the 1920s. A mini-fridge out of a dorm room hummed to itself on the opposite wall. A fireplace had a high, roaring fire in it, and iron fixtures somebody could hang a pot of gruel from. The worn gray couch on the far wall didn't go with the decor, and a small dinner table with a motley variety of straight-backed chairs had been shoved a little to the side to accommodate it.

An older man—fat, but also tall and solid—lay on the couch with his arm over his eyes. Two others were sitting at the little table, an interrupted game of dominos spread out between them. Between the roundness of the table and the weirdly organic shape the tiles had taken, I thought of mold growing in a petri dish. Which made me think of Aubrey and the research biology labs he'd worked in. And then about breaking up with him in the darkened hospital in Chicago. For a moment—less than a breath—I was under Grace Memorial again, my hands bloody and an innocent man begging that I not bury him alive. And then I was back in the real world. Nauseated, my heart racing. But back. No one noticed.

One of the men at the table—thin and Anglo with close-cut sandy hair—yawped with delight and came toward Ex with open arms. The other one—young-faced, with a weak chin his goatee couldn't quite apologize for—looked on in benign confusion. The big one on the couch grunted and tried to turn away from the noise, sleep more important than anything except maybe a fire. Thin Man took Ex in his arms, thumping him soundly on the back. Unfortunate Goatee smiled at me, and I nodded back.

"Chewy was Father Chapin's star student when I first joined up," Miguel was saying to Unfortunate Goatee. I felt like the new kid at school, left out and alone and vaguely threatened by how happy everyone else seemed to be. I balled my fists in my pocket and willed myself to be calm. There was nothing to be afraid of. I was being stupid.

"The prodigal returns, returns, *returns*," Thin Man crowed. "I'd kill you the fatted calf, but we are a strictly lentils-and-greens affair these days."

"Dinner at O'Keefe's?" Unfortunate Goatee said.

"Yes, that!" Thin Man said through his grin. "You'll love the place. Utter hole. Looks like food poisoning on a stick, but they're wonderful. What are you *doing* here? Where have you *been*?"

The sleeping man gave up, rolled to his side, and squinted up at Ex through red-rimmed eyelids.

"Xavier," he rumbled.

"Tamblen," Ex said. It seemed to exhaust the conversation between the two of them, and Ex turned back to Thin Man. "I've been . . . I've been traveling. I was renting a garage in Denver for a few years, using that for my home base."

"Keeping out of trouble, I hope," Thin Man said.

"Wouldn't go that far," Ex said. "This is Jayné Heller."

The men's collective attention turned to me. The

silence was fraught, and I didn't understand the weight it carried. I wasn't the only one to notice either. Unfortunate Goatee was looking at the other priests in confusion. Thin Man let go of Ex and smiled at me.

"Well," he said, "I suppose abandoning one's vows does carry certain benefits."

"Carsey," the big one—Tamblen—said, and the Thin Man held up a palm to stop him.

"Joking, Tamblen, my dear. Only joking," he said, and then held his hand out to me. I expected a false, bitchy smile, and so the naked sorrow in his expression was off-putting. "You're Chewy's girlfriend?"

I shook his hand. He was strong despite his build, and his skin was warm.

"Employer," I said. Thin Man—Carsey—blinked at me as if he hadn't understood. I clarified. "I'm his employer."

"Jayné hired me and a couple of others," Ex said. "We've been helping her put some things together. It's a long story. I talked to Father Chapin about it yesterday, and we came up here to . . . follow up."

Tamblen sat up, chuckling. Carsey's smile warmed and he made a little bow. *Touché*. I didn't know what point I'd scored, but I nodded back.

"He's with the girl," Unfortunate Goatee said. "Him and Father Tomás."

"Out soon," Tamblen rumbled.

"I didn't know that the exorcism had already

started," Ex said. "Or that it was going to be so long."

"This one's rough," Miguel said. "But we'll beat it. She'll be free by Sunday. We've been tracking this demon for months. Its spawn are sent back to Hell. There is only this one left, but it was the source of all the others."

I had to check my phone to be sure, but it was Wednesday. Miguel and the others had been working, and it looked like around the clock, for three days. They were thinking it would be finished sometime in the next four.

Ex stared at the floor, struggling with something. I'd been with him long enough to understand. He'd brought me here to have a confrontation with his old master, and now it looked like said old master had a solid reason for putting us off. He didn't want me to feel like he didn't have my back, but the second thoughts were building up fast. On the timing if nothing else. I let him off the hook.

"Look, why don't we head back down for Taos," I said. "You guys can find us there when—"

Somewhere in the maze of rooms, something banged. A door opening. The sound resonated more than it should have, echoing through the space like we were in a cathedral and not crowded into a tiny kitchen. A girl's voice screamed, fury and violence. The raw power of it washed over me like heat from a furnace. There was nothing human in the roar.

Nothing benign or rational. It was the voice of a rider, deep and thundering and soaked in hatred. A man's voice rose, opposing it.

"—by whose *might* Satan was made to fall from heaven like *lightning,* I humbly call upon your holy name in fear and trembling—"

Unfortunate Goatee blew out a breath. His face had gone pale. Carsey turned to him, nodding, and then back to me.

"Stay a few minutes. Father Chapin's just coming," he said. And then to Unfortunate Goatee: "Rise up, my boy. Break's over."

From the moment he staggered in, I could tell Father Chapin wasn't pleased to see us. He went from surprise to disappointment in a flicker. I could see Ex hunch in a little at the old man's disapproval, like a schoolboy bravely facing his father's punishment.

Chapin looked like crap. Sweat wet his skin, the veins in his temples and neck were discolored and proud as welts. He looked at Ex and then at me. Carsey and Unfortunate Goatee—I really needed to find out his real name—walked out, heading toward the commotion. The unearthly howling kept roaring for a few seconds. Then a deep, resonant boom like the gates of Hell closing. And then silence. Shift change.

Father Chapin walked to the minifridge, took out a bottle of water, and drank it, squatting there on the floor. Miguel and Tamblen watched him. No one moved, waiting for Daddy to say something.

"We didn't know you were in the middle of a thing," I said.

Father Chapin ran a hand over his head and took a long, shuddering breath.

"Come with me," he said without looking back at us. "We can speak."

He walked like an older man than he'd been the day before. It was more than just fatigue. The way his hips tried not to move, the care with which he put weight on his knees. He was in pain. He led us to the room with the window that looked out on the courtyard. A crucifix of carved oak bore a Christ dripping with red paint. His crown of thorns was a real crown of thorns. Father Chapin leaned against the wall.

"I assume you have not done as I asked you," he said.

"I'm sorry," Ex said, and the distress and embarrassment in his voice reminded me of about half of my own childhood. "I only thought—"

"It's not Ex. It's me," I said. "I'm not going to see a shrink. I don't have a psychological problem."

Father Chapin smiled and swung his eyes toward me. A blood vessel in the sclera of his left eye had burst, staining the white red. He looked like he'd been beaten.

"You sound quite certain, Miss Jayné," he said.

"You have murdered. You have compromised the temple of your flesh. You have lost faith in both God and the uncle you most admired. And you tell me you are unscathed, yes?"

"Well, okay, I may have some issues to work through, but I'm not crazy," I said. And then, "Wait a minute. Compromised my temple? Are you talking about sex?"

"There is a reason for the things I ask of you," Father Chapin said, leaning against the wall. "There is a process which we must follow. Not only for you, not only now, but for everyone. Every time. We do not cut corners, take the easy way . . ."

The contempt he shoehorned into the words *easy way* was pretty impressive. Ex was staring at his own toes, his face pale as the snow outside the window. An odd smell wafted through the room, hot and metallic, like a skillet left on the burner for too long.

"Xavier of all men should have explained this. What we do here," Chapin said. "It will not heal those wounds. If you are possessed by the minions of Satan, I may be able to help you to redeem yourself. But to be here now is a distraction, and to commit to these rites without need would damage you and degrade these ceremonies."

I crossed my arms and leaned against the wall next to Jesus. My scowl was etching itself into my skin. The weird smell was getting stronger.

"Well, I don't want to degrade any ceremonies," I said. "But whether I feel emotionally at peace with—"

Something detonated. Dark webs cracked the pale stucco, and the crucifix beside me swung like a pendulum. Father Chapin's mouth was a tiny, surprised O. Ex was the first to recover, but Chapin and I were after him almost as soon as he moved.

The kitchen was in disarray: table toppled and domino tiles scattered on the floor, minifridge door open and its internal light flickering wildly. The others were gone. Someone screamed from the other side of the building. The door Father Chapin had come through stood open. The door Carsey and Unfortunate Goatee had gone out when they were going to take his place in the exorcism. As I paused, I heard other voices—men's voices—raised and shouting as if from a long way away. And something that was like a girl's voice and also like a forest fire roaring above them. The air felt tainted. Something unreal brushed against me and blundered away again like a fish in a pond.

"Possessed girl got loose?" I said.

"Yeah," Ex said.

"Spiffy."

chapter four

Father Chapin limped toward the fight, and we followed, moving through the rooms as quickly as his pained steps could lead us. A black, carved-wood door hung open; the places where its hinges had ripped out of the frame were pale and fresh.

The room beyond had been a chapel or a lecture hall or both. The brick floors were so dark, they seemed to swallow the light. A tiny wooden dais stood across from double doors leading out to the courtyard. Chalked symbols on the floor shimmered like something seen through a heat haze, and the air tasted like hot copper. The priests stood in a circle, holding their palms toward the center or else clutching at black leather Bibles. All of them except for Unfortunate Goatee, who lay unmoving in a corner, limp as yesterday's laundry.

Between the men, I caught glimpses of something moving low to the floor. Ex took my shoulder and pointed toward the bunch of them, shouting, but I couldn't make out his words. Father Chapin hurried forward, and I heard his voice, rising with the others, contending with the demon. Ex went to his side, holding out his hands and shouting down the devil with the others. I went to Unfortunate Goatee. He was breathing, but that was the best I could say for him. His eyes were wide and unfocused. A long, deep cut scored him from neck to belly, but the pink, exposed flesh didn't bleed.

"It's okay," I said, taking his hand. "Just hang tight, and we'll get you to a doctor. Just hold on."

The demon shrieked, the sound sharp and rough as a bread knife. The priests stumbled back. Carsey lost his footing and dropped to his knees. They seemed to be shouting something in Latin, but I couldn't be sure. The thing in the middle of the circle leaped up to the ceiling, clinging there like a spider.

It was a girl, no more than eight years old. Her black hair was in mats and tangles. When she opened her mouth, a dim light spilled out past her teeth, and the same dirty brightness leaked through the sores on her body. The chanting men looked up at her, their voices more strident. They were getting desperate. She sat up, then stood, the soles of her feet on the ceiling, gravity reversed for her and her alone. When she tilted her head back to look down at me, I had the sense of something ancient, maybe something that had been beautiful once but was all septic madness now.

I stood. I was aware intellectually of the fear. My heart was racing; the skin at the back of my neck felt like an invisible hand was stroking it just enough to raise gooseflesh. A wind whirled, stirring my hair and making the black overcoat flap around my ankles. I knew where we were headed. I took a deep breath, let it out, and spread my arms in invitation. *Come on. Let's do this.* The little girl grinned, took two steps toward me, and dropped.

I didn't have a violent childhood. There was anger, yes. There was yelling and accusation and a combination of masculine self-righteousness and maternal submission that I would call less than healthy. But my father never raised a hand in anger, and I had a protective big brother who kept school as benign as he could. The first actual fight I'd ever been in came just after my uncle died, and I'd turned into some kind of ninja, spinning dishware through the air, disarming and defeating gun-toting wizards. Since then, I'd won every fight I'd been in. Oh, it had been close. I'd come out bloody. I'd hung on to the edge of a skyscraper by my fingertips. I'd had a voodoo god beat me until I couldn't stand up. But each time, the sense of being trapped a couple of inches behind my eyes clicked in, and I'd watched my body do things I couldn't imagine or predict.

And so when this demon whirled, her tiny heel slamming into my ribs like a hammer, and nothing happened to deflect it, it came as a surprise.

The impact knocked me back against the wall. I stumbled, my palms against the rough stucco, then slipped and landed on the floor. The left side of my chest felt like broken glass in a sack. Breathing was like being stabbed. She said something in a slushy voice too deep for her small body and pulled back her foot to stomp me like a bug. Tamblen—the big one—tackled her like a linebacker. She didn't fall, but she needed both feet to keep her balance. I scrambled up, one hand pressed to my abused ribs. I couldn't tell if it was the pain or the unearthly, stinking wind, but something roared in my ears. I staggered toward the double doors. Live-wire fear mixed with a sense of outraged betrayal.

I was supposed to be *safe*. I was supposed to be the one kicking ass. I got to the door, my weight more than my strength pushing the release bar. Behind me, Tamblen cried out. The door opened, and the wind spilled out into the world, hurricane strong.

I'd caught glimpses of the courtyard through

the windows. I half fell out into it now. Once upon a time, it might have been a nice little garden for a couple of dozen monks or a place to pray during the bright spring days. In winter, it was brown, dusty earth and dirty, ice-glazed snow. A lone tree stood near the center, branches rising up into the pale sky like a shriek. I pressed my fist into my ribs like I was holding myself closed. The girl—the thing inside of the girl—boiled out past me. I slipped, landing hard on one knee.

She floated in the air, the bare tree behind her writhing in the unnatural wind. Her face glowed with delight and cruelty. She opened her mouth wider than she should have been able to, and I saw her tongue twisting black against the brightness in her throat. She raised her hands, and my ears popped as the air pressure dropped. The sky above me started to change, wisps of cloud twisting in and out of existence like snakes. It sounded like a freight train, and I didn't think I'd make it off the tracks in time.

Please, I thought, pushing the word in toward the thing—magic, rider, whatever—that had always defended me before. Please, now would be a good time.

Father Chapin stepped past me. His Bible was raised in his hand, and he was shouting something in Latin. The black cloth of his pants fluttered against his ankles like a flag in a storm. Close-cut white hair danced on his scalp. Ex struggled by, his arms spread wide against the wind. He matched Chapin syllable for syllable, and for a moment the demonic wind seemed to stutter and fail.

I rose to my feet. The knee of my pants was torn out where I'd landed, and blood was slicking my shin. My ribs ached and my overcoat flapped around me like a cape. The smell of overheated metal assaulted me again, pressing in at my nose and mouth, and I felt the uncanny shifting of the world as the boundaries between reality and Next Door got thinner. I took a step backward. Miguel ran up to Father Chapin's side along with another priest I hadn't seen before, thick-featured and dark-skinned. Tomás, I figured. The double doors leading back inside slammed open and closed and then shattered into splinters and bent metal. A pair of black cellar doors bucked against their chain, like something was trying to rise up out of the earth beneath them.

"Daughter of Satan!" Chapin howled, the first English words I heard from him since the fight started. "You are bound! By the will of God, I bind you! By the will of God—"

The girl screamed, slicing her hand through the air. The gust felt like being punched, and the air was colder than winter. High above us, a branch as long as a spear broke off the tree and whirled down through the air toward us.

Toward Ex.

I tried to scream, tried to warn him. But I couldn't because, with an almost physical click, I wasn't in control of my own body.

Two inhumanly fast, loping strides and I was at his side. The branch was shooting down toward us, but it and everything else seemed to slow. When I put my hand on Ex's shoulder, I felt the heat of his skin and something more too. An echo of his mind, like a voice heard from the far end of a tunnel. His fear and his joy and a deep riptide of longing. His knees were bent against the wind, and I put one foot on his thigh, boosted myself up, twisting to put my other knee on his shoulder. I caught the branch in both hands. The weight bore us both down, but my legs went straight before I touched ground.

I stood in the tempest, Ex sprawled out beneath me. My coat tugged at my shoulders, pulled back almost straight by the wind. The branch was longer than a baseball bat, cold and rough and viciously sharp where it had torn free. I held it in both hands like a staff. The girl floating in the air stared at me, dark lips pulled back in square-gape rage. The sores and wounds on her body oozed black and yellow, pulsing with something like glee. I wanted to step back, but my body ignored me. The wind demon screamed. The power behind the attack was more than physical: raw magic pressed against me. I felt the answering force draw itself up my spine, filling me with a calm that bordered on serenity. I pressed it out from me, expanding it in a sphere that grew from my core. Above me, the tree still whipped and shuddered. The priests staggered under the storm, Bibles fluttering, voices lost in the roar. My coat hung softly at my back.

"Stop this," I said.

The words were no more than conversational, but they carried over the pandemonium. The thing in the girl screamed again, but the attack seemed weak now. Futile. I walked toward her, and the dark, inhuman eyes widened with fear. Too late, it turned and tried to fly away. My body didn't move, but something else did, reaching up for her, pulling her back down to me. The thing's wail was all venom and despair. I dropped the branch and put my hands around her ankles, drawing her to the ground. As soon as her feet touched the dust, she collapsed down, gravity regaining its control. The thing was still in her, and it beat and kicked against me. There was power in the blows, but I didn't feel any pain.

"It's over," my voice said. "You should go."

Her hand shot out toward me, clawed and cat fast. I shifted out of the way, and she spat black bile on my shirt. I gripped the girl across the forehead like her skull was a basketball. The conscious part of me trapped just behind my eyes cringed, expecting something terrible and violent to happen. Instead, my body pulsed once, heat and dryness and solitude filling me, filling my arm, my hand, flowing into the little girl's body. I felt the rider leave her like a joint popping back into place. Painful, a little disturbing, but also now made right.

The world clicked back to normal. The cold air rushed in. I was holding a little girl. Her hair felt soft and hot against my hand. The wounds and sores still marked her, but they were the red and pink of abused flesh now. Her eyes were tea-with-milk brown, and when she opened her mouth, no unearthly light spilled out. The only smell in the air was dust and pine sap. The smell of overheated metal was gone.

"Hey," I said. *I* said. Not something else. I was in control of my body again. "I'm Jayné. What's your name?"

"Dolores?"

I pulled off my coat. I'd been sweating, and the cold against my stained and soaking shirt felt like dipping into ice water. I ignored it. I hung the dark wool over her shoulders. She was weeping. No sobs, no running nose, just tears falling down her cheeks and splashing by her toes. Toes that were starting to turn mottled and dark from the chill. I scooped her up in my arms, my ribs protesting sharply.

"There was a bad ghost," Dolores said. "It smelled bad. It tried to get inside me."

"I know it did," I said. "Now come in where it's warm. I'll make you some tea, okay?"

The priests watched me as I walked back inside: Tomás and Miguel leaning on each other like soldiers struggling back from battle; Tamblen leaning in the doorway with blood on his lips; Ex rising from where I'd pushed him down in the dirt; Carsey with his mouth in a smile that was as thoughtful as it was amused.

And Chapin, flat-eyed and empty. I stopped in front of him, the girl hugged close to my chest. I was starting to shiver and my earlobes hurt. He looked away. I took the girl inside.

UNFORTUNATE GOATEE'S name was Alexander. Ex rode with him and Chapin in the big, beat-up Yukon all the way back to the hospital in Taos. I followed along in Ex's rented sports car. The others stayed back at camp, tending their wounds, fixing the broken doors, soothing Dolores with hot soup, and, I hoped, calling her mother to come take her home now that the worst was over. The good guys had won, demon driven out, like that. Go us.

I cranked up the music, singing along to the songs I knew by heart, even when I didn't know the languages they were sung in. I was starting to feel the effects of the fight. When I got ready for bed that night, I'd have a bumper crop of new bruises. I was pretty sure the wind demon's initial strike had cracked a rib, but I wouldn't be positive until morning. If I could turn to the left, I'd be fine. If not . . . well, it wouldn't be the first time I'd broken a rib. I pretty much knew the routine.

The drive seemed shorter going back into town. Maybe it was just the sense of going back to someplace known. The steering wheel buzzed against my hands, the music celebrated and mourned. Pine trees gave way to smaller, twisted piñons. The dead grass at the side of the road lay buried in drifts of melted and refrozen snow. I grinned at the landscape—distant canyon, snow-clad mountains, pale sun in endless blue sky.

The fight had released something in me. Ever since the night in London when I'd realized that my so-called magical protections might be significantly creepier than I'd thought, I'd been waiting for the thing in my body to take over. I'd been second-guessing every move that I made—had I really reached for the salt, or had it been something else controlling my hand? I'd thought that when it happened, if it happened, it would be the creepiest thing ever. Not the event itself, since I'd been through that before plenty of times, but what it meant. Now that it had happened, I was all relief and rib pain.

When we got near Taos proper, my cell phone

chirped. When we stopped at a traffic light, I checked the log. Chogyi Jake had called again, twice, and left voice mail both times. I'd listen later, when I wasn't driving. I turned right, following the Yukon through the press of ski-racked SUVs and expensive trucks.

At the hospital, three men in white uniforms and a woman in green scrubs transferred Alexander onto a gurney. The long, deep cut wasn't bleeding so much as starting to weep a little blood, but the wounded priest was able to move his arm a little and he was trying to speak. I took those as good signs. Chapin stood next to a doctor whose face made me think of India even though her accent was pure Boston. The sun was already edging down toward the western horizon, pulling our shadows out long and reddish. It wasn't quite four o'clock yet. The night was going to be long.

Once Alexander got rushed inside, Ex pulled himself back into the Yukon and drove it off toward the parking spaces. Chapin and the doctor exchanged a few last words, and the doctor went back inside. Chapin huddled down in his clothes. He looked older than he had before, his skin gray, his eyes bloodshot where they weren't bloody. And there was something else. It was in the way he held his shoulders and the timbre of his voice. Anger maybe. Or fear.

"I will stay here," Chapin said. "Until we are sure

he is stable. Xavier says the two of you will find rooms in the city. We will . . . regroup, yes? Once we have had opportunity to finish here, we will regroup."

"All right," I said.

We stood silently. In the distance, I heard the Yukon's door crash open and closed, and then the almost subliminal sound of Ex getting in the sports car. An old man in a bright green parka walked out of the ER, speaking Spanish into a cell phone. Neither Chapin nor I moved. I figured that was as close as I was going to get to permission to speak.

"So this stuff I've been seeing? The unnatural fighting and weird powers? I'm thinking it's not just a psychological issue," I said.

"I see your point," he said.

"So we can skip the shrink?"

"We can."

chapter five

I never went skiing when I was a kid. Other kids in school did, but only the rich ones. They'd come back from vacation talking about exotic places like Lake Tahoe and Park City. A couple of kids from church—Jacob and Stacey Corman, putting too fine a point on it—always made sure to have a little sunburn when they came back to school after Christmas break. Snowburn, they called it. They'd show off their pinked skin like peacock feathers until their mother got angry, started lecturing about the sin of pride, and threatened never to take them again.

Taos was apparently just the sort of place the

Cormans went to. Finding a place to stay was harder than I'd expected, and Christmas vacation was exactly the problem. A few nights were easy. An open-ended stay-until-whenever started running up against previous bookings pretty fast. Jacob and Stacey were making my world less pleasant one more time. Ex and I sat in the Mercedes outside the hospital, the engine purring away just to keep the heater going, while I made a series of increasingly frustrating calls. In the end, I gave up and called my lawyer's private line. She put me on hold for ten minutes and came back with an address halfway up to the ski valley where I now had a rental condo waiting. When she asked if I needed anything else, I almost laughed. I fed the address into the GPS.

"You want to drive?" Ex asked.

"Really?" I said.

He nodded.

"Are you okay? Did you get hurt?"

"I've had better days," he said, and handed me the key.

We traded places and headed out. Going up the mountain was also more of an adventure than I'd expected. The road was narrow, twisting through the high mountains. It had been plowed and salted, but the ice and snow still clung to the blacktop in places. The falling-rock signs were reinforced by the occasional basketball-sized boulder at the roadside. I turned the heater up to full blast and thumbed on the heating pads hidden in the seats. Ex laid back in the dark leather of the passenger's seat, eyes closed. He looked pale, and I thought he might be sleeping except that when I hit a bump or rough patch, he hissed a little under his breath.

At about nine thousand feet above sea level, there was a turnoff marked by a tiny, unreadable wooden sign. I waited for three sets of SUV headlights and one pickup truck to pass, then made the left turn and headed up the hill. The road twisted and turned among the high, snow-laden pine trees. I could feel the ice in the way the tires struggled to keep their grip. I more than half thought the last little rise was going to strand me or send me backward, but the little car made it. I pulled up to Spirit House Condominiums. It was five closely built structures huddling close enough to make good use of the limited space but with the distance to leave each one private. There were lights on in four of them. The fifth was dark, the windows looking out at the night like blind eyes.

I pulled into the carport, gravel and snow crunching under the wheels. Ex looked ragged enough that I left him in the car while I scouted the place. The wind had been cold before. Here, it was frigid. I left the headlights on while I went out, exploring the front entrance. It had a little alcove, a thick wooden archway, and a bench where people could put on or take off complicated footware. The door was locked, but a key hung from the knob by a thick rubber band. I tried it. It worked. Low security.

Inside, the lights were soft orange-gold glows, barely enough to cast shadows. A little mood-rich, but they worked. Small kitchen, check. Recessed conversation pit by gas fireplace, check. Through the picture window in the back, I could see the dark lump that was probably a hot-tub cover. A thin stairway led to the second floor and more bedrooms. In a pinch, the place would probably have slept eight. It was plenty for us.

When I came back out, Ex was pulling himself out of the car, stiff and awkward. He walked in toward the house, silhouetted by the headlights so that I didn't see how bad he looked until he was almost to me.

"Hey. What's the matter?"

"Might need a little help," he said.

When I put my arm around him, his back was wet. When I looked at my fingers, I saw blood.

"What the *hell*?"

"It's okay," he said. "Just get me inside."

At the little kitchen, I leaned him against the counter and ran back out to shut off the headlights. When I returned, he'd pulled off his shirt. Two deep gouges scored his back, one beginning at the shoulder and digging down to the middle of his shoulder blade, the other starting at the middle of his spine and running down over his kidney. A thin red smear mottled his skin, dark and dried at the edges, fresh and bright where blood still leaked from the wounds.

"Jesus!" I said, shutting the door behind me. "What happened?"

He chuckled, then bent over in pain, resting his weight on the kitchen counter.

"Well, there was this wind demon," he said, smiling through the pain. "We had a little fight."

"You're hurt."

"Little bit. Yeah."

"Why didn't you say something when I asked?"

"Like what? 'Ouch'? That would have helped."

I drew him closer to the sink. The hot water ran icy cold a few seconds before it went warm. I found an old dish towel in a drawer. Water and blood mixed, sheeting down Ex's side. Under the mess, the skin around the wounds was red and angry. When I started cleaning out the actual gouges, he winced.

It felt strange, touching him. We'd been very careful over the weeks together to keep our physical contact down to taps on the shoulder or steadying hands. I was washing him now, my palm against his side, my fingers feeling the ridges and valleys of his rib cage. I pressed the wet cloth against him and watched him respond to it. He wasn't wincing now. Even with the wounds to excuse me, it felt dangerous and sweet, and I found myself being gentler and taking longer than I probably needed to.

"You're going to need stitches," I said. "I can't believe you, Ex. We were just at a hospital. I mean, we were right *there*."

"It would have attracted too much attention," Ex said. "Father Chapin and I agreed that it would be better to keep outside involvement to a minimum. And I don't need stitches."

"Yeah, well, he didn't see your back."

"He did."

I stopped dabbing, but I didn't take my hand away. Ex looked over his shoulder at me. His white-blond hair had blood in it, and his eyes held as much sorrow as exhaustion. I shifted my hand between his shoulder blades, and he looked away. I went back to cleaning up. When I'd done as much as I could, I left him there and went upstairs. There were towels in the two bathrooms, and I used them to improvise bandages.

We moved him to the couch where he could lie on his belly. Between the blood and the water, his pants were sopping, and I put a blanket over him so that he could pull them off without compromising his modesty. He pushed his clothes out from under it and collapsed forward with a sigh. I turned up the thermostat by the stairway, and the gas fire grate hissed to life, orange flames licking the ceramic logs.

"I can call in a doctor," I said. "Seriously, I'll call my lawyer, and she'll find someone."

"And do what?" he asked. "It's all right. I've had my tetanus shots. I'm clotting up. There's nothing to do but wait. What about you? Are you feeling all right?"

I tried turning. The pain was more a deep ache than a sharp stab.

"Bruised," I said. "Not broken, I don't think."

"What about your knee?"

I looked down. I'd forgotten ripping my jeans there, but my kneecap peeked out into the room, grimy with dirt and blood of my own.

"Way better than your back," I said, sitting on the floor. The warmth of the fire pushed gently against my neck.

"Well," Ex said through his smile, "that's a good minimum, I guess."

We were silent for a moment, the only sound the muttering of the flames and the quiet ticking of a clock. Ex put his head down on his arms, his face toward me. He looked tired and distant. His hair was unbound, spilling across his face, softening him. Here I was, alone in a secluded mountain cabin with a man wearing a blanket. I watched the firelight flicker on his skin. It should have felt weird. It didn't.

I knew Ex had a thing about me. Crush, call it. Or attraction or unrequited love. Pick a card. I'd even felt it once when we were doing a ritual that meant blending my mind and his. And my just-barely-ex-boyfriend Aubrey, and his ex-wife and still-significant Kim. We'd been in a lot of trouble at the time, and so all our attention had really been on the battle at hand. Looking back on it from here, it had been intimate in a way that almost nothing else in my life had been. I'd been able to feel Aubrey's confusion from the inside, like it was mine. Kim's desperation and hope. I'd been able to feel them become aware of me. But there hadn't been words. I'd felt Ex's desire and guilt and determination, roaring like a furnace, but not the facts and details of the life that created them.

He sighed. His eyes closed. He didn't look like the passions I'd felt were in him. Even his usual almost-disapproving intelligence was gone right now. I wanted to take his hand, but I wasn't sure what I'd want after that, so I didn't.

"It didn't want to come out this time, did it," Ex said. When I didn't answer, he opened his eyes again, pinning me with them. "When the wind demon attacked you, the rider didn't want to come out, did it?"

"No," I said. "I guess not."

Ex nodded, his cheek brushing against the cushion.

"It's aware, then," he said. "Intelligent. It knew that manifesting would give the game away. More evidence that it's not just spells and cantrips that Eric put on you. They wouldn't have any reason to keep hidden. Or the intelligence to know when they should."

I hugged my knees to my chest. Something in my belly felt cold.

"Did you and Chapin talk about that too?" I asked.

"Yes."

"Great."

"It's what we came here for. To talk about it. He agrees that whatever it is, it's powerful. We'd knocked the edge off the wind demon, but the way you took it out was . . ." He shook his head without lifting it off his arms. "That wasn't small stuff."

"Did he have any idea why we couldn't find anything before?"

"A few thoughts," Ex said. "There are some kinds of riders that survive by stealth. They can live in someone for years and never show any sign, even when you know that you're looking for something. This could be a particularly effective one of those."

"Or?"

"Or the rider may be digging in deeper. Trying to get far enough inside you that we can't see it to pull it out. Or it may be young. Or it may be that the thing where you're hard to see with magic extends to the rider. Or comes from it."

"And no way to guess which one we're looking at."

"Well, there are some other things that point toward it being young."

"Really?" I said, wanting to know and not wanting to know.

"The fact that we're here at all," Ex said. "The rider can take complete control of you. We know that. But it wasn't able to keep us from coming here. That means your will still trumps it most of the time. With a mature rider, you'll usually see it running things all the time. That yours is . . . I don't know. Intermittent? That makes it seem like it's not full-grown."

The warm feelings I'd had before were fading fast, and the hiss of the gas flame started to bother me. Anxiety and impatience nibbled at my skin, and I shifted to sit farther from the fireplace. Ex didn't notice, or if he did, he didn't care.

"Chapin's working hypothesis is that it can't take over for a very long time. A few minutes here and there. And usually in extremis. If you're not threatened somehow, it can't take the reins. Influence you, maybe. Steer you. But not the all-out control like we saw today."

"So as it gets older, it gets more powerful and I get . . . what? Slowly eaten?"

"Maybe. Or maybe it's more like a cocoon. The control dynamic stays right about where it is until the rider's fully formed. Then it breaks out of the chrysalis, and the rules change all at once."

The cold feeling in my gut got worse. I'd had the sense of rider and magic before, and this wasn't it. It was old-school, please-Jesus-get-it-off-of-me fear. I had to change the subject, and I had to do it now.

"So, *Chewy*?" I said, forcing a grin. "What's that?"

Ex chuckled. When he sat up, he winced, but he didn't lie back down.

"Father Ignatius. He was my unofficial mentor when I was a novice. He had this long beard, and when I started my regency with Father Chapin, I tried to grow one too. It didn't go well. One morning, Carsey said it made me look like a Wookiee. I was clean-shaven by afternoon, but it stuck."

His smile was gentle—chagrined and embarrassed, but gentle.

"What did Father Ignatius think of it?" I asked.

"Oh, he never saw it. There are a couple of years of study between your novitiate and regency. The last time I saw him was when I took first vows. I'd have been . . . what? Nineteen years old?"

"What kinds of vows do they make you take at nineteen?"

"The usual ones," Ex said, his voice exhausted and melancholy. "Poverty, chastity, obedience. At the time I thought it was better that way. Disassociate myself from sin before I'd ever experienced it. It's hard to miss a place you've never been. Worked great in theory."

"But in practice, not so much," I said.

"Well, I made it through my first studies and regency," Ex said.

"You keep saying *regency*. Do you have to dress up in a double-breasted tailcoat and an ascot or something?"

"Sorry. It's a Jesuit thing where we were supposed to really commit to apostolic work. Lasts three years."

"You went three years with Chapin?"

"And Tamblen and Carsey. Miguel came in my second year. Tomás finished his regency the year before I came in, and then went on mission. He took his final vows in Japan and came back just before I left, so he was sort of before and after. The new kid. Alexander? I didn't meet him until today."

"Wonder what Carsey calls him," I said. "I mean, I didn't see your attempt, but when it comes to undignified facial hair, Alexander pretty much takes it walking."

"It did look kind of . . . *pubic*, didn't it?"

"Yeah, that's exactly it," I said. "So why'd you do it?"

"Leave them, you mean?"

"That too, I guess. But I meant why did you go in the first place? When I was nineteen, I was about trying to get out from under the church. Anything secular was cool. Why take vows?"

Ex breathed in deeply, held the air inside himself, and then let it seep back out, but it wasn't exactly a sigh. It seemed more like he was steeling himself for something more painful than the wounds on his back.

"I was wondering when you were going to ask me that," Ex said. "God called me."

"Really?"

"Yes. Really."

I tried not to smile or roll my eyes.

"He stopped by the bedroom one night after prayers? I mean, how does that happen?"

Ex shrugged.

"It's different for everyone. When I was ten years old, I wanted to be a soccer star. Didn't have the build for football. That was my brother's thing, anyway. He was on the varsity team at the high school, and he'd have ground me into the turf if I'd tried to horn in on his territory. I went to youth soccer, I watched all the games I could find. I had an old poster of Pelé in my room. And then one morning I got up, and I knew I was supposed to be a priest. I took down the poster, and that was that."

"You just *knew*?"

"I did. I didn't tell my father about it for a few years, but by the time I did, he'd already figured out what I was up to. He didn't like it. Always suspected I was playing some kind of angle. The idea that I'd actually been called just didn't seem plausible to him. But I finished high school a little early, I had good grades, and I'd gotten to know all the priests at church. When I applied to become a novice, it was easy. I taught catechism. I worked with the poor and the homeless. I studied. It was more like being home than being home ever was. When the time came for vows, I didn't hesitate. I was . . . certain. God called me. I answered. Everything was just the way it was supposed to be. I felt blessed."

"Never looked back, then?"

"Not then. During first studies, I found myself drawn to the rites of exorcism. I read about possession, the way the soul can be corrupted. There's a special program for people with a talent for that kind of ministry, and I fought to get into it. I was good. Had a talent for it like no one had seen in a generation. When Father Chapin agreed to take me on, I knew that this had been the plan all along. God had made me to fight the devil and save the innocent, and He'd put me in place so that I could do it.

"I was a weapon in His hand. Tamblen and Miguel and Carsey. Father Chapin. I was going to spend my life with them. They were more than family. They were the other guys in my foxhole. And we saved people. We really did."

Ex shifted his weight and winced. A dark spot was blooming on the towel draping his shoulder where he was bleeding through the bandage. The blanket pooled in his lap, and one bare leg shifted out toward the fire. His pale skin, the angle of his thigh, the distant expression, all conspired to make him seem like a sculpture worked out of marble. Something hard and beautiful and cold.

"And then?" I said.

"And then," he echoed, like he was agreeing with me. "And then we lost one. Badly."

"Isabel?"

His eyes went a little wider, but he nodded.

"The first guy . . . Um. Miguel? He mentioned the name when we got here," I said. "That's all."

"Yes, Isabel."

"You want to tell me about it, or would that be too weird."

"She came to us for help, and I betrayed her trust. I broke my vow to God."

The fireplace hissed.

"You slept with her," I said.

"I did. And because I lost perspective, we lost her."

"I'm sorry," I said, and he shook his head, refusing even that weak comfort.

"It's different this time," he said. "This time, we'll win."

chapter six

When a little before midnight I got to bed, I was asleep almost before my eyes closed. My consciousness fell away like shrugging off a jacket, and I slept through to morning without a single nightmare. I woke up with sunlight struggling in past wooden shutters and only a vague sense of where I was. With all the travel I'd done in the past year and a half, I'd built up a strategy of sorts for waking up in unfamiliar beds. First thing was not to get uptight, this happened all the time. Memory always wandered back eventually. The second was to find coffee.

The upstairs floor was scarred hardwood, and cold against my feet. I dug my bathrobe out of my suitcase, huddled into it, and went down the stairs. Arriving in the dark, I hadn't understood the way the snow amplified light. The sun was hardly visible over the steep, pine-crowded mountains, but it was already bright as noon. I cranked up the thermostat, looked unsuccessfully through the cupboards and refrigerator for anything resembling food, and went back upstairs to raid the emergency supply of coffee from my leather backpack.

The door to the second bedroom stood open a few inches. Ex's snores stumbled out on the air, as disoriented and tentative as I was. I paused in the hallway. His bed sat across the room, against the outside wall. Ex was curled around a pillow, his back to me. I watched for a few seconds as his rib cage rose and fell. The wound on his shoulder had bled a little more in the night, a smudge like a shadow across his skin. Somewhere in the crappy filing cabinet of my memory, a woman said something about falling into bed with a man just because they were alone in a cabin together, that it was the sort of thing men and women do. I wondered if that was true.

I'd lived with my family until I'd left home, and then on campus, and then on the road with Ex and Chogyi Jake. And Aubrey. I wasn't a virgin, and even before I'd passed that supremely anticlimactic milestone, I'd had a pretty graphic understanding of how tab A fit into slot B.

It didn't mean I knew what men and women do together. Not really.

Anyone who'd grown up with any actual experience—even just someone to talk to about it—would have known better than I did. Maybe after you spend a few weeks alone with a man, after you've washed the blood off his back, after he's sat up until dawn with you waiting for the nightmares to fade, something just happens. No one's responsible, and no one's surprised. Was that how it was supposed to be? If I went to him now, slid into bed beside him, would he roll over and smile at me? It wasn't the first time I'd wondered what his lips would taste like. Or what it would be like to slake the longing I'd already felt burning in his mind.

Was I falling for him? Maybe. Or maybe I just wanted to be held, and he was there. I was pretty sure if I pushed open the door and went to him, he wouldn't turn me away. Just knowing that made it more tempting.

Ex shifted, and the movement sent a shock of panic through me. I walked down the rest of the hall as fast as I could on cat toes, my heart racing. I dug the little foil bag of ground coffee out of my bag and went back downstairs. I didn't glance at Ex's door as I passed, but I felt a little twinge of shame at wanting to.

An old plastic drip coffeemaker lurked in one of the lower cupboards, but without a filter. I banged around for a couple of minutes before I uncovered a French press still in the washing machine and a saucepan to heat up some water. When I pushed my hair back from my face, it occurred to me that I hadn't made it all the way into the shower in a couple of days. I'd need to before we went back down the mountain.

On the countertop, my cell phone chirped its little you-missed-something notice. The number was Chogyi's, of course. I'd forgotten to call him back or even listen to his messages. The water started to bubble, rocking the pan on its burner. I picked up the phone, thumbed the call return, and started pouring dry coffee into the French press. It was ground too fine. The coffee was going to be muddy, but it was better than none at all. The phone connection clicked.

"Hey," I said, apology in my voice, "sorry that I—"

"Jayné," Aubrey said. He leaned into the syllables, rushing to say my name so that he wouldn't hear anything that wasn't meant for him. "Hey. He's not here. Chogyi Jake. He went to grab some fresh eggs, and he left his phone."

I felt a reflexive shock of guilt, as if by thinking about Ex I was somehow being unfaithful to Aubrey. Like by answering the phone, he'd caught me at something illicit.

"Oh, right," I said, and nodded even though no

one could see me. "Yeah, okay. He left a message for me, so I was just calling him back."

"I know he was wanting to talk with you. Check in."

"Well, everything's fine," I said.

It was one of those pauses. I picked up the pan of water, focusing on pouring the boiling water into the press. In the glass, black coffee and pale foam mixed and settled. I could feel the pressure building to say something. This was Aubrey. This was the guy I'd been sleeping with for months. He was the guy I'd called for help when things first got weird in Denver. I could tell him anything. I could *trust* him with anything.

He was also the guy who I'd broken up with so he could be with his wife. Ex-wife.

"Everything's fine," I said again. "Everything copacetic over there?"

"Things are going all right," he said. "We're all a little worried about you, though."

Drop it, Aubrey, I thought.

"Nothing to worry about," I said. "Have Chogyi Jake give me a call when he gets back in, okay? And tell Kim hey for me."

"Okay," Aubrey said. I could hear the cool come into his voice. The distance. My chest felt as if someone had hit me right on the sternum. Maybe with a hammer. I fit the top of the press into place and pushed down, the pressure against the palm of my hand slow and steady as the plunger fell.

"Talk to you soon?" I said, falsely cheerful.

"Sure. Anytime."

I dropped the connection before he could. The stairs creaked as Ex walked down them, his steps painful and slow. The coffee smelled a little strong and I didn't even have sugar to cut it.

"You didn't tell him," Ex said.

"It was Aubrey. He answered the phone."

"Ah."

His clothes from yesterday were ruined, but he'd had an extra set in his bag. I was going to have to figure out if this place had a laundry, or if the life of an international demon hunter was about to involve washing my underwear in the sink. I supposed I could call my lawyer, have her arrange a personal shopper to bring me everything I wanted wrapped up in gold lamé. That was supposed to be the charm of too much money, wasn't it? Never having to worry about anything.

Ex touched my hand, and I looked up. I hadn't noticed him coming across to me. I started to pull away, hesitated, and then went ahead and drew back my hand.

"No food in the place," I said. "This was the best I could do for coffee."

"It's great."

"It's kind of crap."

"It's enough."

He poured himself a cup and then one for me, and we stood for a minute in the chill of the cabin, drinking bitter, black coffee. A truck passed unseen on the highway, the rumble distant and softened by the snow and pine boughs.

"We can pick up some donuts on the way through Taos," Ex said.

"Maybe some real coffee," I said.

He smiled.

"Maybe that," he said. "Go hit the showers. I'll get the car defrosted."

"About the others? Aubrey. Chogyi Jake. I just don't want them to get hurt," I said. And it was true, as far as it went.

He nodded, sighed, and drank off the rest of his cup in a swallow.

"I don't either," he said.

Twenty minutes later, my hair still damp, we were heading back down the mountain. Forty minutes after that, we were stocked on cake donuts dipped in powdered sugar. By noon, we were back in San Esteban, parking behind the adobe walls where demons had fought less than a day before.

The town was busier now. An ancient Volvo station wagon scraped down the street, a woman who could have been anywhere between sixty and eighty behind the wheel. Three teenage boys lounged on the street, talking among themselves, not making eye contact, and pretending to be immune to the cold. Ranchero music rolled out of one of the Quonset huts at the far side of town. The signs of actual life left the place seeming a little less eerie. The crows were there, eyeing me from the bare cottonwoods like they remembered me and weren't entirely pleased I was back.

The little cutout where we'd parked before was full. In addition to the sedan and the Yukon, two cars with matching pro-life bumper stickers, and one with a heart-and-cross Marriage Encounter decal peeling in the window. The other had a vanity license plate that said GODSWRK. That was one way to keep from getting rear-ended. Ex parked across the street, and we got out. The air smelled of burning wood. I stopped and looked both ways before I crossed the street, only realizing how ridiculous it was after I'd already done it.

The front door swung open as we came close to it. Tamblen haunted in the doorway, nodding to each of us and stepping back into shadow. Voices speaking quickly in Spanish came softly from the back of the building.

"Is he here?" Ex asked as Tamblen closed the door behind us.

"An hour ago," Tamblen said. "He's with the girl's family."

"How's Alexander doing?" I asked, keeping my voice low.

"Stable," Tamblen said. "Not released yet. They

don't know what they're looking at, so they're being cautious."

"That's probably wise," Ex said.

"You?" Tamblen asked. It was clear from his posture that he wasn't talking to me. "Doing all right?"

"Bloodied but unbowed," Ex said, and Tamblen hitched up a smile.

"We brought donuts," I said.

We walked through the rooms again. They seemed smaller than the day before, the windows narrower, the light that glowed off the pale stucco dimmer. The web of cracks was going to take a lot of work to cover over, and it hadn't happened yet. In the kitchen, Carsey was sitting on the couch with a laptop computer, tapping quietly. The sound of Spanish flowed in from the chapel. Even without knowing the language, I could pick Chapin's voice out of the group. A woman laughed as I set the box of donuts on the little kitchen table.

"Welcome back to Chapel Perilous," Carsey said with a wave. "Are those *all* sugar? Really, Chewy, what did chocolate ever do to you?"

I noticed he was keeping his voice low too. I wasn't sure what it was about the meeting in the next room that commanded a kind of respect. It was in the air, though. The closest thing I could compare it to was being quiet in our rooms while Dad had some of the more respected men from church in the living room. Everything that wasn't the main event became peripheral. I edged down through the rooms until, pausing half in the doorway, I found them.

They were in the room just before the black-floored ritual space. Three women, all with black hair and deep-gold skin and the same squarish nose, sat at a table across from the priests. The oldest of the women was probably sixty, streaks of white at her temples. The youngest was hardly older than Dolores. And also Dolores, sitting at the foot of the table with her hands in her lap. Father Chapin's back was to me, and Tomás and Miguel were at his sides. Everyone seemed to be talking at once, like the end of a particularly successful dinner party. The only one who seemed out of place in the gaiety was Dolores. I edged in a little more, trying to catch her eye. When I did, she waved at me, a small motion and with a weight of desolation in her eyes I didn't understand.

"Don't fuss," the older girl said, slapping at Dolores's arm. It was a big-sister move, and I recognized it because I'd done it. Dolores's gaze went down again, and I sloped back toward the couch and Carsey and Ex. Tamblen was halfway through one of the donuts, sugar spilling down his black front like stars.

"The older sister too?" Ex was saying.

"We thought she was the center of it. The one who was opening other people to demons," Carsey said. "We went to confront Soledad, and she was possessed, but only by one of the spawn."

"Wait," I said. "Dolores's sister was taken too?"

"Soledad and Dolores and a dozen others," Tamblen said. "The beast in Dolores was the oldest of them. The most powerful one. All the others were its children."

"Ah," I said. "That'd be an awkward Mother's Day."

"Victories for the forces of darkness always annoy, don't they?" Carsey asked with a lightness that seemed barbed. "Well, one disaster avoided. Full speed on to the next."

The tone of the voices next door changed. I found I could follow the words closely enough to know they'd moved from whatever the first conversation had been about into farewells, protestations of thanks, and modest denials. I moved toward them. I wanted to see Dolores again, and I also didn't. On the one hand, I liked her and I felt like we'd been through something important to both of us. On the other, she was well now, and I wasn't. Knowing the shame was unjustified only made it sharper, and I covered it up by eating a donut.

The four women passed through the room, escorted by Miguel and Tomás. They nodded to the men but pointedly didn't notice me. We passed in mutual anonymity, like patients at the STD clinic. I laughed at the thought, then swallowed it. Not a joke I wanted to explain to Father Chapin.

And there he was. The night rested hard on him. The eye he'd bled into was an orange-pink instead of full-on bloodred. His skin had the gray, powdery look of exhaustion. His curt bow of greeting had all the certainty and energy of before, but his face couldn't quite carry it off. I hadn't known him more than a few days, and the first thought I had was *He's getting too old for this shit.*

"I'm pleased you came, young miss," he said, pouring himself a cup of coffee.

"Didn't think there'd be much question about it," I said, trying for lightness.

"There are always questions. There are sometimes answers." He offered up a strictly pro forma smile and turned to the men in the room. "Knowing what we do of the young miss, what can we say?"

In the moment's silence, I heard a car engine come to life on the street. Then another. Carsey shifted his weight, but Tomás was the one who spoke. He had a voice like honey glaze and smoke. In a different life, he'd have been Leonard Cohen.

"It cannot stop her. Or it chooses not to," he said. "If the Enemy had been able to keep her from us, she would not have come."

"Yes," Father Chapin said. "It was possible before that the demon had hoped to evade us as it did the group in Hamburg. That after we saw the beast, she could leave and return of her own will is a very good sign."

He stopped here to make eye contact with me and give what was probably supposed to be a reassuring nod.

"And if I hadn't been able to?" I said.

"Then Xavier would have brought you," Chapin said, as if it was obvious.

I looked at Ex. He wouldn't meet my gaze. He'd been waiting. Even as I helped him bleeding over the threshold, he'd been waiting to see if the thing inside me took over and grabbed the car keys or flew up into the air like a Halloween witch. I wondered if he'd really been sleeping when I'd paused by his door. There was an uncomfortable thought.

"We can also say that it likes him more than it does her," Carsey said, waving a hand at Ex. "When the demon attacked Jayné, it didn't leap to the defense. Oh, it might have if pressed, but it wasn't pressed, was it?"

"The attack it defended against was directed against me," Ex said. "I didn't see that branch coming. It would have killed me."

"And what," Father Chapin said, "do we draw from that?"

No one said anything. I finished my donut. The dry cake had sucked all the moisture out of my mouth, and my tongue felt like a desert. I looked around the room at all the men in their dark shirts, saying nothing. Father Chapin nodded once.

"Then it is a thing to hold in mind as we move

forward," he said. "A place to begin. This morning, we perform the blessings and a complete interview with the woman."

"Hey. You know I'm standing right here," I said. Chapin didn't miss a beat.

"This afternoon, we perform de Tonquedec's exercises with her. Once we have a clearer sense of the beast, I will permit a rest. If possible, I would like to force it to reveal its name by the day's end."

"Okay," I said, "when you say 'force it to reveal its name,' how exactly does that go? Because it sounds a little ominous."

"It will be in our control," Miguel said, shaking his head. "There is no danger there, though it may be unpleasant, especially if the beast has hidden itself deep within you. To bring it out by our will instead of its own may cause some discomfort."

I must not have looked reassured, because Carsey cleared his throat.

"Worse than a tummy bug, better than a sick drunk," he said. "Have you ever been sick drunk?"

"No, but I had a friend in college," I said. "Held her hair. That kind of thing."

"Well, better than that," he said with a smile. "The ugly part's not until later. That's worse than a sick drunk."

I nodded. Carsey leaned over and tapped my forearm lightly with the tips of his fingers. For the first time since Chicago, I didn't just half want

Chogyi Jake there; I'd have sacrificed a finger if he'd appeared just then. He'd have been able to tell me just how bad this was about to be and make it all seem possible. Instead, I felt like a child with everyone saying her shots wouldn't hurt. You know. Much.

"All right," I said, trying to sound braver than I felt. "Let's see what we're working with."

chapter seven

When I was growing up, there were two kinds of magic: prayer and witchcraft.

Prayer, we did in church or at the dinner table. We did it at youth group; we did it before class; we did it last thing before bed. The idea that things could be the way I wanted if I just asked hard enough, if I just *wanted* hard enough, was the bedrock of my childhood. And so when my grandmother got cancer, I prayed like my heart was on fire. I knelt by my bed for what felt like hours, hands clenched, asking God to make my Nanna better. At her funeral, the priest said that Nanna had gone to a better place and my mother nodded. I spent the rest of the service embarrassed for having been selfish when I'd prayed that she get well.

Witchcraft was something else. It was the tool of evil. Satan's hand in the world. That didn't stop a few of the kids from making up hex charms. Especially in middle school, girls would sometimes find little drawings stuffed into their lockers made up of what we thought of as occult scratching—yin-yangs, pentagrams, inverted crosses—with their names inscribed. Once a girl in my Language Arts class—Tracey McCort, I think her name was—threw such a violent fit about one that we all had to go see the school counselor.

Before I walked into my uncle Eric's secret apartment and found a desiccated corpse smoking cigarettes, cooking omelets, and cracking wise, the one consistent thing I knew about magic was this: it didn't work.

It turned out I'd been wrong about that. Chogyi Jake, Ex, and Aubrey had taught me a little about how to find my qi, the energy that drove real magic. Right now, I could use it to see through illusions or make someone follow a command, if only a simple one and only for a second. Ex could use it to change what he looked like, if you didn't look hard. Kim could damp down other magic. We could do parlor tricks.

Riders had access to much more power than any

human being. They could fly or change bodies or
toss cars around with their hands. Just a normal
person trying to face down a rider would need a
lot of prep work or a lot of experience or a lot of
friends. Sometimes, all three.

The ritual Chapin ran us through that afternoon—de Tonquedec's exercises—was one of those
preparatory moments. After a lunch of tuna sand-
wiches and stale potato chips, I sat on the floor at
the center of the ritual space, and the men stood
around me. My job, as Chapin explained it to me,
was to draw myself into a place just over my heart,
to retract from my body as much as I could, and
focus everything into a very small place at the center of my body. I'd stay there for about an hour,
then shift myself into the place just behind my eyes
where I went when the rider took over. And then
hang out *there* for an hour.

Two hours sitting on an old cushion while six
men stood around me muttering in Latin. I figured
it would be a little surreal and uncomfortable, a
little boring and a lot goofy. And it was, for about
the first ten minutes.

After that, it was some of the hardest work I'd
ever done.

My eyes were closed, and in the darkness behind
them, I tried to hold myself together. Intangible
things brushed against the tiny, compacted version
of me. I felt Ex among them, his furnace of a mind

comforting only because it was familiar. Each little contact was an echo of a foreign mind like someone in the hallway coughing.

And then, with no trigger I could fathom, I was afraid. Deeply afraid. I was trapped in a haunted house with no way out, and there was something there with me. Something that hissed like an old propane lantern and smelled like burnt cheese. My friends were going to die, and I was going to kill them, and more than anything—more than breath—I wanted not to. I just wanted not to *hurt* anyone. I felt something happening miles overhead and was disturbed to realize it was me, crying. The sensation I felt so far above me was the thickness of sorrow in my throat. I had the powerful sense that my hands were bleeding. Not my real hands, out there impossibly far away from me, but these small, invisible ones. They were bleeding because I'd used the palms like hammers, driving in the nails. I was killing him. I was killing him again.

Something in my belly moved.

Something that wasn't me.

I came up gasping. Around me, the six priests stood in pairs: Carsey and Tamblen, Tomás and Miguel, Chapin and Ex.

"Bathroom," I said. "I need the bathroom."

"You have to hold on a little longer," Ex said. "You can—"

"Let her go," Chapin said. "We've seen enough for now."

The bathroom was tiny. I could put my hands out, pressing palms against both walls at once. The light came from a tiny window, no more than four inches square, outlined in deep-blue tile. The toilet was undersized, and it ran a little. I stood until I was sure I wouldn't pass out, then slid down, my back against the wall, and cried for a while. I was shaking badly, and I felt light-headed. I briefly reconsidered vomiting, but decided against it. When I rose to my feet again, I didn't know how long I'd been in there. Five minutes or five hours both seemed equally plausible. I washed my face in the tiny, mineral-streaked sink and looked up into the mirror. In the dim, I looked older. Worn-out. My eyes were puffy and red. My hair was frizzed out like a black cloud. My skin was pallid. There were raw, rashy-looking spots at the corners of my nose.

My right hand rose up without my knowing it was going to. My fingertips touched the mirror gently, caressing the girl in the glass. I shook my head and stepped back. When I went out, the priests were sitting around the big table where Dolores and her family had been before. Their conversation went quiet as I stepped in, and Tomás stood up. Someone had old-school ideas about etiquette. Outside, the light was slanting down from the west with the red-gold glow of evening. It was probably half past four. The dark came so *early*.

"Hey," I said. "Sorry about that. Hit a rough spot."

"It is fine," Father Chapin said.

"Do we—" I started, but the question stuck in my throat. I actually had to swallow twice before I could talk again. "Do we dive back in?"

"I think that we do not," Chapin said. I felt a tension between my shoulder blades ease, and at the same time a flush of shame. I hadn't made it halfway through the first step without freaking out. I wondered how Dolores had done. My guess was better.

"Sorry," I said.

"You did fine," Ex said, and I saw Carsey and Miguel exchange a glance I couldn't parse.

"We know considerably more than we did this morning," Chapin said. "I do not believe that we have anything more to learn from de Tonquedec. Tell me, Miss Jayné, do you know the word *larva*?"

Tomás nodded toward his chair, and I sat down gratefully.

"Sure," I said. "It's like maggot, right?"

"Linnaeus took the word for this meaning, but it is an older term than the biological sciences. The word is Latin, and before it became another word for grub, it meant a specter. A spirit. And also—this is telling—a *mask*. The taxonomist wished to describe the fashion in which the form of the young insect masks its adult body, you see? And so he took a metaphor. He took the word that sorcerers and diabolists had used for centuries before. Do you see?"

"So because it's young, it's hard to tell what it's going to be when it grows up?" I said.

"Yes," Chapin said. "But more than this, it is *subtle*. It has hidden itself in you as it grows in power. From what we have observed, we know it to be very potent. But from its actions and nature, we can deduce that it is also still vulnerable. And in this we must take hope."

"It seems unlikely that it is less than the second hierarchy," Miguel said. "A prince of Dominions, perhaps."

"I'd have said a Throne," Carsey said. "The way it crawled up Chewy like a tree? And the wind demon may have been weakened, but our new visitor still swatted it down like it was a schoolgirl. I'd say it's a *gressil*. Possibly *sonnenelion*, but my first thought's *gressil*."

"No," Ex said, "Not *gressil*. I've been in her company for over a year, and she hasn't shown anything like that kind of impurity."

"Maybe not to *you*," Carsey said.

"There is no room to speculate," Chapin said, a sharpness in his voice that made Ex and Carsey both go silent. "We will know its name when the time comes. To pretend knowledge we do not have leads us astray."

"Are we sure it's bad?" I asked.

Chapin looked at me. I hadn't realized until just then that he hadn't been. His eyes were unreadable as stones. In my peripheral vision, Ex looked embarrassed.

"I mean, there are riders and there are riders, right?" I said, willing myself not to talk so fast. "Some of them are stone-cold killers. Some are . . . not so bad. This one's never tried to hurt anybody. It stepped in with the wind demon. I mean, it's probably saved my life six or seven times. Are we sure it's one of the bad ones?"

"She may have a point," Miguel said. "When the spirit has taken control from her, it hasn't acted against her."

"That we know," Tamblen said, shrugging his wide shoulders.

"A subtle beast is more dangerous than one with mere brute power," Tomás said. He sounded smug.

Chapin hadn't looked away from me. If his gaze was supposed to make me uncomfortable, it was working like gangbusters.

"That it has appeared to help you means only that you remain useful to it," he said in slow, measured syllables. "If it were a holy thing, it would have no need to hide from us. Do not hope to befriend it. Whatever it seems, in truth it is your enemy."

"Right," I said. The tears and trembling I'd

thought I'd left in the bathroom threatened to come back. "Point taken."

Chapin's smile was warm, but it didn't quite reach his eyes.

"Perhaps it would be best if you permitted us to consult," he said. "The terminology we employ can be confusing. Alarming, even. And, through no fault of your own, it is not possible to include you fully without also including the enemy."

I wiped my eyes with the back of my hand, but my voice was steady. I got up.

"All right. That's cool. I'll go get some dinner or something. You guys do your thing and let me know what's next."

"I'll come with you," Ex said. His chair scraped against the brick floor when he stood.

"I will need you here, Xavier," Chapin said. "With Alexander in the hospital, we will need you actively involved."

"It's cool," I said. "I can drive myself."

"Point of clarification," Carsey said, lifting one finger. "Are we sure it's a good idea to have her wandering about the world unchaperoned?"

"You know what? You can have me here, or you can not have me here, but I can't do both. I thought the whole point of sending me and Ex off on our own last night was to see if I'd come back. Well, I did. So forgive the language, but what exactly the fuck do you want from me, buddy?"

I was shouting. I didn't care that I was shouting. I kind of liked that I was shouting. Carsey shifted uncomfortably. Tamblen made a deep chuffing sound, his face darkening. It took a second to figure out he was laughing.

"Don't think that was the beast talking," Tamblen said. "Think that was the girl."

"Agreed," Ex said. "That was Jayné."

"She can go," Chapin said. And then, to me, "Please return to us this evening."

I got the car key out of Ex's coat pocket. It wasn't actually a key at all but a little magnetic fob that made me think of a thumb drive. When I stepped out into the twilight and closed the blue double doors behind me, the cold seemed a little better than it had in the morning. In the west, clouds glowed gold and pink and gray. In the east, the sky was almost black. The little house down the road had its television on again. The Quonset huts were closed and quiet, and the boys who'd been lounging on the street were gone. The clock in the car said it was 5:32, but it felt later. I started the engine, cranked up the heat, and leaned back into the soft leather. Part of me wanted to get on the highway and keep on driving south until I hit someplace warm. Brazil, maybe. I was almost sure the part that wanted that was me. Almost.

I didn't know where I was going, but the GPS had a menu option to find nearby restaurants. It cycled for almost a minute before the map pulled back and a half dozen red dots appeared on the face of northern New Mexico. The closest was a cluster of fast-food joints fifteen minutes away. They were at the highway, and pretty much screamed truck stop. More dots stippled the map near Taos. One, off almost by itself, was labeled O'Keefe's. I remembered Carsey saying it was good, tapped the dot, and let the car figure out how to get there.

I didn't like who I was being. Yelling at Carsey had felt good when I'd done it, but the truth was I hated being on a hair trigger. Once upon a time I'd been calmer. Less anxious all the time. Less likely to freak out.

I wanted that Jayné back, and I didn't know how to get her.

Twenty minutes later, O'Keefe's was a light in the darkness. A gravel-and-ice parking lot with a half dozen trucks in it. An old sign painted in green and gold and lit with the kind of exterior light you can get from Wal-Mart for twenty bucks. When I got out of my car, an ancient black Labrador appeared at my side, wagging and sniffing at me. The wooden stairs that rose to the front door were warped and uneven. A girl who could have been fifteen greeted me when I walked in the door and pointed toward a table at the back. The walls were wood and hung with hunting trophies and old rock posters: Rush 2112 tacked up next to a bear's stuffed head. The tables looked like they'd been gathered from estate sales, no two the same. The chairs were all random sets too, and the heat came from a potbellied stove in the middle of the room. Six men in Day-Glo yellow safety jumpsuits sat around a table next to mine, speaking Spanish. Two old men sat together across the room, leather cowboy hats hung on the backs of their chairs, and talked in low voices. Apart from the world's youngest waitress, I was the only woman there.

The menu was printed on white copy paper. I picked the steak because it was at the top. The girl brought me a Coke and a glass of water and then went away.

Sitting there, alone and not alone, I wondered whether the rider was aware of my thoughts. I didn't know if it could pick through my mind like a kid in a sandbox searching for treasure or if I was as hidden from it as it was from me. But I hoped that it couldn't. I wanted—maybe needed—something that was my own, and if it wasn't my body, all that was left was my thoughts.

Because my body wasn't mine. The fact sat there like a toad, malefic and poisonous. Something was inside me, and had been since who knew when. I couldn't get it out, not by myself.

And that was why I was gnawing at myself like a wolf caught in a trap. Father Chapin and Ex and all the others were there to help me, and so I was going to give my body over to them. I wasn't taking control. At best, I was choosing who got to control me because I was too weak to do anything for myself. I needed Ex and Chapin, and I resented them because I needed them, and above anything, I just didn't want anybody else to *know*.

The shame pulled my shoulders in, thickened my throat. All my secrets pressed down on me—I was a killer, I was the puppet of a demon, I was a stupid little girl playing at games she didn't understand. If I'd been stripped naked in public, it wouldn't have been worse than this. I felt like I was going for an abortion.

"You okay, lady?" the girl said, sliding the plate in front of me.

"I'm fine," I said, not meeting her gaze. "Thanks."

When she retreated back through the kitchen door, I picked up the knife and fork and cut joylessly through the meat in front of me. It had been cooked in red wine and black pepper and onions grilled until they were sweet, and the first bite exploded and melted and brought me suddenly back to myself. The greens on the side were squash and broccoli with butter and garlic that made them taste more like themselves.

I know this, I thought. I've had this before.

I stood, my breath fast, adrenaline speeding the blood through my veins. Three steps to the door, and I pushed through. The kitchen was small and sauna hot. The smells of garlic and meat, tomato sauce and basil, wine and cigarette smoke, were like walking backward in time.

A vampire stood at a narrow prep table, his flesh ropy and desiccated, his eyes the yellow of old ivory. The mouth was a ruin and his skeletal hands were the dark of dried meat. For a moment, we stared at each other, unmoving. When he took the cigarette from his mouth, I swear the skin creaked.

"Jayné Heller. As I live and breathe," Midian Clark said, smoke curling out from behind stained teeth. "What's the matter, kid? You look like shit."

chapter eight

"Lemme get this straight. You broke up with Captain Milquetoast, killed some poor bastard, and figured out your body's got a dual-boot operating system all in the same *week*?" he said with a sticky-sounding chuckle. "No wonder you're looking rough."

I didn't know where to start. *Aubrey isn't milquetoast* or *How do you know about dual-boot computers* or *How many cigarettes do you smoke in a day anyway?* Instead, I shrugged and leaned back on the little vinyl couchlike thing that was the closest Midian's RV had to guest seating. Over the last half hour, I'd told him everything—the thing with the guy in London, our adventure in New Orleans, the catastrophe of Grace Memorial, each bit of my last year spilling out like I was talking to my best friend.

The RV was parked out behind the restaurant, and probably had been for the last decade. The tires were gray and tiny; dead-twig weeds had lived and died where the missing hubcaps let dirt accumulate. The interior was clean and neat apart from the patina of cigarette tar that turned the white surfaces amber. The combined scents of old smoke and coffee and garlic oil made me think of my grandfather. Midian stood in the tiny galley as if the four feet between us really made it a different room. His tiny espresso machine hissed and burbled as he steamed the milk for me. He still wore the white shirts and forties-style high-waisted pants he'd had in Denver. Zombie Bogart.

"What about you?" I asked. "You're looking . . . wetter."

He grinned, ragged lips exposing teeth like old stones.

"I try."

"What happened to you? I had a plane ready for you at the airstrip. When you didn't show up, I thought the Invisible College caught up with you after all."

"Yeah, I appreciate the thought, but I figured it'd

be better if I just took off. Headed south, kept my head down, stayed off the grid. Northern New Mexico's not a bad place to vanish if you're looking to. All the locals know you don't belong, but they aren't generally talking to anybody else, so it doesn't get out far. And if you pull your weight, speak Spanish, and don't start off every conversation with an Indian by pumping their hands, making eye contact, and asking 'em to tell you how they're feeling, you can make a niche."

"Even with the looks?"

"Yeah, well. I told 'em I'm a veteran. Burned in Iraq," Midian said, then took a long drag on his cigarette, the cherry blooming red and fading to gray. "Actually, I feel kind of bad about that. But I figure passing myself off as a serviceman isn't exactly the low rung in my hierarchy of sins, y'know?"

"You mean feeding?"

"I mean feeding," he said. "I'm still trying to get my feet under me on that score. Turns out if you fast for a couple of centuries, it takes it out of you. I've been pretty much keeping to goats and rats."

"Really?"

He looked over at me.

"That was a joke, kid."

He poured the steamed milk into the espresso, the careful shaking of his hand forming a perfect rose in sepia and white on the surface. When he passed it over, the ceramic was hot against my fingers. His voice made me think of Tom Waits in the later part of his career.

"I've been trying to keep a low profile. Mostly I'm just harvesting the kinds of guys nobody misses. Some guy deals smack to middle school kids, no one really cares when he drops out of sight, you know?"

"Misdemeanor murder."

"Yeah. I love that term," he said, then turned and leaned against his counter. It creaked under his weight. His eyes flickered over me with something like sorrow.

"So you want to finish the latte and we can get this over with?"

"Get what over with?"

"I know why you're here. We don't have to dance around it. You came to kill me, and I'm not up for dying just yet. So—"

"I didn't come to *kill* you. I came for dinner. I didn't even know you were here," I said. "Besides, I wouldn't do that. You're my friend."

I had never astonished a vampire before. He crossed his arms. A gust of wind pushed against the RV, rocking it gently on its ruined springs. I felt the breath of cold through the cracked window at the back of my neck.

"Damn. You *have* got it bad. I figured we were doing that moment of camaraderie for old times' sake thing before we went all Bushido on each other," he said.

"Just wanted some coffee," I said.

"So if you weren't hunting for me, what exactly brings you to the ass end of nowhere?"

"A bunch of Ex's old priest buddies are up here. He was hoping they could scrape me clean." The words came out more bitter than I'd intended them. I took another sip of the coffee. It was rich and warm and soft. Like a coffee-flavored cloud. Midian must have seen my reaction.

"Pretty good, eh? I get the milk straight from the dairy. Makes the difference," he said. "So that bunch up in San Esteban are Ex's crew, are they? Makes sense, I guess. I knew he fell from grace right around here somewhere. Add that things have been a little rowdy since we kicked over the Invisible College's anthill. Anybody around here who's in the habit of dealing with folks like me's been doing bumper-crop business."

"Folks like us," I said.

He paused, considering.

"Yeah, you put it that way. Folks like us. What does Tofu Boy think about the whole exorcism thing?"

"Nothing," I said. "I haven't told him. Can I ask you a question? What does it feel like?"

"What does what feel like?"

"Being a rider."

He took a long breath and let it hiss out between his teeth. The body he was in had died sometime in the nineteenth century, so I had to take his breath as an editorial statement. I looked down at my hands. I had a scab across the knuckles that I didn't remember. Something from the fight against the wind demon, maybe. I couldn't keep track anymore.

"Should I not have asked that?" I said.

"No, no. It's all right. Just kind of a personal question is all. What's it feel like? Well, it feels . . . It's like putting your face underwater. Look, imagine you're by a lake or something. Nice blue water stretching out to wherever, right? Now you lean over, put your face in water, and open your eyes. Boom, there's this whole other place with fish and plants and whatever junk the kids threw off the dock last year. This whole world you weren't part of, but now you can see it. Be part of it. And everything there's amazing, you know? There's light and thoughts and sex and hunger and . . . *being*. Things *exist*. It's gorgeous."

He rubbed his ear, grinning. I'd never heard him sound excited or passionate about anything before. Maybe food, a little, but this was different.

"And so you dive in," I said.

"No, kid. You want to. Worse than anything, you want to. But the only thing I can do is push in a little. I'm like an iceberg. Some of me's in this body, sure, but most of me's in the Pleroma. I don't fit here. I don't belong," he said. Then, a moment later, "Why do you want to know?"

"Because I wondered. What if . . . What if I'm not really Jayné Heller at all? I mean I don't know how long this rider's been in me. Maybe it always was. What if the real Jayné never took a breath. Never had a thought. What if *I've* been the rider all along."

"You're spilling your coffee, kid."

I righted the cup.

"Sorry," I said.

"It's all right. But anyway, the theory doesn't wash. Who comes and kicks ass when you're not calling the shots? Who does all this weird magic shit that you can't? You're not a rider, kid, no matter how pretty it'd be to think so."

"*Pretty?*"

"Sure, that's the point, right? If you're the nasty evil boogum, then Jayné still gets to be clean. She didn't kill that guy. The exorcism comes, and you get cast into the darkness where you belong. She gets to live her life innocent and free of sin. That's what you'd be hoping for, right?"

The blush started at my neck and crawled up toward my forehead, feeling like a sunburn. It was a dumb idea, and I felt like a stupid kid for having said it.

"It was just a theory," I mumbled. "Never mind."

"Nah, I get it. You kill someone the first time, it's traumatic. And then you find out you aren't even in control of your own body? That takes a lot away from you. Makes a hell of a one-two punch. I figure you've got a right to be on the ropes."

"Thanks," I said.

"So how're you gonna get off 'em?"

The silence lasted a few seconds.

"I don't know."

"Ah, jeez. Don't start crying. Look, you had a bad run. You did your *Oh, poor me*, and that's fine. We all get those sometimes. It's just that being a victim gets to be a habit. You stay there too long, you get comfortable. Gets to where a victim is who you are. So game-plan it. Put on your big-girl panties and tell me what're you gonna do."

I took a deep breath. What did I need?

"I need to be all right," I said.

"Good start, but maybe a little vague, right? How're you going to get there from here?"

"I don't know," I said, choking a little at the end.

I couldn't help it. I started crying in earnest. Tears and sobs. Head in hands. The whole thing. Midian's sigh was like gravel sliding off the back of a pickup truck. The cheap, stinking cushion of the couchlike thing shifted under me as he sat down beside me. His arm around my shoulder was weirdly hot and hard as concrete. The smell of his cigarettes almost covered the garlic and onions and fresh basil. Kitchen smells. I leaned against his shoulder.

"It's okay, kid," he murmured. "You go ahead if you need to. It's all right."

It was bad weather. A storm that came up fast and washed away thought and awareness and then broke. I might have been there, curled up against him for a couple of minutes. It might have been half an hour. I couldn't have told the difference.

When I pulled myself back together, he stood up, fished around in his pocket, and pulled out a linen handkerchief. I wiped my eyes, blew my nose. When I spoke, my voice was thick and wet.

"I need my body back," I said. "I can't have this *thing* living inside me."

"Okay, then," he said, walking the three steps to the back of the RV. "You've got a plan for that. What else?"

"I want to never hurt anybody again ever."

"Tall order, but worth aiming for," he said, grunting. I glanced over. He was pulling on a fresh shirt. I'd left a wide damp spot on the old one.

"I need to figure out who I really am," I said. There was a weird sense of déjà vu in saying the words.

"Yeah, well. That's never wrong. So here's what I'm hearing you tell me, okay? No matter what comes next, the first step, you're finishing up with the papists. After you're calling the shots on your body, you're spending some time actually getting your shit together. Which means not running around the world like a decapitated chicken all the time. Slow down. Figure out what your next step is. And—this is me talking now—no more stroking your inner victim. Bad for your skin."

"Yes, Oprah," I said, but I smiled when I said it.

"Hey. Fuck you too," he said, grinning. He teeth were black where they weren't yellow.

My phone rang at the same moment that something scratched on the thin metal and plastic of the doorway. I turned toward the sound of claws, ready for a threat, but Midian waved me back. I pulled my phone out of the leather backpack I used as a purse. It was Ex. Midian opened the RV door and the ancient Laborador from the parking lot hefted herself up the stairs on arthritic hips. I answered the call.

"Is everything okay?" Ex said instead of hello. His voice was tight as a wire.

"Sure," I said, trying to keep the aftermath of tears out of my voice. "Everything's copacetic. Why?"

"You've been gone a long time. We were starting to worry."

"No, I'm at O'Keefe's," I said. "You wouldn't believe—"

Midian coughed. He stood in the galley, scratching the dog between its ears and looking at me. His yellow eyes were empty, and I understood. If I told Ex he was here, he would tell Father Chapin. If Ex told Father Chapin, the exorcists would come after Midian. If not now, then later. Maybe I should have felt some conflict about lying to Ex, but I didn't. It was *Midian*.

"You wouldn't believe how good the food is," I said gamely. "I'm just luxuriating over a little coffee."

"Did anything happen?" he asked. The tension in his voice sounded like a small accusation.

"I haven't been taken over by the rider and hijacked to Juárez," I said a little sharply. "I'm fine. I'll be back in a little bit."

"All right," Ex said, backing down. "We've got a game plan and a schedule. When we've gone over it, we can all call it a night."

Meaning that until I showed up, Father Chapin wasn't going to let himself rest. It was like looking forward in time to who Ex was going to be at sixty. His cranky, paternalistic streak shifted into a different frame. It wasn't that he wanted to control how long I took eating dinner. He just wanted to take care of his uncompromising old teacher, and this was the closest he could come to saying that out loud.

"I'll come home soon," I said. "Promise."

"Thank you," Ex said.

We paused for a moment, neither of us with anything to say and neither one hanging up first. I could hear him breathe like he was sitting beside me.

"Thank you," he said again, and dropped the connection. I put the phone back in my pack a little more gently than I'd taken it out. Midian stopped scratching the dog's ears, and it turned to me, pushing its nose under my hand and wagging. It had gray on its muzzle and around its black, watery eyes.

"Vatican's junior hit squad wants you back, eh?" Midian said.

"Guess so," I said, petting the dog's head, then scratching its breast. The dog smiled and turned to look over its shoulder at Midian. *See, this is how you're supposed to do it.* "This one's yours? I never saw you as a pet kind of guy."

"Ozzie's not mine. She came with the job. I don't know how she got here originally. Being loyal to disloyal people's my bet. Lived by catching rabbits and birds. When she got old and weak, she started hanging out at the back door, stealing scraps."

"And now she's part of the place."

The dog chuffed happily.

"Sort of," Midian said. "The guy that owns the place still wants to shoot her, but I let her come in when it's cold out. I've got a soft spot for down-on-their-luck predators. Don't know where it comes from."

"Can't imagine."

"So we're good?" he asked.

"Of course we're good," I said, but when I stood up to go, I found I didn't want to. I wanted to sit back down and pet the dog and drink the coffee and talk all night. I had a powerful flash of resentment toward Ex and Father Chapin and all the rest. Men who were risking their lives to help me. I looked down.

"You want to talk about Eric, don't you?" Midian asked.

"Yeah. And about a million other things."

He lifted his beef-jerky arms to the RV like he was displaying a treasure.

"You know where to find me," he said.

"All right, then."

"Yeah," he said. "All right. 'S good seeing you, kid."

The wind outside was biting cold and it smelled like snow. Low gray clouds had rolled in while I wasn't watching, smothering stars and moon. I wrapped my coat around me and ran around the side of the restaurant. The parking lot was nearly full now, and it took some maneuvering to get the car to the ragged blacktop. The heater roared discreetly, and I turned up the music to carry over it. China Forbes sang "Let's Never Stop Falling in Love" and I sailed through the darkness, feeling something like peace for the first time in weeks.

I cried after Chicago without knowing particularly what I was crying about, but I had been alone and there hadn't been any catharsis in it. Tears wouldn't clean me. I'd thought at the time it was only because I was so thoroughly blackened. Now I wondered if it was just that I'd done it alone. If Chogyi Jake had been there instead of recuperating in Chicago, if I hadn't broken the thing off with Aubrey, and there had been someone to talk to. Someone to confess to. Would it have been different?

I tried to imagine what it would have been like if I'd gone to Ex. On the one hand, it was kind of unthinkable. From the moment I told him I had a rider, he'd been focused on fixing the problem. If I'd talked to him about guilt, he'd have handed me over to God, and it was a long time since I'd taken comfort there.

But on the other hand, what if he'd listened? What if he'd put his arm around me and let me cry *his* shirt wet. Would it have stopped there? Would I have wanted it to? Maybe the kind of intimacy where I could tell him about what I was afraid of and guilty over would have led to the other kind. And maybe that was where we were going anyway.

The road went under the highway, and I reached the ramp up, signaling my lane change even though there was no one in sight. I swung the nose of the car to the left, crossed the oncoming lanes, and flew up toward the interstate like a crow taking wing. The first fat flakes of snow spattered against the windshield, and the car knew to start the wipers without my touching anything. The GPS glowed, guiding me. There was more traffic, and I checked my blind spot as I merged.

"Please don't do this to me," something said with my mouth.

My heart started spinning like a bike wheel. My hands dug hard into the wheel, white-knuckled. I drove eighty miles an hour down a dark, mostly unfamiliar road, waiting for my body to speak to me again.

chapter nine

The crows were there when I pulled up, watching me from the dead branches. The snow was coming down harder now, grabbing any stray ray of light and trading it back and forth until the world was a deep gray that never quite made it to black. I trudged up to the blue double doors through half an inch of fresh snow, humming the melody to "White Christmas" without any particular pleasure. My jaw ached with the tension of the drive. My hands were balled in my pockets. Winter drifted down around me.

I opened the blue doors, and the light spilled

out. Behind me, the crows lifted into the snow-heavy air, their caws like threats and accusations. I walked into the warmth and shook the snow and water off my coat. In the darkness, the electric lights seemed even more out of place strapped on the ancient adobe walls. Jesus was staring down from his cross or collapsed on his mother's lap in every room. I found them in the kitchen. Tamblen squatting like a bear and poking at the fire. The whiskey-voiced Tomás sitting across a checker-board from Ex. Miguel looking even more like Benicio Del Toro sitting on the same gray couch as thin-bodied, thin-faced Carsey. And Father Chapin standing by the tiny window, looking out into the snowy courtyard.

He looked terrible. Shadows hung around his eyes, seeping into his skin. His hair was so short it could barely look disarranged, but it managed. The square of his shoulders and his upright head made me think less of strength and more of bloody-minded endurance. Yesterday, he'd been fighting a demon. Losing to it. And for weeks before that, tracking down the thing's spawn. What Aubrey would have called the daughter organisms. And now, me. No rest for the wicked, no peace for the good.

"Hey," I said, trying for a lightness I didn't feel. "How's it going?"

"Good that you've come back, young miss,"

Chapin said. "We have a schedule set. If you are willing, we will begin tomorrow. The rite itself."

"No more prep work?" I said, my stomach tightening and hope soaring up my spine. Nothing more to do, no more hoops to jump through, just getting whatever was in me back out and taking my real life back.

"None. Only, I must warn you of one thing. If we are to attempt this, you must be constant in your own rejection of the beast. Knowing as little as we do of this infesting spirit, there are longer paths we can take. Paths that are more certain, perhaps, but at the cost of time. But I believe, and my good friend Xavier agrees, that you are strong enough to reject the evil in your heart. If we are wrong about you, the rite will fail. Time and effort wasted."

It felt like a challenge. I felt the distant touch of anger. I'd come here for help, not a lecture on how I needed to really mean it or else everything would be my fault.

"I can do it," I said. "I mean, I'm not sure exactly what *it* is, but whatever I can do to make sure this works, I'll do it."

"Your resolve must not waver," Chapin said.

"Won't."

He smiled and reached out, putting a hand on my shoulder.

"Then tonight, rest. We will all rest. And in the

morning, we will begin. We will find its name, and then God will free you of this burden."

I took a deep breath.

"Thank you," I said. "I appreciate what you're doing. For me."

"Well, this should be quite the event, shouldn't it?" Carsey said. "Once more unto the breach, dear friends, once more."

"You should rest now, Father," Tomás said, rising from the checkerboard, red and black disks abandoned behind him. "We all should."

Ex appeared at my side. I'd seen him look worse, but only a few times. And besides the fatigue—within it—there was something else. A fierceness.

"We'll be back in the morning," he said.

We walked out to the car together. The snow was still falling, and there was already a scattering of white on the black of the car, the heat of my drive not enough to defeat the cold. The priests huddled in the doorway behind us, watching us go.

"For that, he made you wait?" I asked.

"Chapin wanted to see you when he asked if you'd keep your resolve."

"Why?"

"He wanted to see if he believed you."

"A little creepy, but okay, whatever," I said. "How's your back?"

"Hurts. Why? You want me to drive?"

"Yeah. It talked to me. After you called, before I

got here. Makes me a little nervous about having the steering wheel."

I passed him the key chain. We got to the car, and I slid down into the passenger's seat. Ex closed his door, put the fob in place, and the engine purred to life. In the headlights, the snow was pure and perfect.

"What did it say?" he asked.

"It asked me not to do pretty much exactly what we're about to do," I said.

"Ah," he said.

"Yeah," I said. "Let's go."

The road conditions were awful. I turned off the music and tried not to talk just so that Ex wouldn't be distracted from the slush and ice and the New Mexican drivers trying to take the highway turns at seventy. In Taos, we stopped at a drive-through, fueling Ex on a greasy burger, fries, and a diet soda. Then it was back into the treacherous black.

When we reached our place, we didn't even try driving up the hill; we parked at the bottom and walked up. The other condos were lit up, glowing in the dark. Someone in a bright green coat the approximate proportions of the Stay Puft Marshmallow Man was hooting and twirling around outside of one, his arms out to embrace the sky. I hadn't thought about it, but it would be a pretty good night for skiers. He waved at us as we headed in toward our door. I waved back. He shouted something I couldn't make out, but it sounded happy.

Once we were inside, Ex cranked up the heat. The gas fireplace ignited with a soft huff, then hissed. The sound left me anxious. I washed my hands more for the sound of the water drowning out the voice of the flame. Ex groaned and lay down on the floor, his feet to the grate.

"Did you get any food down there?" I asked. "Or was that burger the only food you've had since lunch?"

"I'm fine," he said. "I'm just . . . tired."

"Council of war took it out of you?"

"It was a little fraught. You can't have that many men working together on something this hard without some fault lines. They're all dedicated to the work, and they all love Chapin."

"So if he says, it goes?"

Ex chuckled.

"With some grousing and argument, yes," he said.

"You want to let me in on anything about that conversation? Spread out the inside dirt? Or would that be telling?"

"There are some things about this you shouldn't know," he said.

I thought of Midian, leaning against his RV's galley. It wasn't like I was sharing everything either.

"Yeah, all right," I said. "Maybe after. When it's over."

He sat up. The shadows of the fire shifted on his skin. A few strands of white-blond hair had escaped his ponytail, draping down the side of his face. He looked up at me almost grimly.

"Jayné, when this is over . . . when you're safe . . . there's another conversation we need to have."

My breath caught. I was very aware of being alone in a house with a man, away from the world, away from everyone I knew, and halfway to snowbound. With a hot tub three feet out the back door. I imagined what it would be like to sit back in that steaming warmth with the snow shawling down around us. I felt an echo of the furnace of longing and guilt that I'd touched back in Chicago when our minds had been less separate than they were now. Adrenaline was leaking into my blood, and this wasn't even fear. Wasn't anything like it.

It occurred to me for the first time that my shame about the rider really wasn't the only reason I hadn't told Chogyi Jake to rejoin us.

"Then we should probably get this over," I said, my voice carefully even. "Right?"

"Right," he said softly, and let gravity pull him slowly back down. "Oh yeah."

"You really should have seen a doctor about that back," I said.

"I'll be fine," he said. "Once you're safe, I'll be perfect."

THE BAD dreams came fast that night, but at least they weren't the vicious reenactment of past events I sometimes had. Instead, I was lost in a city I didn't know. I was supposed to have studied the local language, but I'd blown it off. Now I needed to get somewhere, but I couldn't find anyone who could understand me. Sometimes I had a phrase book but couldn't read the script, sometimes I was just trying to string syllables together and hoping. There was always a sense of being late for something I couldn't afford to miss. And of being alone in the middle of a crowd. Every time I thought I was about to get there, the dream reset, and I started again.

And then, like waking up without waking up, I was in the desert.

For as long as I could remember, the desert had been one of the constant areas in my personal dreamscape. The wind-paved emptiness, the mountains rising on the infinitely distant horizon, the quiet. And as often happened, there were two of me. I saw the paired Jaynés from outside, like I was watching a movie, and I noticed that one of me was actually a mask. With the clarity that comes in dreams, I could see the hairline crack that ran around her face. The place where it would separate, and whatever was inside would come out.

She was looking at me now. Looking into me. A profound grief washed over me, like I'd lost someone I loved. Like someone died. I tried to speak, but I couldn't move my mouth. The other Jayné put a finger across my lips.

Shh, she said. He'll hear you.

I knew she meant Ex. A frigid wind came across the empty plain. I smelled the weird burnt-cheese smell of exploded cyclopropane, heard the hiss of the fireplace and it became the hiss of the lantern under Grace Memorial, and I was being buried alive. I was in the coffin and I was shoveling dirt onto it. I wanted to stop, but I couldn't. The world got smaller, darker. I was trapped.

"Jayné!" Ex screamed from a different continent. "Stop!"

The dream shifted. I was running, only it wasn't me running. I was in the small, still place two inches behind my eyes, and my body was moving of its own accord. Bare feet skidded on the new-fallen snow, and fresh flakes drifted down like ashes from a fire. I was wearing my big black coat and my pajamas. My hair blew into my mouth and I spat it out without being aware I was going to do it. I leaped over something big and black and half-encrusted in white. The car. I'd just vaulted over the car at the bottom of the hill, and I was sprinting toward the highway.

I wasn't dreaming.

"Jayné!" Ex screamed again, his voice growing fainter. "Fight it! Fight against it!"

I panicked. I tried to scream. I tried to force my body to stop or slow or do something. I felt paralyzed, except that my body was moving frantically. My breath was a white cloud. Trapped inside myself, I thrashed, pushing out with my will against whatever I could find. Nothing happened. My body skittered down to the bottom of the hill and paused to look back. Ex was running after me: black clothes and white hair in a world of snow and winter-black trees. The rider bolted into the forest, working my legs faster than I could have. I didn't just run, I bounded. Under the canopy, the snow was a little thinner, the carpet of pinecones and needles hushing under my steps. My feet avoided the snow, my footprints all but invisible. Ex wouldn't be able to find the trail, not in the darkness. And even if he did, he couldn't keep up.

My body slid gracefully down a steep gully, and then clambered up the other side. I'd reached the road. Pale ice snaked up toward the ski valley and down toward Arroyo Seco, the little town at the base of the mountain. The rider paused, crouching at the shoulder. There were stones under the snow now, and a high bank of slush and ice where the plow had come through and scraped the worst of the snowfall to the side. A wide, low SUV trundled past, skis sprouting from the rack on its top like horns. My body waited until the red taillights vanished around the curve, then turned down the hill and started an easy loping run. Not sprinting anymore. Going for distance.

Stop, I tried to say. Turn back. Stop running.

Nothing.

So okay, stomping at the problem like I was killing snakes wasn't going to help. I tried to calm down, to find a still point in my tiny prison. I'd had a year of practice meditating, focusing my qi, doing small magics. It ought to be good for something. I tried to put aside the fact that every second was taking me farther from safety. I focused on the desert of my dreams, the stillness of it. The calm.

I found I could feel my body a little bit, but everything was muted. My feet were screaming in agony, but from a long way away. My lungs hurt too. I had a stitch in my side I hadn't known about; the rider was powering through the pain. It wasn't the same as controlling my own flesh, but the fact that I was getting reports—even secondhand ones—felt like a start. Slowly, I brought my focus to my right hand, not trying to do anything with it. Just being very, very aware of it. How the fingers curled into a fist. Where the skin tugged at the scab across the knuckles. The numbness across the back where the air was icing me down. My body kept its rhythm. I poured everything I could into thinking about my right hand.

And then I opened it. I did, not the rider. It closed again almost immediately, but for a second and for a few isolated muscles, I called the shots. It was such a small victory, but I rejoiced all the same.

Behind us, there was a roar of an engine. My head turned back. Ex's cute little sports car was somewhere on the road behind us, hidden by the curve of the road. Headlights caught the trees, and the rider shifted, sprinting toward the drift at the side of the road. Running for cover. I shifted my awareness to my knees, trying to bend them double. The rider stumbled, fell, slid against the frozen asphalt.

Ex's car came around the bend, fishtailing a little, and caught me in the headlights. The rider sprang up, arms wide, mouth a feral grin. I plucked at it from inside, but my body was still as stone now. The brake lights flared, and the car started to spin, back tires drifting toward the far side of the road. It righted suddenly, jerking toward me. Faster than a thought, the rider danced out of its way. The car stopped, the door spilled open, and Ex jumped out.

"I command you to stop, devil," he shouted, running toward me. In the headlights, something in his hand glittered.

The cry that came out of my throat was rage and despair and grief.

Get back, I thought, pressing the words out through the air. It's not me anymore. It's not safe. Get back.

But Ex kept coming. His eyes were wide and wild, his jaw set and angry. He lifted his hands, and I felt the power coming off him when he spoke.

"In the name of Christ, I command you. Release this woman."

"I *saved* you," the rider said.

Ex was in front of me now, the headlights silhouetting him. It made the steam of his breath look black as smoke. He lifted his hand. The glittering thing was a medallion, not more than two inches across. My gaze fastened on it like it was a snake. I could feel the rider trying to turn away, but the medallion held it.

"I said *release her*!" Ex screamed, and it was more than sound. His raw will was in the word, pressing out of his body and into me. I felt the rider shudder, and then my body was mine again. The agony was transporting: my feet were freezing and cut bloody by running, my hands and face burned with the cold. I blacked out for a second, and when I was aware of myself again, Ex had his arm around me. I limped to the car, groaning and weeping with every step, then huddled in the passenger's seat, curled in a fetal ball. The pain was immense.

"It's okay," he said, tucking the silver medallion

into my hand. "Hold on to this. It'll make it harder for the rider to come back."

"What . . . is it?"

"Sigil of St. Francis of the Desert. Tomás put it together."

"Couldn't give it to me before?" I managed through clenched teeth.

"It only lasts for a while," he said as he started the engine and put the car in gear. "I was hoping we wouldn't need it. Try to keep it against your skin."

The tires hissed and spun, but we turned around. Sensation was pouring back into my fingers and toes, thawing the places that were numb. I cried out, banging my fist against the door.

"I can't move," I said. "I can't. Oh God, why didn't it stop to put on some freaking *shoes*? I'll never get up that hill."

In the green of the dashboard light, Ex smiled wearily.

"It's all right," he said. "If I have to, I can carry you."

I lay back on the car seat, letting the engine murmur to me, and thought about how nice it would be to have somebody to carry me safely home.

chapter Ten

"This is good," Chapin said. For the first time since I'd met him, he seemed really happy. "Its fear is a *good* sign."

"Plus which, we brought more donuts," I said, a little bitterly. "Chocolate, even."

The night hadn't been much kinder to Chapin than it had to us. His skin was still pale. The darkness under his eyes looked less like a bruise, but it was still there. The other four looked a little better, though Tamblen's hair was standing up awkwardly in the back, like he'd just gotten up from his pillow. Outside, the snow had stopped and the clouds thinned to a colorless haze. The whole world from my little place up near the ski valley down to Taos proper and out to San Esteban was wedding-cake white, and where it wasn't—bark, asphalt, the crows that huddled on the branches and wheeled across the sky—it was utterly black by contrast. All shades of gray were gone.

My feet still hurt. When we'd gotten back to the hill, I had felt a little better. Ex and I sat in the car at the bottom of the hill for a while, letting the heater run. I'd thought about asking him to go up and get me some shoes, but I was pretty sure that leaving me alone in a running car wasn't going to be high on his to-do list. Rather than put him on the spot, I'd gotten out of the car and done my best sprint for warmth. In the little kitchen, I sat on the counter running warm water over my ankles and feet until the cold stopped hurting. Once I saw that I'd avoided frostbite, I started feeling a little better. Ex went upstairs and came back with a first aid kit. We'd dabbed the cuts and scrapes with antibacterial goop, and Ex used an Ace bandage to press the little silver medallion against my arm, the metal securely against my skin.

Twice in the night, the magical icon had woken me up, burning, but I'd managed to steal a couple of solid, dreamless hours before dawn. Sinking into the gray couch at the sanctuary now, I'd have been perfectly happy to tip over and sleep away the morning. Except, of course, that wasn't going to happen.

"Did you learn anything about the demon?" Tomás asked in his lovely whiskey voice.

"Hints, maybe," Ex said. "One thing that stood out was—"

Chapin made a sharp sound somewhere between a cough and a shout.

"Not before it!" he said. Then, to me: "Miss Jayné, you will excuse us. We are about to enter a very dangerous place in our battle. We must know all that we can, and we must allow the devil no entrance into our council."

"None taken," I said. "You guys figure out what you need to do, and I'll wait here. I just want to get this over."

"Very soon," Chapin said, nodding solemnly. "Miguel, please sit with Miss Jayné."

"Yes, Father," Miguel said.

The others followed Chapin out, closing the doors behind them. I lay my head against the back of the couch and groaned. Miguel chuckled.

"It's been a rough week?" he asked.

"Has," I said. "And I haven't even started my Christmas shopping."

"There will be time."

"You're sure about that?" I said. "Because that last rite looked like it was aiming for days. And I don't think the thing inside me is weak."

"Different demons take different times to mature. The thing in the girl—"

"Dolores," I said. "Her name's Dolores."

"In Dolores," he said with a gentle smile. "It was very old and very sure of itself. The devil within you is still young. Your soul is, for the most part, intact."

I looked at him, sitting at the little table. His eyes were dark enough to pass for black, his face sharp at the edges but round in the cheeks.

"Meaning hers wasn't?" I asked.

"Not entirely, no," he said. "We saved her and the others the devil inflicted with his power, but exorcism doesn't leave anyone entirely whole. She will be vulnerable for the rest of her life. There will be scars upon her that only God can heal."

He must have read my expression, because he nodded as if I'd spoken.

"I forgot," he said. "You haven't accepted Christ."

"That's not exactly right," I said.

"No?"

"I spent most of my life accepting Him. It just didn't take. I probably clocked as many church hours as you when I was a kid, and I held on to my faith as long as I could. And then . . ."

I shrugged.

"Can I ask you what happened?" Miguel said, speaking each words softly, like a doctor probing at a wound.

"I stopped believing in hell," I said. "I wanted to. But I couldn't square up a God that loves us and cares for us and a place of eternal damnation without the hope of being redeemed."

"There are many people who consider themselves Christians who agree with you," Miguel said. "You weren't brought up in the Catholic Church?"

"Evangelical," I said. "Evangelical but pro-Hellfire. But when I started doubting Hell, that was just the first part. I started wondering about that, and then everything sort of came into question, you know? And the more I looked at it, the more it seemed like there were problems. I mean, did you know there's no archaeological evidence for exodus of the Jews from Egypt? You'd think if a whole nation of slaves decamped after a bunch of serious God's-wrath plagues, there'd be some record. There's not."

"And that's important to you," he said. His voice didn't make it a question.

"Yeah, it is. It's kind of the difference between truth and a pretty story. Doesn't it matter to you? I mean seriously, you've given your life over to this. What if it turned out that the Bible was all third-century political metaphor and propaganda?"

"That would be disappointing," he said. "But I have seen too much with my own eyes that confirms my faith. I have felt the presence of God, and I have seen His work in the world. The evidence of Providence is all through my life, and I can't doubt it any more than I could doubt the sunshine. Take you."

"Me?"

"Yes. We lost Chewy years ago. He was the best of us, but his soul was tested and he suffered. It was terrible for him, and it was terrible for all of us. We couldn't help him."

"You mean with Isabel," I said.

"You know, then?"

"A little," I said. "She came to you guys for help. Ex fell for her. When it all went pear-shaped, he blamed himself. Felt like he'd let down God."

Miguel's gaze focused on the empty air, and he crossed his arms. Outside, the crows called to one another. The little refrigerator hummed to itself.

"It was a terrible thing," he said. "She took her own life. He was with her when she did. After that, he couldn't stay with us. Father Chapin only asked that he renew his vows and never again transgress against them. Did he tell you this?"

"No."

"I was there when he was to take his vows again. He couldn't. Father Chapin led him in it, but the words would not come from his lips. He wept silently, but he could not dedicate himself to the purpose again. Ever since, I wondered why God would have permitted it to happen. We are His loyal servants, and Chewy most of all. What reason could there be for him to suffer what he did? Chewy cast himself into the world. And then he returned. With you."

I shifted, the couch springs creaking under me.

"So you think this was part of a *plan*?" I said. "That this other girl died so that Ex would drive himself out of the group here, go work with my uncle, and be around to find me?"

"Chewy brought you here. You look so much like her, she could have been your sister. You are in need of our help, and you would not have found us if things had not happened exactly as they did," Miguel said, spreading his hands as if offering something invisible to me. "What is that if not providence? I don't know what God meant by bringing you here. I may never know. But I cannot doubt that He intended it."

"Really? Because I can doubt the hell out of it," I said. "If it hadn't happened that way, something else would have, and then that would be God's will. With that kind of logic, any coincidence is evidence of God."

Miguel's smile was bright as sunlight on snow.

"Yes," he said, and without intending to, I laughed.

"We're just not going to agree about this, are we?" I said.

"I have some hope," Miguel said. "I believe that

Hell is the absence of God. God doesn't cast us into the fire. We cast ourselves there. And we hold ourselves there. It is not His fault that we burn, but the consequence of our own choices. I think you have turned away from God, and you live in the living shadow of Hell. And so I am glad you came, and that you will let us help you. And that you've brought Chewy to us, even if it is only for a little while. I pray that casting Satan out of your flesh will change your mind about the merciful nature of God."

"I don't think it will," I said. And then, "But thank you for helping me anyway."

"Of course," he said. "What virtue is there in helping only the people you agree with? Are there any donuts left?"

When, a few minutes later, the doors opened and Father Chapin led his cadre back in, Miguel and I had moved on to talking about the relative merits of the Swedish and American versions of *Let the Right One In* and breaking the last donut between us. The fatigue had fallen from the old man's shoulders, and even Ex looked actively hopeful. I stood up.

"Thundercats are go?" I asked.

"I believe we are prepared, Miss Jayné," Chapin said. "If you are ready to reject the demonic power within you, we will free your soul."

I almost said *Nifty*. Smarting off was a reflex now. It was the way I told myself that I could deal with whatever made my heart race and my mind

start to fishtail under me. Just then it felt disrespect-
ful and small.

"Thank you," I said instead.

"WHEN THE time comes, you must reject it utterly," Tomás said, squatting beside me on the floor.
"It will try to trick you, but whatever happens, you
must not waver. Be your strength."

"Stone strong and waver-free," I said. "That's me
in a nutshell."

He patted me gently on the back of the neck
as he rose to take his place, and I tried to smile.
I felt like I was about to jump out of an airplane.
My chest was tight, and I didn't want to breathe
so much as pant. The place at the back of my neck
where Tomás had touched me tingled, and the small
of my back where the tattoo was itched like I'd sat
in poison oak. I had to put it all aside.

I knelt on the floor more or less where I'd first
seen Dolores. The six priests were all around me:
Father Chapin in front of me, Ex to his right, Carsey
to his right. Tamblen was directly behind me, and
Tomás and Miguel to either side. We'd covered the
windows, but the midday sun pressed in at the
edges. The only other light in the room came from
the single white candle. A single stick of incense
gave the room a sweet smell. The bricks under
me were cold. I wondered whether a space heater

would have been too secular for the occasion. It seemed like it might be worth trying.

The consecrated ceremonial robe was rough cotton cut like a sack, and since I was only wearing it and the medallion-enhanced Ace bandage, I was pretty cold. I stared at the still, yellow flame, focusing myself like a meditation. The energy of magic—my qi, my soul, whatever name it goes by— was narrowed to that one bright spot. I could barely see the faces of the priests past it. When Father Chapin lifted his palms toward me, they were pale spots in the darkness.

He began reciting the names of saints, the others echoing him. After the first five or six, the flame began to shift back and forth—toward him and away and toward him again like seaweed in the waves. I'd been part of magical rituals before, and I could feel the combined will of men around me starting to cohere. By the time Father Chapin ran out of saints, the air around me was about equal parts oxygen and raw magic. Time seemed to stretch. I didn't know how long they'd been chanting, but the candle had burned lower than just a few minutes could explain. I felt disoriented and had to work to pull my qi back into place.

"I come in the name of Christ, and in His holy name I command you, beast. Reveal yourself!"

It was like a bus speeding by, missing me by inches. The combined will of the men pounded past me, violent and intense and hot as a burning coal. In my gut, just below my navel and about three inches in, something shifted. Writhed. I gritted my teeth.

"Reveal yourself!"

Another hit.

Come on, I thought, pressing the words toward the thing living inside me. It's going to happen anyway. Fighting's just going to make it hurt worse.

"Reveal yourself!"

The candle flame in front of me ballooned, fire bursting up and out. By the light of it, I could see Chapin's face clearly. He was smiling like this was exactly what he'd wanted. I felt my fists clench, but I hadn't clenched them. The growl came from low in my throat, and it sounded like despair.

"In the name of God," Father Chapin said, and the others repeated it. The words had a pressure like diving too deep underwater. My ears ached. "In the name of God, I command you. Reveal your name!"

"Why are you doing this to me?" my voice said without me.

"Reveal your name!"

"I am innocent."

Father Chapin shook his head. The darkness around us weighed in against me, and I knew that whatever I was feeling, the rider was suffering a hundred times worse than I was.

"Innocence is the claim you make. What is your name?"

I felt my jaw clench. I had the sense that the rider had already made a mistake, already given up more than it had meant to. The candle sputtered, the flame fading to a pale blue sphere with a glowing ember at its center. I wondered, when this was over, whether I'd ever dream about the desert again. Was losing that emptiness and stillness part of the price of being just Jayné?

"Reveal your name!" they all shouted together. I could feel each of them. Chapin was like a strap of leather, hard and unforgiving. Carsey was like a knife, cold and focused and precise as mathematics. Tomás's will was wide and deep and strong, like a pillow over the face. Tamblen—strong, silent Tamblen—felt like a request, the weakest of all of them, but implacable and patient and unbreakable. Miguel's voice had the raw tenacity and violence of a bare-knuckle fighter's jab.

And Ex.

In the midst of the riot of personality, I felt Ex. His guilt and his longing, his deep internal pain carried in silence and forged into a weapon. For a moment, I caught a glimpse of a girl who looked a little like me: dark hair cut in a bob, mouth a little wider than mine, cheeks a little more generous. Isabel, I thought. He was using Isabel, and I realized that I could follow his lead. I brought the night in Grace

Memorial, the guilt and horror of killing someone who didn't deserve to die, and I wrapped myself around it. It was the most painful, terrible thing I ever experienced, and I held it like a knife so hot it burned me.

"Reveal your name!" they shouted again, beating at the rider. I stabbed at it too, adding myself to the assault. The thing inside my skin shrieked, but only I could hear it.

Something cold brushed against my neck, surprising me. I smelled sewage. *What the hell was that?*

"Reveal your name!"

"I am my mother's daughter," the rider said, almost too softly to hear. But Chapin had been waiting for it. He pounced on the words, pointing a finger at me—at it—as if in accusation.

"That is the path by which you have taken this woman. Reveal your name!"

There, trapped in my skin with the rider like we were sewn in the same sack, I lost my balance. The bus didn't miss me this time. The room spun around me. A part of me that wasn't my body hurt. The sewage smell was getting worse.

"Beast, in the name of God and all His saints, in the name of Christ and His apostles, I command you! Surrender your name!"

My head lifted, and my body stood. I felt the effort it took, like a giant rising against a mountain of chains. When it spoke, my voice trembled with defiance and fear.

"I am Sonnenrad, the Voice of the Desert," the rider said. "I am the Black Sun and the Black Sun's daughter."

Silence fell on the room. I saw triumph in Father Chapin's expression.

"Yes," he said. "Yes, you are."

chapter eleven

I'd seen exorcisms before, mostly as performed by Ex going it alone in the field. I hadn't understood how difficult the rites he'd performed were. He was the expert. I made sure he had what he needed, and he did the rest. If afterward he'd seemed a little sapped, he hadn't complained about it. So I had figured that, taxing as it might be, it couldn't be *that* punishing.

Bad call.

I had thought forcing the rider to give us its name had been bad, and it had been. The next part was worse. The combined will of the six men around me was a constant source of pain, even though the burning and nausea and disorientation I felt was just the spillover of what the rider was absorbing.

"... *qui ambulavit super aspidem et basiliscum, qui conculcavit leonem et draconem, ut discedas ad hoc hominae* ..."

After the second hour, time had stopped having any meaning. The candle I'd used at the ceremony's beginning was gone—kicked over and stomped into the brick under my feet. I didn't remember doing that. My skin felt hot, like I had a bad sunburn. My vocal cords strained with screaming. At one point, the rider had fallen to the ground, writhing in a pain that felt like bathing in acid even secondhand. The fall left my lip bleeding, and the taste of blood hadn't left my mouth since.

"*Ecce Crucem Domini, fugite, partes adversae!*" Chapin shouted, waving a crucifix at me. It was enchanted like the medallion that still burned and blistered my arm. The rider couldn't look at it.

"Stop this," it cried. "You don't know what you're doing. You don't know what this *means*!"

The Latin kept on beating at it, the syllables a medium for the power behind it. It didn't feel holy. It didn't feel like the cleansing power of a glorious God. It felt like violence, but I'd put in for this, and I was going to see it through. Caught in the space behind my eyes, I pressed myself hard as a stone and endured.

For what seemed like weeks, the rider didn't shift. It just took the abuse like a mountain in a windstorm. But slowly, at first by degrees so small I could barely feel it, they started to pull it away. It felt like someone ripping off a scab. Something I'd always thought was part of me started to ache and then burn and then—painfully—to lift at the edges.

And once it started losing, it kept losing. I felt its frenzy, its frantic search for something in me to hold on to. I kept my will tucked tight, small and safe, and put everything I could spare into pushing it away.

When it came for me, I knew we were close to the end.

The desert had changed. The stones bore long, black scorch marks. The sky, usually vast and blue, was hazy with smoke and a shining curtain like the aurora that hurt to look at. We stood there, the two of us. We were both bleeding from the lip, but mine was red where hers was white. She held her hand out to me, begging me to take it. And despite everything, I wanted to. I put my hands behind me, locking my fingers around the opposite wrist. The wail of despair wrenched itself out of the desert to the room where my physical body shook against the floor like someone in a seizure. For a moment, I could see it all at once, and I knew the rider was losing its grip.

I felt it fall away. There was space between us. The rite was going to work. It was going to be cast out. It was going to die.

The mixture of elation and regret was the last thing I felt before the new attack came.

I smelled sewage again. Something touched my belly, wet and soft, and I wasn't sure if it was in the desert or on the brick floor. I tried to sit up, but then I wasn't anywhere. The rider screamed, but it didn't use my throat. No one else could hear it.

Something foul slid into my mouth. Not my real mouth, but mine all the same. It tasted like salt and rot. The outhouse stench was overpowering. I choked, and the thing pushed deeper into my throat. It wasn't just the two of us. There was something else.

Something else was in there with us.

Another rider.

"Stop!" I shouted. I did, with my own flesh. Chapin ignored me. The desert spasmed, and the other me was falling away, her hand out toward me. "I said stop! It's me! Jayné! Something's wrong!"

"I adjure you, ancient serpent—"

"I said something's wrong! You have to stop!"

The thing in my throat thickened, pulsed once. I couldn't speak. My throat froze open, and I heard myself retching. It was shutting me off, silencing me. With my real eyes, I looked up at Ex. His palms were toward me like he was taking heat from a campfire. Look at me, I thought. See what's happening. *Save me*.

He didn't. A sense of Novocain-like numbness was spreading from my mouth out through my body. For a strange moment, I was in control of my arms and legs, but not my breath or neck. The other thing—the *invader*—pushed out, trying to fill me. I felt a sense of triumph, deep and powerful and unfamiliar and threatening as a strange man's cough in my bedroom.

I reached out to the desert, to my other self. I felt my rider grab on to me, and I pulled her in with all my strength. The numbness faded. The foul smell receded. In my real body again, I rolled onto my side and vomited. The cold, hard bricks under me felt as comfortable as a feather bed. It took me a while to realize that no one was shouting in English or Latin. I looked up. They were all around me. The sunlight pushing in around the window shades glowed gold and red. Sunset colors. We'd been going at this hammer and tongs for hours. No wonder I felt like this. I tried to talk, coughed, and tried again.

"Different rider. It was trying to get in me while the other one got pushed out."

"No, Miss Jayné," Chapin said. His voice was almost as weary as mine. "There was not. Satan has a thousand tricks. We were making great progress.

We might very well have succeeded, had your will not broken."

I forced myself up to sitting. My muscles ached and trembled. I was cold.

"Didn't break," I said. "There was another one."

"Not actually possible," Carsey said. "You're in a circle of exorcists, in a consecrated building, and you've got the Mark of St. Francis of the Desert clapped up against your arm. You're in more danger of being eaten by an alligator than being attacked by a demon you didn't bring in here yourself."

I hung my head. My ribs hurt when I breathed too deeply. One of the scabs on my feet had ripped open during the rite; my right leg from knee to ankle was red with blood. What he said made sense. Of course there couldn't be another rider. Of course the thing inside me would do anything it could to keep its grip on me, to survive. Of course Satan had a thousand tricks.

And yet . . .

"It's okay," Ex said. "We'll get it next time."

"Yes," Chapin said, with a long sigh. "We will take a few minutes to recover ourselves. Then we will begin again."

"We won't," I said. "I don't understand what's going on here. Until I've got a handle on it, we're stepping back."

"That isn't an option," Chapin said.

"Really is," I said.

He knelt by me. His eyes were calm and implacable. He put his hand on mine, and he felt icy.

"The beast inside you, Miss Jayné? It is a Prince of Hell. That the Black Sun has spawned at all is of great significance. And that you have brought its larva to me is, I am certain, the benign hand of God. If you had come to me when it was fully mature, I might not have been able to help you."

I wiped a thread of puke off my lips and tried to find the words to say I wasn't feeling particularly helped just at the moment, but I couldn't string the sentence together. And there was some point I wanted to make that flickered in and out of my mind too quickly to quite hold on to. Something about the sewer stench.

"You must not let yourself be tricked by it," Chapin went on. "You must gather up your will and reject Satan."

"I can reject Satan just as much as the next guy," I said. "There's something else going on here."

"There is not. It is trying to distract you. You must not let it."

"Be strong," Tamblen said from behind me.

"Jayné. Please," Ex said. He really was begging. That, more than any of the God-and-Satan talk, made me want to keep going. I didn't want to let Ex down, embarrass him in front of his friends. I stood up, Chapin helping me to my feet. The white ceremonial shift looked as if I'd rolled through a bar's parking lot after closing. They were all around me, silent and expectant. Waiting for me. I found Ex. His ponytail was coming loose, white-blond locks of hair draping to his shoulder. I wondered whether Isabel had been in love with him.

I was about to say okay. I was about to start it all up again when the memory flitting around the back of my head clicked into place. I'd been kneeling in the courtyard, gathering the little girl—Dolores—up. She'd said something. *There was a bad ghost. It smelled bad. It tried to get inside me.*

It had happened before.

"No," I said. "We're done here."

Chapin sighed, his head sinking toward his chest like a defeated warrior. Ex looked pale and stricken. I wanted to touch his arm or hug him or something. I wanted to tell him it was going to be all right.

"I'm sorry, Ex," was the best I could manage.

"Xavier assured us that your will was strong, but even so, we knew this was a possibility," Chapin said. "A likelihood, even. I had hoped . . ."

"Don't put this on Ex," I said. "This is my choice."

"No," Tomás murmured in his beautiful whiskey voice. "There's no choice here."

My throat went tight and the hairs on the back of my neck stood up.

"When your mind is your own again, you will thank us for this," Chapin said.

A thick arm wrapped around my throat. Tamblen's, I thought. The Mark of St. Francis of the Desert, still bound to my arm, flared hot. I tried to twist around, but there were other hands on me, snatching at my arms and legs. Someone grabbed my waist, lifting me off the ground. I thrashed and tried to scream, tried to kick out. The charm on my skin felt like the surface of the sun, and I expected to smell my skin burning.

"It's going to be okay," Ex said. "I'm right here, Jayné. I'm right here with you."

I got a leg free for a second. I hit someone with it, but it was less a kick and more an unfriendly bump. I was one woman who'd just been through the wringer. They were six men. If my rider had been at full strength—not assaulted and bound by magic—I might have stood a chance.

They carried me outside, into the courtyard. The late afternoon air felt like a freezer. Their feet crunched in the snow as if they were walking through Styrofoam. I heard the rattling of a chain, and the creaking of hinges. The cellar doors. They were taking me underground. The wild, irrational certainty that they were going to bury me alive rushed through me, and I fought back with all the strength I had.

I might as well not have bothered.

They carried me down into the musty, cold darkness. I'd never seen the room before, but everything about it was familiar. A wide concrete slab with a wide steel ring set in it. Chains were attached to the ring. I'd helped Ex build something like this before. A prison for the possessed. They put me down, belly to the ground, and Tamblen shoved his knee into the small of my back, pinning me. Someone else—Carsey, maybe—had my elbow locked, bending it back until it hurt. I felt the manacles close around my wrists and ankles. There was power in them that didn't have anything to do with the strength of the metal.

Ex was beside me, holding my arm steady while someone else fastened the locks. His eyes were hard, his lips a line so thin they could have been drawn on his face with a pen. His eyes flickered up at me and then away. Behind him, I saw the bare earth walls, pale as bone, with a single bulb hanging from a wire in the corner. The concrete slab under me was icy. The steel chains clicked and slid, link over link. The soft, rolling, final sound of the padlocks closing on my restraints was like a nail hammered into a coffin lid. The priests stepped back from me all at once, like it was something they'd rehearsed. They probably had.

Light the gray of twilight spilled down the concrete steps. I could see a bright line where the cellar doors stood open, the white of the sky. The crows called to one another. I lay on the floor, stunned. Chapin stood beside the bulb, hard shadows marking his face.

"You will wait here, beast," he said. "We will return with rites less pleasant than those we have employed until now. This woman will not be lost to you."

I swallowed. I wanted to say they were wrong, that it was me and not the rider, to for Christ's sake let me go.

"Ex," I said. "You have to trust me."

He crouched down, his head on the same level as mine. Distress was drawing lines in his face. Carving him.

"This is how they work, Jayné," he said. "This is how they trick you into fighting on their side. Against us. Against me."

"Why?" I could hear the whine in my voice, and I hated it. "Why don't you believe me?"

"If you had a fever and it made you hallucinate, believing your visions were real wouldn't help you. It'd be letting the fever win. The riders trick people. It's what they do. And I won't let the rider win. Not with you."

He was so certain that he was being my strength when I was weak, my protection when I was vulnerable. He couldn't hear me, and I couldn't reach him. He couldn't even see the betrayal.

"Don't turn off the light," I said. "Don't leave me in the dark."

"I never will," Ex said even before Chapin nodded. I closed my eyes, listening to the soft footsteps.

At least one of them was limping. That was all I'd managed.

The cellar doors creaked when they closed, and the voices of the crows grew fainter. I was alone and numb. I felt myself start to shiver like it was happening to somebody else. I didn't feel anything, not hope, not despair, not even betrayal. My heel had started bleeding again. I was thirsty.

In the harsh light and black shadows, I took inventory of myself. Feet all messed up. Bruises on my arms and hands. Cracked rib. Filthy hair. Smelled of puke.

I rose to my knees; the chains wouldn't let me stand all the way up. The light from the cellar doors was gone. Night fallen or just decent weatherstripping. No way to know from here.

I thought about shouting until someone came, telling them that whatever it was had come after Dolores too, but I already knew what Ex and Chapin would say. The thing inside me had latched onto something the girl said, exploited it, used it to fool me. And I didn't have any way to prove otherwise. No one would believe me.

I was trapped with one rider in my body, and another one no one believed in stalking me like a fox walking around a henhouse. I was in chains, and the only one of my friends who knew where I was had helped put me there. My family didn't know me anymore. The uncle I'd idolized was an evil bastard.

My lover was back together with his wife. My feet were cut bloody and my ribs hurt.

Something shifted in my chest. Not the rider, but an emotional tidal wave rising up from the deepest part of myself. I expected weeping and rage and sorrow as deep as an ocean.

And so the laughter surprised me.

It was a deep sound, rich and warm and rolling, and it didn't belong to anyone but me. I laughed and I laughed and I laughed. When I spoke, my voice sounded hoarse but surprisingly strong.

"Well. Hel-lo, *bottom.*"

Slowly, I sat up. My mind felt weirdly clear, like I'd just woken up from a long sleep or come back from a good vacation. My body might be trembling-tired, but I could think.

I wasn't going to be able to get Chapin and his crows to believe me. I wasn't going to be able to get out of the chains here in the basement and make a run for it. But if I didn't do something, the sewer-stench thing was going to slip back through whatever chink it had found in Chapin's defenses, and sneak into my body as the Black Sun's daughter was ripped out of it. I couldn't call for help. The cavalry wasn't coming.

I took one deep breath, and then another, gathering my qi the way Chogyi Jake had taught me. Chogyi Jake, whom I had gone out of my way to exclude from this. Who would have believed me and taken my side if he'd been there. I pushed the thought aside. I didn't have time for guilt or regret. Might-have-beens later. Right now, I had to focus.

Put on your big-girl panties, Midian said half in my memory, half in my imagination, *and tell me what're you gonna do. Because if you're getting out of this one, you're doing it on your own.*

chapter Twelve

"Hey," I said. "Are you there?"

By now, it would be dark outside. Starlight on
snow. In my little oubliette, the lightbulb was the
closest thing to a heater. My nose was running, and
no matter how I curled up, I couldn't get warm. I'd
been there for what might have been an hour. Long
enough that the cut on my heel had clotted again. I
waited. Nothing happened.

"Hey," I said again. "So, listen. Here's the thing.
We both know there was another rider. And I
think we're both in trouble. I don't like having
something inside me that's not me, but since it

looks like that's kind of nonoptional, I've got a proposal."

The rider didn't do anything. I imagined it listening, aware but unable to act. Buried inside of me.

"The way I figure it, we don't have much to work with except each other. So how about a truce? Just between us. We work together, you and me, until we can get our necks out of this noose. And then I promise I'll try to find a way to get you out of me that doesn't . . . that doesn't kill you. But I'm the one who makes the decisions. No more running out into the middle of the night without me. That's the deal. We work this together. I'm the boss, and I'll make sure you don't get hurt. Sound good?"

It didn't sound good. It sounded weak. I'd come here of my own free will. I'd sought out Chapin so that he could do exactly what he was doing now. If I were the rider, I wouldn't have trusted me. But on the other hand, I didn't see what options it had either.

"Okay," I said. "That wasn't a no."

I squeezed my hands into fists, working the blood into them until the numbness went away. I pulled back the little Ace bandage on my arm. The hard metal of the medallion felt sharp against my fingertips. I hesitated. If Ex and Chapin were right, if the second rider was a trick, I was falling for it. But at least it was my mistake to make. I plucked the Mark of St. Francis of the Desert out. As much as it had hurt, I thought there would at least be a rashy spot, but my skin was unmarked. I let a couple of layers of bandage fall back in place and slipped the metal in over it. It looked more or less the same. If Ex or Chapin glanced at it, they probably wouldn't see a difference. But the Mark wasn't touching my skin.

"All right," I said. "I'm just going to put my arm down here at my side. I'm not going to move it. See what you can do."

I waited. Nothing happened. I tried to relax my arm, willing the muscles to be soft and calm. I breathed deeply three times. Four. Five. Six.

Sometimes, right on the edge of sleep, I would twitch. It was just once, and it always meant I was almost down. When my arm moved, it was almost the same. I didn't do anything, and then the movement just happened, sudden and sharp, sending the arc of steel chain undulating like a snake, and then gone again. I let out my breath.

"Good," I said. "That was good. Just hang on, little tomato. Things will be all right."

After that, I waited. There was nothing else I could do. Screaming wouldn't help. I didn't want to cry. Mostly I wanted to get warm, get my own clothes on. Maybe find a hot tub somewhere with my name on it. Sweet dreams. Instead, I sang through all the songs on *Hey Eugene!* and a couple from *Splendor in the Grass,* slapping the concrete and rattling my chains as musical accompaniment.

Then I segued over to some of Pink Martini's Christmas music, slapping out the percussion and doing my best China Forbes imitation for "Little Drummer Boy" and "Santa Baby." Singing, I could see my breath.

It was only a couple of more weeks until Christmas. With the strange tangle of spirits and darkness, demons and angst, that my life had become, the idea of normal holidays seemed to belong to a different world. I wondered what I would have been doing if not for the money and trouble that Eric had left for me when he died. I imagined myself working in a supermarket in Tucson. Arguing about who had to work the holiday shift and going back to a little apartment I'd probably have to share with someone just to make rent. Compared to what I was really doing, the grubby little kitchenette in my imagination seemed impossibly romantic.

It was weird to think that back home, Mom and Dad and my little brother, Curtis, would be putting up the tree, hauling the same ceramic nativity scene out of the attic and putting it on the lawn, going to the extra prayer meetings on Wednesday nights to beg that the Jews see the error of their ways, and I was here, doing this. I had the powerful memory of the smell of the mulled wine we kids weren't allowed to drink. If I'd stayed home, been the girl they wanted, I'd probably have been able to have a cup by now.

If I'd been who they wanted, I'd probably be married to someone from the church singles group. And pregnant, so maybe no wine after all. Probably all the girls I'd gone to high school with had families of their own now. It didn't seem right somehow that they still existed. They belonged to a different world, in some past life. And God help me, right now it seemed like a better one.

The truth was, I'd never really had a plan for my life. My whole childhood had been programmed and controlled by my father and the church, and my adult demon-hunting career had followed along the tracks that my deceased uncle Eric had laid down right up until it all went wrong. The only accomplishment that hadn't been in the shadow of one older male relative or another was making it through two semesters of a secular college before I dropped out. It wasn't much. But my life was mine, and I wanted it.

The cellar door creaked open. I stopped singing and shifted to sit cross-legged beside the concrete-set ring. Father Chapin, Ex, and Carsey came down, one after the other. They looked deathly solemn.

"Hey," I said. "I don't guess you guys brought a space heater or anything?"

"Who am I speaking to? In the name of Christ, I demand you answer with the truth, deceiver!"

I felt a pulse of something pass through me. Will, magic, qi. Whatever I wanted to call it. It didn't have the raw, screaming power of a rider's magic. It could have been just the focused power of a really well-practiced human being. I wondered if the other thing might be hiding inside Chapin and pulling its punches to keep anyone from noticing. It was one of them. If not Chapin, then one of his cabal.

Right now, though, it didn't matter. Wherever the invader was hiding out, my job was the same. Put everyone at ease, let them relax the security protocol a little, and then get out of Dodge. The first part, at least, wasn't something a rider could do for me.

I was the one playing this game.

"It's me," I said. "Jayné. The real one. I had one little twitch a while back, but things have been really quiet otherwise."

The three of them exchanged glances. Chapin had the best poker face, but I grew up in my father's house. I'd been faking contrition since before I could fit all the right consonants into *Sorry*.

"Look," I said, "you were right. It had a trick. I fell for it. It was just that right there, in the moment . . ."

"Satan is the lord of lies," Chapin said. I could see he was choosing his words carefully. "There is no shame in being fooled by him."

"Maybe not once," I said. "If it gets to be a habit, that's more of an issue."

Chapin knelt just far enough away from me that if I made a break for him the chain would pull me up short. I felt like a Doberman. Chapin rubbed his palm across his chin, the sound of skin against whiskers like wind moving sand.

"I am not certain what you mean by this, Miss Jayné," he said.

I sighed, looked down, hoisted an eyebrow. I couldn't say "All better, trust me again." It was the sort of thing you'd do if you were planning to make a break. Since that's exactly what I was planning, this was when to look different. I had to be the smart-ass girl struggling to admit she wasn't so smart after all. Bluff and bravado over a creamy center of vulnerability.

"I went into this pretty sure I wasn't going to slip," I said. "Turns out that was optimistic. Right now, sitting here? Yeah, I don't think it's going to happen again. Fell for it once. Know the score. Ready to take it on, right? But I was wrong then, and I might be wrong next time we go in."

Ex nodded almost subliminally. A tiny ghost of a smile touched Carsey's lips. I smiled, a little nervously. They'd want to see a little shame. Nothing says sincerity like eating crow. And since I was putting all the stress on what happened after we started the next rite, I was also taking the focus away from what happened between now and then. I felt a pang of guilt at the deception, but I'd killed an innocent man. Lying to Chapin—as the man said—wasn't exactly the low rung in my hierarchy of sins.

"What do you suggest?" Chapin asked.

"Well, I'm not going to insist we keep the chains on, but I think we're going to have to treat me as a hostile witness. I don't think it's safe to assume I won't break when the pressure's on. So we kind of have to assume I'm going to, right? Then if I do hold it together, pleasant surprise."

Chapin didn't smile so much as shift his eyes. The effect was the same.

"I believe you are correct," he said. "We have been preparing a slightly different ritual. Harder and longer, I think. If you can reject the spirit during this, it will be better. But it is not required."

"When do we start?" I asked.

"Right away."

"Cool," I said, locking my jaw. I couldn't let them take me back there. I couldn't let them start. If I didn't have time, there couldn't be an opportunity. Which was probably why Chapin had arranged it this way. He was a professional. I had to give him that. "Any chance I could hit the bathroom? Maybe get a fresh outfit? This one's kind of stinky."

I saw him hesitate. It was like watching a movie with one skipped frame, there and gone before I could quite register it.

"Of course," he said. "But under guard."

"Wouldn't have it any other way," I said.

They took off the manacles. Outside, the sky was clear. The stars filled the sky like smoke from a fire. I hopped across the snow, yipping as the cold bit at my toes. Inside, Tomás and Miguel were kneeling before a circle chalked on the floor. Tamblen stood at the doorway, quietly apologetic. Candles the off-white of fresh cream burned all around, and sweet incense thickened the air. As I stepped through the double doors and into the warmth of the room, it occurred to me that for *sure* the other rider was in the room with me right now. I didn't let myself look at them and wonder. I couldn't let anyone see I was thinking about it. I had the powerful physical memory of smelling sewage and the numbing thickness forcing itself down my throat. I hoped the moment of fear read as dread of the punishing ceremony we were all about to begin.

"Just stopping by the little girls' room," I said. "Then we'll get the party started."

"I'll take her," Ex said, putting his hand on my elbow.

I had maybe five minutes. To the bathroom, back from it. I thought about crawling out the bathroom window before I remembered how small it was. Something else then. Whatever happened, I couldn't step into that circle.

I walked through the kitchen, past the box of donuts that I'd bought years ago, in some different lifetime. I passed a crucifix. The Christ figure's face seemed turned away from me in particular.

"Don't be worried," Ex said as we came to the bathroom door.

A surge of hope rose up in me. He knew about the other rider. I was going to be all right. And then he spoke again, and the hope went away.

"Lots of people fail the first time out. It's not that bad. We will beat this thing. I promise."

I opened the door. Inside, the bathroom was tiny. If I went in, there was no place to go but back out. So this was it. My opportunity. My moment. I looked at Ex and smiled with a brick of lead in my gut. He was doing this—all of this—because he needed redemption for the girl he'd failed before, and because he loved me. It was written in his expression. I hated what I was about to do.

"You know I really appreciate all this," I said, meaning every word. "Facing up to Chapin for me. Chasing me down in the middle of the night. All of it. You've been a really good friend to me."

"Jayné—"

"I mean it. It's meant a lot to me."

His eyes met mine. There were tears in them.

"I couldn't do anything less. I won't say it's all been easy. Or fun. But if I had it to do again, I would."

"You say the sweetest shit," I said. And then, regret in my chest like a tumor, I turned my attention inward. "All right. Now."

My left hand took his wrist, snapping it down,

and my right rose to clamp his throat, turning him. My body slipped in next to his, my arm around his throat and my rider pulling him off his feet before he had the chance to scream. His feet touched the wall, and he kicked off awkwardly, trying to break my grip. My rider rolled with the motion, using it to shift my hand off his throat and lock my forearm in its place. Then, his head pressed against mine, I rocked back a few degrees and cut off his air.

You'll snap his neck, I tried to shout. Don't hurt him. But the rider was in control now, and I might as well have been talking to the thin fella on the crucifix. Ex batted at me awkwardly, tried to flip around, and then convulsed. My arms held him for a few seconds after he went limp, and then lowered him softly to the floor. My rider paused long enough that I could see Ex was still breathing, and then she turned, padding through the brick-floored rooms like a cat. At the blue front doors, she paused, gathered herself, and threw my body out into the snowbound night, sprinting through the high snow with an intensity that could have been fear or joy or both.

THE HIGHWAY barely deserved the name. Two lanes stretched out in the darkness, no wider than a residential street. The snowplows had been through, clearing the asphalt and throwing walls of snow up at the shoulders. I stood in the middle of the lane, my hand up, and hoped that the oncoming headlights would stop. And that my ragged white ceremonial gown wasn't too see-through. No way around it, this wasn't going to be a high-dignity day.

The headlights slowed, shifted to the side like the driver was thinking about going around me, and then stopped. I couldn't see the vehicle itself past the glare, but it was big enough to be a truck or SUV. The passenger's door opened and a wide, burly man stepped out toward me. He was wearing a black puffy coat with iron-on patches at the elbow and sleeve and a baseball cap that had *Guajira* printed on it in fading red letters.

"Hey," he said, and then paused. "You okay? You got car trouble or something?"

It was a pretty obvious assumption to make. Inappropriately dressed, somewhat bloody woman in the middle of a lonely stretch of country road. Car trouble. Sure.

"Something like that," I said through my chattering teeth. "I could really use a lift."

A voice came from the driver's side, a low masculine voice speaking Spanish. The man in front of me shouted back into the light. I promised myself that if I didn't collapse from hypothermia and die here in the wilderness, I'd make a point of learning a language besides English. The driver shouted something short, and the man in the hat shrugged and turned back to me. I noticed he had a thin mustache and a tattoo on his neck. If I'd seen him at a bar or walking along a street, I'd have been wary of him.

"We can give you a ride, sure."

"Thanks," I said, and walked to the passenger's door before he could change his mind. It was a pickup truck, white where it wasn't muddy. The man behind the wheel was bigger than the one who'd gotten out, and older. Gray at his temples and thick, callused hands. I hauled myself up and scooted into the middle of the long bench seat. The man in the hat got in after me. The cab smelled like WD-40 and pot, and the back window was covered by Gothic-lettered stickers in loving memory of someone who'd died three years ago and young. I thought about all the stories I'd heard about girls going hitchhiking and coming to bad ends. I thought about all the stories I'd heard about people picking up mysterious hitchhikers who turned out to be more dangerous than they seemed. The truck's heater was running full blast, and nothing in my life had ever felt better.

"Me llamo Ramón, y este pendejo llame Marcos," the driver said. *"Como te llamas, eh?"*

Even I knew enough to make sense of that.

"Jayné," I said. "I'm Jayné. And thanks for this. Seriously."

The driver shrugged—*It's nothing*—and we started down the dark road. The passenger crowded himself against the door, trying not to touch me.

He took his hat off, fidgeted with it, and put it on again.

"We're heading for Peñasco," he said, "but the cops got a station in Carson. We could drop you off there."

"No," I said. "No cops."

The two men exchanged a look over my head. I felt the driver shrug again.

"So where you going?" the passenger asked, and as soon as he did, I knew the answer.

"You ever been to a place called O'Keefe's?"

chapter Thirteen

When we pulled into the slush and gravel of the parking lot, I was amazed by the number of cars. It was eight o'clock, and apparently still the height of the dinner rush. Ramón and Marcos let me out and headed back to the road with my gratitude and a sense of being relieved to be done with me. I turned and considered the front doors. I knew I looked like hell. I didn't want word of me to spread back to Ex and Chapin, so marching straight in seemed unwise. Freezing in the parking lot was also not a great plan. I walked quickly around the side of the building. I could hear voices from inside the restaurant, shouting over the radio. The truck's heater had taken the edge off my cold, but I was still barefoot in the snow. I needed to get into shelter.

Midian's RV was dark but unlocked. I didn't know what it used for a heater, but the air was warm and close. The only light was a tiny fluorescent bulb over the stovetop. Clean dishes were stacked beside the sink. A magnet with a scorpion encased in plastic pinned an envelope to the fridge. Somewhere under the sink, a water heater burbled and hissed. No one else was there.

I sat down on the little couch and cradled my feet. After a few minutes, I stumbled to the back and pulled a comforter off Midian's bed to curl up in. I was shivering hard, my body reacting to the cold and abuse and hellish day I'd just suffered. I didn't figure Midian would mind if I messed up his bed. The cotton and down stank of old cigarettes, but I didn't care. I folded myself onto the miniature couchlike thing, pulled the comforter around my head, and waited to get warm. Twelve hours ago, I'd been driving in toward San Esteban.

I thought about the little condo near the ski valley. It had my clothes. My laptop. The leather backpack I used as a purse was with Ex and the priests, along with my wallet, my credit cards, my cell phone. I wondered what they were doing now.

Searching for me, no doubt, but I'd always been hard to locate magically, everything I owned with a GPS chip was somewhere else, and the trail of my footsteps in the snow ended at the highway. So far even Midian didn't know I was here. The ashtray-stinking darkness was about as safe as I was going to get.

When Midian's shift was over and he came back home, I could talk to him about it. Make a plan. I kept telling myself that. Feeling seeped back into my arms and legs. My toes hurt like hell, and one place near my little toe was still numb. But everywhere I pressed white went pink again when I let up the pressure, so I seemed to have avoided frostbite. I took the Ace bandage off of my arm, throwing the exorcist's medallion in the sink.

Part of me wanted to keep going, think everything through, take action, but exhaustion and the slowly growing warmth scattered my thoughts. I was only vaguely aware that I was falling asleep, and then the sound of claws against metal woke me up.

It was daylight outside, and not the blue that came before dawn either. I'd slept through the night on the little not-quite-couch, and Midian hadn't come in. Claws scratched against the door again, and I levered myself up, muscle-sore and aching, to open it. The Labrador chuffed at me, her breath white, and wagged her thick tail.

"Yeah, sure," I said. "Come on in."

As she clambered up the steps, I looked around. The snow-covered ground was so white it had flecks of color—blue and purple and pink. Icicles hung from the restaurant's eaves while meltwater from the roof dripped down them, making little caves of ice by the wall. The sky was huge and blue and marbled by cloud and contrail. And Midian hadn't come home last night. Ozzie the Lab sat on her graying haunches, looked at me, and wagged. I scratched her ears absently. Maybe he was out feeding. Or maybe he'd come in, seen me, and made other arrangements for himself. I was still wearing the white shift from yesterday, and it was starting to reek. My rider was quiet. I figured she had had at least as rough a time as I had. I didn't know what kind of damage the near exorcism had done to her, or even what kind of shape I should hope she was in.

"Hey," I said. "Are you there? Truce is still on as far as I'm concerned."

I might have been talking to myself. I didn't know. My stomach growled, my hunger level going from background noise to ravenous in about ten seconds. I tried to remember the last time I'd eaten anything. Something like twenty-four hours ago, and that had been donuts. No blood sugar probably wasn't helping me think. I leaned over, reaching the refrigerator door easily from where I sat. The light took a second before clicking on. A glass bottle of milk, three apples, half a loaf of bread, four eggs, and a hunk of cheese. I took an apple, the cheese, and the bottle of milk. I didn't figure Midian would mind. When I closed the refrigerator door, I noticed the scorpion magnet again, clipping its envelope to the door. With the daylight, I saw there was a single word written on the pale paper like an address: *Kid*.

Taking a long drink of milk with my left hand, I plucked the letter out from under its scorpion with my right. A single sheet of paper. The note was in perfectly clear handwritten letters, tiny and flowing. Almost like calligraphy.

Hey, Kid.

> *I'm going to be a little vague here. I don't know for sure who's going to be reading this. Figure you'll get what I'm talking about. You're smart that way.*

> *I make it the chances of your coming back here are pretty good, or I wouldn't be leaving this. And probably you won't have anybody of a clerical bent with you. But if you do, that could make for a really bad day. No offense meant, but I didn't make it this far by taking risks that weren't strictly necessary. Sorry to let you down and all. You're a good kid and I like you, but I don't see how you and me get to spend a lot of time hanging out. It's a lifestyle thing. Dietary. You know what I mean.*

I've been thinking about that guy you did wrong by in Chicago. I've seen a lot of people struggle with exactly that kind of problem over the years. Thing is, what you did comes pretty naturally to me. I know what you're going through, but I don't really get it. So maybe that's what I've got for you. Some folks it bothers, some it doesn't. You're one of the ones it does.

And I've got to tell you, I think it's a good thing Capt. Milquetoast's out of the picture. I know how this sounds coming from me, but the age gap between you two was always a problem. He's just at a different place in his life. And this work you've been doing? He's not cut out for it. Twice now he invoked the abyss. Plus which what you said about him getting ridden in New Orleans? Getting a rider's like a drinking game. Once you start losing, you keep losing—getting ridden opens you up and getting closed again is tricky. That's something you're probably going to have to deal with too, now that you've gotten the thing shucked out of you. So, you know, good luck with that.

Okay. My ride's here. I know you've got a metric shitload of questions about your uncle. I wish I could help you more, but hey. We do what we can, right? Here's what I've got for you in three sentences or less: He was a sonofabitch. He never did anything without a reason. The reason was always that it made things the way he wanted them.

You've got a rough road, kid. Good luck with it.
Don't come looking for me.

Your pal, Midian.

I read it over twice more, waiting to see if I felt betrayed, but all that was there was vague disappointment. Yes, he was a vampire. Yes, he killed people. Ex and Chapin and all the others would have wanted him destroyed, and for good reason. But I liked him. I wondered if my willingness to give him a free pass might not be another step down the path toward not being one of the good guys. I put the letter back in its envelope. Ozzie looked up at me with black, watery eyes, her tail thumping heavily against the floor. I sighed and headed for the back.

Midian hadn't cleared everything out when he went. The tiny closet had a pair of paint-splattered men's jeans that I could just about squeeze past my hips, and I found a gray sweater with a stain across the front that might have been blood, but smelled like barbecue sauce and cigarettes. The shower was almost too small to turn around in, but it was there. No shampoo, but I used the bar of soap. Lousy for shine and body, but plenty good enough for getting the worst junk in my hair out of it. The water was hot enough to scald, and ran out after about two minutes. Still, pulling on Midian's hand-me-downs, I felt better than I had in days. I still didn't have shoes. Or money. Or anything of my own.

So, that was what I needed to fix next.

O'Keefe's was open for breakfast. I didn't go around to the front. I'd done terrible things to my feet in the last two days, and sleeping through the night seemed to have gotten the blood back to every single nerve ending I had. The snow felt burningly cold. I hopped quickly to the kitchen door. The man who opened it was maybe eighteen with hair cut close to his scalp and an ornate cross hanging at his collarbone. He was wearing an ironic Santa hat complete with white pom-pom at the floppy tip, and he was smoking a cigarette.

"Hey, I'm a friend of"—I gestured back toward the RV—"of his. Could I use your phone?"

The guy looked from me to the RV and back, then stood back and let me inside. The kitchen was hot, and the smell of cooking chorizo sausage and freshly brewed coffee was like a postcard from a better world. The man gestured me toward a thin green door. I nodded my thanks and ducked through. The office was tiny. The phone was a cheap cordless with a huge chrome-and-red logo on the mouthpiece for a company I'd never heard of. It took me a couple of tries to remember how to call information, and then how to call information in Denver. All the numbers I needed were in my cell phone, and I didn't know the actual numbers. Eventually, I got the listing I needed.

The first call was disheartening. I'd forgotten it was Saturday, and all the businesses were closed. But the message left an emergency contact number, so I wrote that down, called back, and waited, biting my lips while it rang. Once I got someone to pick up on the other end, it was a question of minutes while the call was transferred. The clicks and hums made it sound like I was going through about a dozen exchanges.

"Hello, dear," my lawyer said. "How are you?"

"Little rough," I said. "Trending up, though."

"What can I do for you?"

I paused. I'd gotten this far without knowing exactly what my plan was, except that I had resources there and I wanted them here. A crowd of things all came at once: shoes, shampoo, proof that the Black Sun's daughter hadn't tricked me into running. My backpack. My friends. Lunch.

The truth was, the answer depended on what I meant my next move to be. I'd gotten out, I'd made it to safety. Ex and Chapin and the others were certain to be out looking for me, but if I wanted to, I could head out of the country on my own. Or go to ground behind the best-paid security that money could buy. Flee or hole up. Or something else.

I took a deep breath and blew it out.

"I need a car. Something big with four-wheel drive. No GPS on it, though. And a cell phone with the GPS taken out or broken. And a couple of outfits. I'm wearing borrowed clothes right now. With good shoes. And really thick socks. And maybe a few thousand dollars in cash. Oh, and . . . Hey, is there a way for me to get a replacement driver's license without actually being there? Because I can't really get to mine right now, and I don't want to explain that to the highway patrol or the TSA or anyone."

"I'm sure we can arrange something," my lawyer said. "Is there anything else?"

"I need Chogyi Jake's cell phone number. I've got it in my old phone, and I don't remember it."

She gave it to me, and I dug around in the thin gray metal desk drawers until I found a pen that worked and a piece of paper. Behind me, the kitchen rattled with cutlery and the sounds of frying meat and eggs, loud Spanish and quieter, more distant English. I shifted the phone to my other ear.

"That's enough for now," I said.

"Where would you like to take possession?" she asked, and I smiled but didn't laugh.

"I'm staying in an RV behind a roadside restaurant called O'Keefe's outside Taos, New Mexico. They should bring everything there."

"O'Keefe spelled like the painter?"

"I didn't know there was a painter."

"Don't worry. We'll find it. How soon do you need all this?"

"As soon as you can," I said. "Today would be good."

There was a pause. I heard keystrokes as she typed something on her computer.

"I don't think I'll be able to do that. Weekends make these things difficult," she said. "I can manage tomorrow early afternoon for the license and the car. I could have the rest of it to you earlier if you'd like."

"No, I don't want a lot of different deliveries. It'd call attention to me." I tried to remember how much food had been in Midian's RV. Could I really even stay there? It had to really belong to someone, and that almost certainly wasn't him. Well, I could cross that bridge when I found it. "Bring it all at once, but don't spare money making it happen fast. If throwing cash at it will help, go wild."

"Understood," she said cheerfully.

"You may be hearing from Ex. Whatever he tells you, ignore it. If he asks for anything, don't do it."

"Yes, dear. And should I take him off the payroll, then?"

"No," I said. "He thinks he's doing the right thing. He's just wrong and he's not listening to me right now."

I could almost hear her eyebrow go up, but her voice didn't give her away.

"Whatever you think is best," she said.

"All right, then," I said. "I think that's got me covered."

"If anything else comes up, don't hesitate to call, dear."

"Won't," I said. "Thanks."

I hung up, turned, and leaned against the desk. Something was bothering me, and it took me a few seconds to figure out what. Eric was saving me again. When he'd died, he had left everything he had to me, and his personal empire was huge. If I'd come running to Midian's RV with only what I'd actually earned myself, I wouldn't have been able to afford my own lunch, much less new clothes, a new car, and a semilegal driver's license. I didn't know what I would have done. But I didn't have to know, because I did have Eric's money.

He was a sonofabitch. He never did anything without a reason. The reason was always that it made things the way he wanted them.

I hadn't stopped to ask myself what Eric had meant by bringing me into this secret world. Riders, magic, spirits, wealth. All of it. When it had first happened, I'd thought it was because he'd been my own personal support team. He'd always been there. Not at center stage since he and my Dad fell out, but waiting in the wings. There to catch me when I stumbled. After the drunken lost weekend of my sixteenth birthday, he'd nursed me through my hangover and helped me hide the new tattoo from my parents. Now it seemed like he had to have known. All that time he had to have known there was something growing inside me. That I was infected.

And still, he'd put everything he'd built up into my hands. From beyond death, he was saving me again right now. And he was doing it because somehow, it made things the way he wanted them.

"I don't suppose you have anything you'd like to tell me about why Eric would have wanted me rich after he died," I said, but if my rider heard me, she didn't respond.

I was going to take the money anyway. Even with this suspicion that it might all be poisoned, I would take it and spend it to get myself out of a tight spot, because I didn't see any other option. For the first time, it made me uncomfortable.

In the kitchen, a woman's voice rose in fast, annoyed tones. The cook who'd let me in the office answered. I couldn't understand any of the words, but the tone was dismissive. The woman signed percussively, and a door opened and closed. I picked up the telephone handset, smoothed down the scrap of paper, and punched the code to block caller ID—just in case—and then the rest of the numbers.

The phone on the far end rang three times. Chogyi Jake picked up.

chapter fourteen

"Hello?" he said. I'd forgotten how gentle his voice was.

"Hey. It's me. I'm sorry I didn't call before. And by before, I mean weeks ago. I've actually been pretty messed up, and I didn't want anyone to see me like that," I said, and then when he didn't reply right away, "Also I was still freaked out over you getting hurt because of me, and I was having a really hard time talking myself into putting you back in harm's way on my account."

"I see," Chogyi Jake said carefully.

"Anyway, I don't know if Ex called you yet, but

I figured out why I have all these weird powers that are getting stronger when they should be getting weak. I've got a rider. It's called Sonnenrad or the Black Sun. Apparently it's really powerful, but it's young. Ex took me to New Mexico to find his old mentor, who's this kind of intense guy named Father Chapin. Only, when they tried to exorcise it, there was another rider. It was trying to get in while the old one was being forced out? And I . . . I took off. I mean, Ex thinks I'm being played by the rider I *do* have, and so he chained me up, and they were going to try again. Only I kind of called truce with the Black Sun thing and I got out before they could offer me up to this other whatever-it-is. So I'm pretty sure Ex and his old posse are out hunting me on the assumption that I'm in the grips of the devil."

"Okay," Chogyi Jake said. I felt a moment's fear. He was being so distant and withdrawn, and I interpreted his reserve as anger. And then I didn't. I closed my eyes, chagrined.

"Only Ex called you last night and told you all of this. And you flew out," I said. "He's standing, like, *right* next to you, isn't he?"

"Yes," Chogyi Jake said.

"Well, that's awkward."

"I was thinking the same thing."

We were both silent for a moment. In the kitchen, something fell. The clatter of metal spilling on the floor made me jump a little.

"I'm not coming back in," I said. "There really is another rider."

"Okay."

"Only they're not going to believe that. At least not coming from me. So . . . yeah. I'll check back in later."

"I'm glad to hear that," Chogyi Jake said. I could hear him smile.

"It's good to hear you, though," I said.

"You too," he said. "We'll talk again soon."

The line went dead, and I put the handset down on the desk. I didn't know if I was disturbed that Chogyi Jake was with Ex and trying to track me down, or glad that he was in the neighborhood even if he wasn't by my side. Both, maybe. It was interesting that he hadn't wanted Ex to know it was me on the phone. I tried to imagine what Chogyi Jake would see, looking at Father Chapin's cabal, and I failed. Warriors against the army of the unclean. Unhealthy religious zealots. Something else. It all seemed equally plausible.

I stepped out of the little office and back into the kitchen. The guy with the cross was scraping a steel spatula over the grill, the muscles of his arm tense with the effort. Voices and the clinking of knives and forks against plates came from the front like it was a different planet. I waited until he looked over his shoulder at me.

"Thanks," I said.

"Yeah. You know when he's getting back? I don't want double shifts my whole life."

"I'm not sure," I lied. "Couple of days at least."

He said something casually obscene and turned back to the grill. I slipped out the back. The cold was vicious and the jeans-and-sweater outfit, while better than a ceremonial shift, still counted as underdressed for the occasion. I ran across to the RV, opened the door, and hopped up. Ozzie the Labrador bumped against me, pushing out through the door I'd come in. I watched for a few seconds while she peed, scratched gleefully at the snow, and trotted back to me. I wondered whether Midian had housebroken her or if she'd come that way. I let her clamber back in beside me.

It took me a few minutes to figure out the stove. There was a switch that turned the whole thing on and off separate from the controls for the individual burners. I assumed it had something to do with safety and not having your apartment catch fire while you were driving it. I scrambled one of the eggs and ate it while sitting on the couchlike thing, petting the dog with my feet to keep my toes warm. After a while, my nose became accustomed to the ashtray smell, and I didn't even notice it.

I was alone, or as near to it as I'd been in years. I didn't quite have enough food to make it through to tomorrow afternoon without a few hours of mild hunger. I still had a foreign thing living inside of me, ready to take over at any moment. The guilt and horror of Grace Memorial were at the back of my head like a headache that wouldn't quite go away. I didn't have shoes or a coat. I didn't have chains on me, but I was almost as trapped here as I had been in the basement in San Esteban.

It should have felt like a prison, but it didn't. It felt like a retreat. The cheesy, decrepit RV was where they couldn't find me. There was nothing to do but listen to the radio, doze, and watch the late afternoon sunset turn the snow from white to gold, gold to unearthly red, and red fading to gray under an unimaginable spread of stars. I could feel the cold radiating from the windows, but the heater was working just fine. I found a spare fitted sheet stuffed in a cupboard, stripped Midian's bed, and made it my own. Ozzie went out just after dark and didn't come back for a couple of hours.

Hundreds of miles away, my little brother, Curtis, was getting ready for what was going to be his last Christmas at home. Next year, he'd graduate high school and go off to Bible college or a job, if he could find one. My older brother, Jay, was probably still getting ready for his shotgun wedding. I hadn't spoken to him about it, hadn't met the girl who was going to be my sister-in-law and the mother of my nephew or my niece. I knew her family was Mexican and that my mother was embarrassed. I wondered if Jay was in love with her or seduced and trapped or something else that I hadn't even imagined. The wind started to pick up, the RV creaking and rocking under the pressure.

In Chicago, Kim and Aubrey would be getting home from work. I'd set them up with enough money that they could make their own research plans. I'd never thought about the questionable joys of parasitology before I'd met them. Now I was going to be responsible for funding some good basic research about *Toxoplasma gondii* that I probably wouldn't understand. Closer to hand, Chogyi Jake and Ex were looking for me, both worried about me, probably for totally different reasons.

I couldn't do anything about any of it. Not now, and not until late tomorrow, and I didn't feel powerless. I felt relieved. If great power brought great responsibility, then being totally impotent meant I was off the hook, at least for a while. Tomorrow would come, and I'd need to make some decisions. I'd have to find a way to prove that there really was another rider. I'd have to figure out how it had gotten past a circle of exorcists and explicitly rider-proof magic. I'd have to decide what I was doing about having a Prince of Hell sharing my body. All of it tomorrow.

I wondered, nestled in the little metal and plastic shell, whether this was how my rider felt. Just before midnight, I heard claws at the door, stumbled out of bed, and let the dog back in.

"You are a pain in the ass," I said sternly. "I was comfortable."

She chuffed happily, jumped on the couchlike thing, and fell instantly to sleep. I went back to my bed—I already thought of it as mine—and curled up under the blanket. I remembered the first time I'd seen Midian, stretched out like a corpse on a bed in the apartment Eric owned. I'd been sure he was dead until his eyes opened. And then a couple of hours later, we'd been attacked, and I'd felt my rider for the first time. I tried to pull back from the memory, but sleep-soaked as I was, I couldn't help it. I saw Midian walking over the fallen wizards, a Luger in his hand. He'd told me at the time that they weren't people, just qliphoth. Shells. That the riders in them had displaced anything human. Probably, he'd been lying.

From there it was a short step into nightmare. I was in Grace Memorial, burying the black coffin with an innocent man inside it. I was crying. I wanted to stop, but I couldn't. I drove the nails into the coffin with the palm of my hand.

And then I was outside myself, watching. That was new. The dream never went like that before. I was in a theater, watching myself twenty feet tall. A beam of dusty light hung in the air above us, connecting the projectionist's booth to the screen. Beside me, my rider took my hand.

"I had to," I said.

"I know," she replied. "I was there too. We did it together."

"If I hadn't—"

"Shh."

I turned back to the movie. It was just like all my other nightmares except for the distance that came from watching it all from outside. I felt the same sickening grief and guilt and fear, but maybe not as vividly. When I woke up crying, it was just weeping instead of the violent sobs I was used to. Ozzie was at the bedside looking concerned. Her breath was warm and stank. I scratched her between the ears, and, reassured, she went back to her place on the couch.

I WAS sure when I went back to sleep, I would dream of the desert. Instead, I spent the rest of the night talking to my boyfriend from college about his plan to start a business delivering ice cream wirelessly over the Internet and walking through a cathedral-sized shopping mall trying to return a cookbook my mother had written for me while sparrows did complex mating dances with bits of trailing ribbon and twine. I woke up to the yellow-blue light of approaching dawn, feeling more rested, peaceful, and calm than I had in weeks.

I got dressed in yesterday's clothes, cooked the last eggs, and scouted around the RV for paper and something to write with—a stub of dull pencil and the back of the envelope Midian had left for me. The radio muttered the best of the nineties, bringing with it some surprisingly vivid memories of my church preschool classroom and Mrs. Springsteen, who'd taught it. I couldn't think she'd ever played Nirvana during our nap time, but the two things had become conflated in my memory. I let Ozzie out, and she bolted after a half dozen crows that were going through the restaurant's trash. I still had a few hours before I had to do anything, but then the new car would come—the new shoes—and break time would be over.

My first order of business was the other rider. I couldn't leave things with Ex and Chogyi and Father Chapin the way they stood. I had to find proof that there had been another rider. How to go about that . . .

I took the pencil stub and wrote *Dolores*.

If she could tell them what had happened to her, it would give my story some weight. The problem, of course, being that what I knew about her was her first name, that she'd had an exorcism go south on her four days ago, and that she probably lived somewhere in northern New Mexico or southern Colorado. Or maybe farther afield. I didn't really know how wide an area Father Chapin covered, but I, at least, had come to him from Austria. I didn't have the impression that Dolores's family was quite the jet-set type, given their cars . . .

Their cars. There was something about that. It took me a couple of minutes before my subconscious handed me the thing I'd been trying to remember. They'd had a vanity plate. I picked up the little stub of pencil and wrote on the back of the envelope: *GODS-WRK*. I felt pretty good about that, which was nice because I didn't get much further on that track.

I turned to how another rider could have been there in the first place. If I'd been a rider, a circle of exorcists was pretty much the last place I'd want to be: the sanctuary was consecrated, and I'd had the rider-stopping medallion on during the rite. When I started listing the reasons that the sewer-stink thing really couldn't have been there, it was a pretty strong argument. I wrote my questions on the envelope: *Why/how can it live with the enemy? Why didn't the medallion stop it?*

I sat looking at the words for a long time, wondering what I'd do if I found Dolores and she didn't know what I was talking about. It was possible that the Black Sun really had been tricking me. Footsteps crunched through the snow, and I shoved the envelope into my pocket before the knock came. The guy was midtwenties, wearing jeans that actually fit, a thick flannel shirt, and curly dark hair that had been gelled to within an inch of its life. He had a black suitcase in his hand too big to be called an overnight bag, but too small to hide a body in. His smile was cautious.

"I'm looking for Jane Heller?" he said.

"Close enough," I said. "Tell me those are my new clothes."

He handed up the suitcase.

"I have the car out in the parking lot," he said. "There's some paperwork I need you to sign."

"No problem," I said. "Give me ten minutes to change, and I'll meet you inside."

"That'll be great," he said with a bobbing, deferential nod.

I put the case on the kitchen counter, unzipped it, and popped it open. The top of the pile was fresh underwear, two different sizes of sports bra, and thick white wool socks. I couldn't stop grinning. Tights that were right on the line between panty hose and thermal underwear. Two pairs of slacks, one black and one tan. Low-heeled boots that zipped up the side that could pass for businesswear, but had enough tread and arch support to take hiking. A pack of undershirts still in their plastic, three blouses, a dark overcoat not that different from the one I'd left behind, a package of ponytail holders, a black baseball cap with insulated foam lining, a pair of sunglasses, a discreet emergency pack with a variety of feminine protection products, a wallet filled with hundreds and twenties, a New Hampshire driver's license with a picture of me I didn't remember seeing before, and a black case with a smartphone in it. I pushed the power button, and the little thing sprang to life. It was thicker than the other ones I'd seen, and the matte black case had an almost military feel. The opening touch screen was filled with application icons. The address book had only one entry: my lawyer's private line. I could have kissed her.

It took me twenty minutes to change, and when I stepped out of the RV for the last time, I looked like someone from a SWAT team. My hair was pulled back through the adjustment band of the baseball cap. I had the dark slacks, the black overcoat, the sunglasses. The shoes were a little too big and the sports bra was still a little too tight, but walking around to the front of O'Keefe's, I felt more comfortable than I had in days. Just before I turned the corner, I looked back. The snow was mostly melted off the RV. Its sides were scabby with sun damage. I still smelled like Midian's cigarettes and probably would until my hair grew out.

"Thanks," I said to the broken-down old vehicle and the vampire I'd borrowed it from.

My car was a blue SUV with the dealer's paper-work taped to the back window. It stood out in the parking lot because of its lack of mud and wear. I walked into O'Keefe's to find Mr. Hair Gel chatting up the underage waitress I'd had the first time I came in. He looked pleased and nervous when I sat down across from him.

"I just need a signature on a few things saying

you took possession," he said, setting a pack of legal-sized papers in front of me with neon-green sticky notes showing me where to sign. He also handed me a really nice ballpoint pen.

"Thank you," I said, and started making all the right marks. In the corner of my eye, I saw the waitress trying not to stare at me.

"Excuse me," Mr. Hair Gel said. "I'm sorry for asking, but are you a movie star or something?"

"Nope," I said, putting my initials on an insurance policy for the new car.

"It's just we don't usually get this kind of service request. I mean, there was this one time Julia Roberts had a bunch of people out in Arroyo Seco, and—"

"I've never met Julia Roberts," I said. "I think we travel in different circles."

"Right. I just had to ask," he said. "You looked like you could be."

I glanced up. His smile was bashful and cocksure at the same time. I was being hit on. I smiled back.

"Anything else you need me to sign?" I asked. He shook his head and passed a single key on a remote control fob across the table. I picked it up, weighing it in my hands. All right, then. Time to hunt down demons. "Thanks. You do have a ride back to town, right?"

"He'll be along shortly," Mr. Hair Gel said, but his

tone suggested that he'd be open to the offer of a lift back in my car. For half a second, I was tempted.

Once I was in the SUV, I cranked up the heater, letting the engine run. The cell phone had great reception, even here. I called my lawyer.

"Jayné!" she said, answering before it could ring. "Is everything all right, dear?"

"It's great," I said. "You're a miracle worker. But I need something else. Can we get an address for a someone if I give you a license plate? I'm not sure if it's New Mexico or Colorado plates, though."

"Of course, dear. Give me what you've got, and I'll be right back."

I spelled out GODSWRK to her and waited while she repeated it all back in military code. *Golf Oscar Delta.* Then we dropped the line. The SUV said I had a full tank of gas, the built-in GPS was disabled and couldn't find a signal, and it was a few degrees below freezing outside. I took a deep breath and leaned back. Jayné Heller, international demon hunter. Well, all right, then.

As I pulled out to the road, Ozzie trotted into the parking lot. I saw her dark eyes looking up at me, her tail wagging. The little chuffed bark was white in the cold. I stopped and opened the passenger's door. She looked at me.

"You coming?"

She trotted over, hauled herself up the step, and sat in the passenger's seat, panting through a canine smile. When I reached across her to close the door, I got a cold earful of damp nose. I took us out to the highway.

Jayné Heller, international demon hunter, and her dog.

Even better.

chapter fifteen

"Hey," I said. "Can you talk?"

"Yeah," my little brother, Curtis, said. "They're all out doing stuff. What are you up to?"

"Surprisingly difficult question to answer," I said. "I just got a dog. What's going on at home?"

For twenty miles, Curtis filled me in on the gossip at home. Our older brother, Jay, had gotten his girlfriend pregnant, and now my future sister-in-law and her whole extended family had descended to prepare for the wedding. Mom had given up all hope of keeping the bun-in-the-oven issue quiet, and was now explaining to everyone at church that the new in-laws only *looked* Mexican, but were really Brazilians who'd just been living in Mexico before they came to the United States. In her mind, this was apparently better. Curtis was wildly amused by the whole thing, and his schadenfreude was a little infectious.

Before he hung up, I got Ozzie to bark hello to him a couple of times.

My new cell phone had a web browser that promised me a hotel with a real shower and hot water if I drove back in toward Taos proper. My other option appeared to be heading north into the Carson National Forest and staying there until spring, so with a little trepidation, I headed south.

The sky was enormous, the horizon seemed to fly out before me snow-white and earth-brown and the gray-green of piñons. Clouds draped the overwhelming blue like lace pulled to breaking, and the air smelled of cold and smoke and pine. For all my moving around the world, I'd spent very little time driving, and almost none by myself. I found myself humming, and then singing. Ozzie didn't object.

There were a few cars and trucks on the highway, zooming along regardless of the ice on the pavement. I passed the turnoff to San Esteban with a little shudder. I kept waiting for Ex's little black sports car to zoom up alongside and force me off the road. Once I got in close enough that there was traffic and an almost urban concentration of buildings, I actually started feeling better. I had cover and the anonymity of the crowd.

I made it to a little hotel just after three. It was two stories, with low scrub pine around the perimeter and a gravel parking lot mostly buried under ice and snow. We were a long way from the ski valley, and even so, there was only one vacancy. The guy at the desk balked at Ozzie until I gave him an extra hundred. The room was on the second floor, and it would have been physically impossible to do a hundred dollars' worth of damage to it. The carpet was damp and stank of mildew. The bed sagged visibly in the center. The windows had scallops of dust running down them. At that moment, the honeymoon suite at the Bellagio wouldn't have been better. I took a hot shower, washing my hair three times to get the last of the cigarette stink out. When I toweled off, my toes were pale and prune-wrinkled. The scabs and cuts that cross-hatched the soles of my feet burned, the water loosening the clots, but I didn't start bleeding again. When I probed my rib, it still hurt, sure enough. In the mirror, my skin was bright pink from the hot water where it wasn't white with old scars: my arm, my side. I stretched out, and the vertebrae between my shoulder blades cracked pleasantly.

Ozzie had curled up on the bed and wagged

heavily as I got dressed again. I was going to need a place to use as my base of operations. This wasn't the little condo halfway up to the ski valley. It didn't have the gas fire heater or the hot tub or the little kitchen. If I wanted food, I'd have to head out to the convenience store or a tiny diner a few blocks down the road. In the next room, two women were shouting at each other over the yammering of their television cranked to eleven.

"Okay," I said. "I know it's not the best accommodations in the world, but it's what I've got for now. Just don't take off running down the road with me like last time, okay?"

My rider didn't reply, but Ozzie sighed and let her head loll down on the bedspread. So I figured that made two out of three in favor with one abstention. Not great, but until I had better, it'd do. I put my few belongings in the closet and bathroom counter, pulled my hair back into a ponytail, and went out for supplies. The convenience store was called Allsup's, and it was entirely covered in Christmas decorations—tinsel icicles, printed cardboard reindeer, even blinking colored lights strung around the cash register. A weak version of "Little Drummer Boy" was leaking out of the radio, reminding me that I wanted my own music back. But they had dog food for Ozzie and some snacks for me. I bought enough granola bars, sunflower seeds, and Diet Coke to keep body and soul together for a couple of days. Ozzie stayed in the car. As I walked out, flimsy plastic bag on my wrist, my new phone rang, a chiming tritone.

"Hello?" I said, fumbling to get the SUV's back door open and talk on the phone at the same time.

"Jayné, dear? I have the information on that license plate you wanted me to look for," my lawyer said.

"Spiffy. Give me just a second, and I'll . . . Okay. Got a pen. Go ahead."

The car was registered to Eduardo Garcia with an address in Questa, New Mexico. I was reasonably sure that none of the women I'd seen sitting around Chapin's table had been named Eduardo, but apparently someone knew him well enough to borrow his car. It was a start.

"Also I had a call from our friend Ex," she said. "He seemed a bit upset."

I closed the rear door and leaned against the SUV. An ancient-looking station wagon pulled up to the gas pumps, an old man at the wheel and three young children mashed close together in the backseat. A fire truck cruised by, slow and stately as a sailboat.

"Dear?"

"What did he say?"

"He seems to think you've had a psychological crisis of some sort. Run off in the night. He wanted me to look into getting you an evaluation. Against your will if necessary."

"Great."

I waited for the next comment, certain she'd ask what was really going on and unsure what I'd say.

"Are you certain you want to keep him on the payroll?" she asked.

I smiled.

"Yeah, for now. He's overreacting to some disagreements we had. We'll figure it out."

"He's a darling boy, and very intense, but he seems a bit histrionic sometimes."

"He just hates not being the one in control," I said.

"Well, that's true of us all, I suppose. Is there anything else I can do for you right now?"

"Nope," I said. "I'm good."

I got in the SUV, started up the engine, and paused. It was Sunday afternoon, with a couple of hours still before sundown. Questa was half an hour away. If it all worked out right, I could find Dolores tonight and get her back to Chapin and Ex in the morning with her story to back up mine. Except . . .

Except she wasn't the only one who'd gotten an exorcism recently. Was it her sister? Someone else in her immediate family had been ridden and cured before she had, and I was pretty sure it had been her sister. And if all of Chapin's exorcisms came with a secret toy surprise like mine, that meant at least one person in Dolores's household was being ridden right now. Or maybe everyone. Hell, all of Questa could be one big rider colony for all I knew.

And for that matter, I was making an assumption about Chapin too. I was thinking there was only one ringer in the circle. What if that wasn't true? What if all of them were under the control of something else? I leaned against the steering wheel. I couldn't go running after this like I was chasing fireflies. I had to think it through. Ozzie yawned massively and lay down on the passenger's seat.

Being with Aubrey for as long as I had, I'd learned a few things by osmosis. Things like this: parasitic systems have structure. By watching what a parasite did, you could figure out something about its life cycle. A mycoplasmic infection made mice seek out the smell of cat urine? Pretty fair bet that the parasite wants to get inside a cat. A carpenter ant crawls down out of its nest in the forest canopy and latches onto the bottom of a low-hanging leaf? The fungus that's about to pop its head open would probably like to rain its spores down from about that height. So if a rider is taking the risk of hanging out with exorcists in order to get fresh victims, that meant something. Specifically, it meant that the benefit it got from being around exorcisms outweighed the risk of being discovered by the kinds of guys who were professionally not in favor of spiritual parasites. Which meant . . .

I sat back and pulled the folded envelope from my pocket. Midian's letter was still inside. I plucked it out.

Getting a rider's like a drinking game. Once you start losing, you keep losing—getting ridden opens you up and getting closed again is tricky.

So this particular rider needed people who were easy to possess. People who were already vulnerable. I remembered something that Aubrey had said once about hospitals being a great breeding ground for infection because there were so many people there with crappy immune systems. An infection that wouldn't be able to survive in a normal person would have all kinds of room to grow if you gave it a community of people who couldn't fight it off. And if that was the kind of rider I was looking at, then what it was doing made sense.

So unless Questa was hip-deep in people who'd already been ridden by something else, Stinky's pool of possible victims was going to be limited.

And it meant something else.

I pulled up my phone and turned the envelope over. I took the extra minute to put Chogyi Jake's number into the address book before I called. It rang five times and rolled to voice mail. I growled in frustration and waited for the beep.

"Hey. It's me. Find out if any of Chapin's boys has had a rider. It may be important. But be discreet about asking. Don't be obvious. I'll check back in later."

I dropped the connection and sat back. Ozzie considered me with wet eyes.

"I think it's going pretty well," I said. And then, still out loud, "Okay, listen up. I'm heading toward Dolores and her family. Chances are pretty good that there's going to be a rider there and it won't want us to take her back. If you think you're too weak to take this thing in a fair fight, tell me now, and we'll find a different plan."

I waited. The guy with the kids finished gassing up his station wagon and pulled out. A girl maybe thirteen in a huge blue down coat walked across the street and into the store. A car drove by slowly, thumping out a bass line that was rendering anyone inside it deaf and sterile.

"I can," I said, unaware that I intended to until the words came out. The voice had an exhaustion I didn't feel myself.

Ozzie scrambled to her feet, whining anxiously. Her head was tilted.

"Yeah, I know," I said, scratching the dog between the ears. "It freaks me out too. But she's on our side."

For now, anyway, I thought while I started the engine.

THE ROAD to Questa was lousy driving—hard-packed snow where it wasn't ice. I took it slow enough that I didn't feel the immediate danger of skidding into the oncoming lane but as fast as I could manage. The sun was sliding close to the horizon, and people were already turning headlights on. I wasn't sure I'd make it back to the hotel outside Taos if I could find a room on Questa that kept me from driving back in the dark. Or one with a dry carpet. Part of me rebelled at the idea of having two hotel rooms at the same time, but with a few thousand dollars in my pocket, it was hard to get too worked up over the loss.

All through New Mexico, I'd passed little houses sitting back off the highway. Sometimes they were by themselves, sometimes in clumps of three or four sharing the same mile of asphalt. Except for a car-parts store and the whitewashed and ominously named Sangre de Cristo motel, Questa seemed less like a town than a few of those random, lonely, improbable buildings that had landed together. The main street was the highway, and the two lanes divided by the broken yellow line looked cosmopolitan compared to the side streets. Sidewalks would have been an affectation. Yellow-gray grass and scrub pressed in on the road, none of it rising much above knee-high, and the difference between a road and a driveway wasn't immediately obvious. Leafless cottonwoods, some chopped back so viciously it was amazing they'd lived through it, stood in the snow, and huge hills rose up to the east. I squinted through the rose and orange light of a glorious, gaudy sunset, looking for road signs and comparing what I saw to the map on my phone. Cisneros Road. The corner of Cisneros Road and Cisneros Road. *Old* Cisneros Road . . .

The house sat back from the road. Pitched roof, pale stucco, with a raised wooden deck for a front porch and a dish antenna aiming its gray platter at the sky. The sunset reddened the house and left everything in the shadows gray. The flickering blue and white of a television lit the windows. At the side, a familiar car assured me from its bumper that I couldn't be Christian and pro-choice. The plate was GODSWRK. So bingo.

I hopped out of the car. The air was cold, and only getting colder. I considered letting Ozzie out to sniff the local fire hydrant equivalents and decided against it. I wanted the option of a fast getaway if things went poorly, and whistling for the dog while unholy spirits attacked me sounded like bad tactics. The snow was solid as rock under my feet. Road salt covered the deck. I took a deep breath and knocked on the door. Inside, a little dog yapped and growled. A man's voice snapped something I couldn't make out, and the door opened a crack.

He was maybe sixty years old, white hair with a

sprinkling of black. The wrinkles in his face looked like they'd been carved there by a sculptor who'd gotten a little carried away. A gold crucifix hung at his neck.

"Hi," I said. "Eduardo Garcia?"

His eyes narrowed, but he didn't close the door.

"I'm not buying anything," he said. "Fixed income."

"I'm not selling. I'm looking for a girl named Dolores. I think you might know her."

He paused. I could see him thinking. I smiled, doing my best innocuous.

"You got the wrong house," he said and closed the door.

Inside, the little dog started barking again. I stood silently for a few seconds, wondering what to do. My first impulse was to keep pestering the guy until he admitted that he knew Dolores and told me where she lived, but the small, still voice of wisdom suggested that strategy was more likely to end in gunplay that I wasn't really up for. And I didn't even know if I was looking at small-town suspicion or demon-cult stonewalling. I walked back to the SUV, got behind the wheel, and sat for a few minutes. The curtains shifted open an inch and then closed. I figured he was on the phone right now, warning Dolores's family that a twentysomething Anglo girl was looking for them.

Okay, so no element of surprise, but at least I'd

shaken the tree. What was going to happen next? He'd warn Dolores. If the rider had gotten into Dolores in the time since her exorcism, it would see me as a threat and either run like hell or come after me. If it hadn't gotten into Dolores, it was still almost certain to be in her sister, and *she* would hear about it and either run like hell or come after me. If it ran, the chances were pretty slim I'd be able to catch it. I didn't even have a last name to work with, and they had a massive home-court advantage.

If it attacked, I'd be able to fight it off or else I wouldn't. I needed backup. I needed Chogyi Jake or Aubrey. Or Kim. Someone who already knew about riders and how they worked. Someone who Ex and Chapin would trust, since anything I said was going to be discounted as a propaganda leaflet from the Black Sun. Here I was, spitting distance from one of the most experienced groups of exorcists in the world, possessed, and still totally on my own. Water, water everywhere, and not a drop to drink.

Unless . . .

I paused, turning the new idea over slowly. There were holes in it. Risks. But even if I failed, I wouldn't be any worse off than I was now. I got back out of the car, walked back up to the door, knocked again. The little dog inside sounded like it was about to have a seizure. Eduardo didn't open the door. I knocked again, and kept it up every few seconds for what felt like an hour but was probably three or four minutes. When the door opened, he had a rifle in his hand, so I'd called the gunplay thing right.

"If you don't—" he started.

"My name's Jayné," I said. "You just tell her I'm in town and that I want to talk. I haven't told anybody what they are, but I still can. I'll get a room at the Sangre de Cristo. They can meet me there in the morning if they want to negotiate. If no one shows up, I'll start spilling beans."

"I don't know what you're talking about, you crazy bitch."

"She will," I said, then turned and walked back to the SUV. The back of my head itched like someone had painted a bull's-eye on my hair, but when I got into the car and started the engine, he still hadn't shot me. I took a long, shuddering breath, started the engine, and backed out.

Five minutes later, I was at the hotel. I booked a room for three nights, got the key—a real key on a real key ring—and then took Ozzie out for a quick walk before she peed in the car. I'd been lying, of course. I didn't have anything to negotiate. There was nothing that I wanted from the other rider apart from evidence that it really existed. But now they'd know where to find me.

And when they got there, I hoped to have a

witness. Someone whom Chapin and Ex would trust. Or at least listen to.

When I got on the road, it was almost six o'clock and dark. Ozzie lay on the passenger's seat, her nose tucked under her tail. The moon lit the night around us an unearthly blue as I headed back south toward Taos, and—*maybe*—help.

chapter sixteen

Unfortunate Goatee—Alexander—sat in his hospital bed, playing solitaire with real cards. In a flimsy blue and white gown, he looked younger than he had in his priestly black. The other bed in the room was empty. The wound that the wind demon had dealt him was almost invisible apart from a bright pink dent at his neck that ran down to disappear under the cloth. A little white board on the outside of the door had KOPP written in looping purple letters. I didn't know if that was the nurse on duty, the doctor, or Alexander's last name. Not that it mattered.

I'd dreaded walking into the hospital, expecting the memories of Grace Memorial to haunt these hallways too. But the architecture here was so simple and clean, the colors so different, that it almost felt more like going to a dentist's office than a hospital. The nurse at the station outside Alexander's door was typing something and trying not to make eye contact with me. Her nails were bilious green and her makeup almost hid how tired she looked. I didn't bother her. Careful not to pass in front of Alexander's door, I walked down the hallways with a confidence I didn't feel. Two turns later, a radiology waiting room had three people sitting in uncomfortable plastic chairs and watching a sitcom on a television that hung from the ceiling. A wheelchair waited by the door marked WARNING: RADIATION HAZARD. I went up to it, clicked off the brakes, and walked it away with the same bored air the nurse had used. Yes, I was stealing from sick people. It wasn't the worst thing I'd ever done. And anyway, it was a hospital. They'd find another.

When I wheeled the chair into Alexander's room, he looked up. His expression cycled through shock and fear to the wariness of a hostage negotiator in less time than it took to wave hello.

"So," I said. "I'm guessing you remember me."

He nodded. I closed the door behind me. His hands were flat on the little rolling table, the forgotten playing cards sliding onto the sheets.

"Who are you?" he said. There was only the slightest trembling in his voice. "I mean, who am I talking to."

"Janyé," I said. "The other one's still here. The Black Sun. But I'm the one calling the shots right now."

"Have you come for my help?"

I spread my palms.

"Yeah, but not exactly the way you're thinking. I need you to come with me."

"I'm not going to do that." He didn't miss a beat. I tried to look at this from his perspective: demonically possessed girl walks in, says come with me. It did seem like the kind of beginning that ended with the gruesome details of finding parts of his body. The set of his chin and the calm facade over raw panic didn't remind me of Chapin so much as someone doing a decent Chapin imitation.

"Okay, look," I said. "I know this is freaky, but I'm actually on your side. At least for right now. They told you what happened? How the exorcism went south and I got fooled by the devil into not rejecting it? Like that?"

"Yes."

"There really was another rider that tried to get in during the exorcism. No. Stop. I know. Not possible. I got that. But it was there, and now I'm trying to track down proof. So here's my deal. I think your group's been infiltrated by something nasty. You think I'm under the influence of the devil. One of us is right, so let's you and me get some evidence. I think I can show you that I'm not just making it up. If I can't, you take me back in and we'll do this the hard way."

"I don't think that would be—"

"If you don't come with me, I'm walking out, and none of you are ever going to see me again. You know that, right? You didn't get into this job to let demons walk away. So come with me."

He bit his lip. He couldn't have been more than a year or two younger than me, but he looked like a kid. A siren rose in the distance, the wail growing louder by the second until it cut off. He shifted his weight, the bed creaking under him. Somewhere nearby, a monitor chimed a low, steady alarm. He was wavering.

I had one more card to play.

"Alexander, what if there's a *reason* you got hurt? You believe in God's plan? Well, here it is. There's a reason God took you out of the group when He did. You are the only one who wasn't there when it happened, so I can trust you. Mostly. Some. God made it so that you could be the instrument of cleansing the group of its corruption. And He sent me too, so I could be here and now telling you to put aside your fear and do the right thing."

"You don't believe that," he said.

"Not even kind of. But my faith's not the one in question here."

He swallowed, wincing a little. I wondered how deep the wound from the wind demon ran. I'd assumed it was just on the surface, but the damage could have gone all the way to the bone. It was bad enough they still had him as an inpatient, so it had to be serious. I wondered how much I was really asking of him, but not enough to stop.

"The danger," he said, each word slow and considered, "of the beast inside of you . . . The power it wields could be—"

"If it wanted you dead, you'd be dead by now. Seriously. Neck broke, and me halfway to Phoenix. That's not what this is about," I said. And then: "Look, I know you don't want to do this, but when God says go to Nineveh, you're going, right? You came to fight demons, and you're not doing it in here."

He took a breath. His eyes were focused on nothing. Or maybe on something I couldn't see.

"You really think you're the whale to my Jonah?"

"No," I said. "But that doesn't mean I'm not."

Alexander closed his eyes, his brow knotting. We were silent for a few seconds. His lips twitched like he was talking to himself. Praying on it. I wanted to interrupt, to make my argument, to convince him. I held back and tried to be patient. My fingers tapped nervously at my thigh. It seemed like forever before he heaved a sigh and opened his eyes. He looked a little nauseated.

"Let me tell Chapin where I'm going."

"Leave him a note?"

Alexander nodded. I hopped out of the room to the nurse's station for paper and a pen, glancing back over my shoulder every couple of seconds. Alexander didn't go for the phone or try to make a run for it. I got two sheets of plain white printer paper and a pen with a huge purple pom-pom on the end that I assumed was there so no one would walk away with it. When I got back to the room, Alexander had pulled on a pair of black pants and was stripping off the gown.

The scar marking his body was as fresh and ugly as when we'd brought him in.

"Yeah," he said, seeing me react.

"It hurts?"

"Oh yeah," he said, pulling on his shirt. I handed him the paper and pen, and he sat on the bed, clearing away the cards. He took paper and pen, leaned over his little desk, and wrote. It didn't take very long, but it did seem to eat up a lot of his energy. He sat down in the wheelchair carefully, sucking in his breath with pain. I pushed him into the corridor and turned toward the front.

"Excuse me," the nurse said. "Where are you—"

"Lawyer needs to see him in the admin office," I said, not breaking stride. "I told the attending about it. We'll be right back."

The hallway turned twice, then emptied into a

larger waiting area. Alexander sat forward in the wheelchair, unconsciously guarding his wounds. I felt a twitch of concern. Maybe I should have tried to get a look at his medical records before I hauled him out into the middle of another fight. Now that I thought about it, they'd kept him in the hospital for an awfully long time. I was about to ask him how he was doing when we made the turn toward the front doors and the parking lot.

The doors were two sets of wide glass that slid open with a little airlock-like space between them. Ex and Chogyi Jake were just walking up to the outer pair. I saw them like a still frame, like something caught in a lightning flash. Ex's hair was uncombed and rough. His hand was out to Chogyi Jake like he was making some kind of rhetorical point. There were dark bags under his eyes, like sleeplessness had bruised him. Chogyi Jake wore his usual sand-colored shirt under a denim jacket that looked too light for the cold. His scalp stubble was just getting long enough that you could see the gray coming in at the temples. His head was a degree forward and tilted in toward Ex, the platonic image of listening.

Joy and fear leaped up at the same time, and I turned the wheelchair around, pushing fast back around the corner. I wanted to run to the pair of them, but I didn't dare. Not yet.

"What's the matter?" Alex asked.

"Slight change of plan," I said. "Nothing we can't handle. Just hang tight."

In the distance, I heard the sliding doors open. Ex's voice was too faint for me to make out the words, but the cadence of his speech, the roughness in his voice, was perfectly familiar. And then Chogyi Jake's reply, asking something. I paused. I couldn't go back to Alexander's room. I couldn't face my friends and former allies. I pushed the wheelchair briskly, not running. They'd be able to hear my footsteps, and it would have sounded weird to have someone running. I turned down a corridor leading toward Pediatrics and Nuclear Medicine. My hands were shaking, and my heart felt like it was about to force its way out between my ribs and leave on its own. I got about twenty feet down the new corridor. The voices were getting louder. It was hard to breathe. They were behind me. They were right behind me.

"Are you okay?" Alexander asked, his voice barely a whisper.

This is an anxiety attack, I thought. I saw Chogyi Jake in a hospital, and the last time I did that was in Chicago. So now I'm having an anxiety attack.

Great.

"I just *really* hate hospitals," I said, trying to keep the tremor out of my voice. Ex's voice started to fade. They'd gone past the turn. I flipped Alexander around. "Okay. We should be good now. Just stay calm."

"Calmer than you," Alexander said, and it took me a few seconds to realize he'd just made a *Big Lebowski* joke.

I walked fast. The irrational, unbending fear was still alive in me, but I was holding it together so far. At the corner, I caught a glimpse of their backs disappearing down the hallway toward Alexander's room. I had maybe a minute before they got there. I walked fast. Out through the waiting room, out through one set of doors and then another, out to the biting cold of the open air. And then I ran, pushing Alexander before me. When we hit the asphalt, the wheelchair bounced and jittered in my hands. Alexander leaned back into the seat like he was afraid of falling out. The SUV was fifty feet away, Ozzie already standing up in her seat, wagging and barking like she was my cheerleading section. I didn't know if the raging urge to flee was sensible or an absolute overreaction. The plan wasn't changing either way.

I unlocked the doors with the button on my key ring fob, the red brake lights flashing twice. Ex's little black sports car was across the row and about eight spaces down, mud spattered on its side up to the windows. As I helped Alexander up into the backseat, I wondered where Ex had been driving. Where he'd been looking for me. Ozzie stood awkwardly on the passenger's seat, wagging and looking back at Alexander like I'd brought him as her new toy.

"You're good?" I asked him. In the pale light of moon and streetlight, he looked a little gray.

"I'll be fine," he said. "Just a little more activity than I've had lately."

"Okay," I said, and closed the door with a satisfying clump. I felt a little guilty about leaving the wheelchair in the parking lot, but I didn't see an alternative. I lost a second peering around the dark parking lot before I realized I was looking for something like a shopping cart return at a grocery store. I opened the driver's door and stepped up.

"Jayné! Stop!" Ex shouted, and I turned to look. He was sprinting out from the hospital. From where I was, the dome light was probably silhouetting me perfectly. I hesitated. Part of me wanted to wait, to let him reach me. If he was with me—he and Chogyi Jake both—the next part would be easy. I wouldn't have to worry about Alexander's health. We could all track down Dolores together. We could prove I was right.

"Ex!" I yelled.

"Fight it! You can *fight* it!"

Or he could lock me up in the cellar again. Right.

I closed the door and started the engine. I pulled out of the parking space too fast, wrenching the steering wheel hard to the right and gunning the engine. In the rearview mirror, Ex glowed red. Chogyi Jake was ten or fifteen feet behind him, and darker. I sped toward the end of the row. There wasn't a cutout, only a gray concrete stretch of curb. If I wanted to get out, I'd have to turn back toward them or else jump the curb.

"You might want to hold on to something," I said.

The SUV bounced up with a sound like a car wreck, but it didn't stop. The back wheels hit the curb just as the front ones came down. Ozzie slid to the floor, her claws scrabbling at the plastic mat. The steering wheel spun out of my hands. I wasn't the one who grabbed it, but the rider kept control only until we crossed the sidewalk and thumped down onto the street. I was the one who turned us to the right, cutting off a white Nissan and heading toward the traffic light. I couldn't see Ex or Chogyi Jake, but I figured they were grabbing Ex's sports car, heading for the actual driveway. Coming after me.

"You solid back there?" I shouted.

"I'm all right," Alexander said.

I didn't have time to figure out how badly he was lying. Half a block ahead of us, the light turned red. Two ranks of cars hit their brakes, but there wasn't a median, so shifting left into oncoming traffic—headlights almost blinding me—was easier than it probably should have been. I leaned on the accelerator and hoped there weren't any police at the intersection. That the cars heading toward me would stop. That I wasn't about to kill myself or Alexander

or some poor bastard who just happened to be turning right at the wrong time.

I reached the intersection, cutting hard to the
right. Someone honked from much too close, and
I passed in front of all the cars that had stopped for
the red. I was pretty sure I was going exactly away
from Questa, but my plan was to just keep going
straight until I was sure Ex wasn't behind me, and
then figure out the navigation later. Ozzie got back
up in her seat. In the permanent twilight of traffic it
was hard to be sure, but I thought she looked indig-
nant. I took a deep breath and let it out slowly. The
steering wheel was pulling to the left. It hadn't done
that before. Alexander's voice was more composed
than I'd expected.

"Are you doing all right up there?"

"Yeah," I said. "I'm good. A little freaked out, but
holding it together."

"Where are you taking me?"

I thought about it for a few seconds, but I
couldn't come up with a reason not to tell him.

"Questa," I said. "Where Dolores was."

"You think that the wind demon took her
again?"

"No, not the wind demon. The other one. I
think when you guys were trying to kick out the
wind thing, she felt the same thing I did. The other
rider. And I think her sister probably got taken
over when she got her treatment. Maybe they got

Dolores when she went back home. I don't know. But if we find her, we'll find the other rider. Or, well, it'll find us."

There was a long pause. A small car with four teenage boys zipped around me, music blaring from it. So I wasn't the only maniac on the road. Nice to know.

"It'll find us?"

"Yeah," I said. "I didn't know where to find Dolores, so I went to Questa and stirred things up. The next part of the plan is that we hole up there and wait for the rider to come to us."

"And why will it do that?"

"To get rid of me. Because I know about it and can rat it out to you and Chapin and the rest."

"Only now, I'll be there too."

"Yeah," I said.

"All right," Alexander said. "Just wanted to make sure I understood what we were in for. You're driving too fast."

I looked at the speedometer and slowed down. My knuckles ached from gripping the wheel, and it was hard to get them to relax. When the streetlights started getting fewer and farther between, I pulled over, got out my cell phone, and dug around until I found where we were and a route back to the hotel. And, I hoped, Dolores. I twisted around in my seat. Behind me, Alexander still had his hand on the oh-shit handle. His eyes were closed. I felt a stab of sympathy for him. Being the chosen of God always did seem to suck.

"You want me to stop for coffee or something?" I asked. "Could be a long night."

He opened his eyes, tried for a smile, and shook his head.

"Take me to Nineveh," he said.

chapter seventeen

The Sangre de Cristo motel office was dark by the time we got back. The place was built like a strip mall: a long parking lot along the front, a small covered walkway, with numbered doors leading into all the rooms. I pulled in at mine and killed the headlights. The window to the left showed the flicker of a television, the one to the right was dark. A light wind had picked up, and dry snow blew across the blacktop like sand in the desert, making patterns like snakeskin.

"Wait here," I said.

The air was cold and dry and smelled of wood

smoke and pine. I unlocked the door, pushing it
open gently. The room was dark. The bed—just
one—lurked against the far wall. The dresser was
nearest me with a television on top it so wide and
thick, it was probably older than I was. I stood in
the doorway for five long breaths, waiting. I'd been
gone for a couple of hours. If Dolores and her sister
had gotten my message, they could be here waiting.
But the only things that came out of the darkness
were the ghostly scents of spent cigarettes and old
perfume and the muffled voices and canned laughter from the television next door. I flipped the light
switch, and muddy yellow light filled the room. Pin-
striped wallpaper, fake-quilt print bedspread, carpet
that showed the years of strangers' feet. A single
chair huddled apologetically in the corner and the
bedside table had lost some of its veneer, the par-
ticleboard showing through. The heat came from a
little electric unit along the floorboard that clicked
to life in the cold draft seeping in past me. I checked
the closet—empty except for an ironing board, an
ancient-looking iron, and a half dozen coat hang-
ers. The bathroom was also empty. White porcelain
sink and a toilet small enough for a five-year-old, a
tub and shower with a white plastic curtain on a bar
that bent out to make the tub seem bigger than it
was. On the way back out, I looked under the bed.

At the door, I gestured to Alexander. He opened
his door, let Ozzie clamber past him, and eased

himself to the ground. He walked slowly, like a man in pain. Ozzie pushed past me into the room, wagging and sniffing everything she came to. When Alex got to the door, I took his arm and helped him to the bed.

"You're still pretty messed up," I said.

"Yeah, I am," he said. "On the mend, though."

He lay back, his head on the pillow, palms pressed to his neck and chest. He took a few long, careful breaths. I sat on the little chair. Ozzie came and sniffed at my knees, turned around three times, and lowered herself gingerly to the floor with a long, contented sigh. She, at least, was having a great night.

"What did the doctors say about it?"

"They decided it was a lightning strike," he said. "Ball lightning. The kind that wanders around looking for something to bump into. I just told them I didn't remember what happened, and they seemed comfortable with that."

"Yeah. I can see that."

"They don't know how well it's going to heal, or over what kind of time period. It looks like it didn't kill the bone, though. That would have been bad."

"That was an option, was it?"

"It was a fear. But at least I know where my first scar's coming from. Father Chapin always says the people with the scars on the outside are the lucky ones. It's the ones on your soul that hurt worst."

"Well, there's a cheerful way to look at it," I said. "I've got a few scars too. I had this rider in Denver stab me with its fingers. And then this one?" I held up my arm and pulled back my sleeve, showing the long knot of white. "Voodoo god in New Orleans popped me open like a ballpark frank."

"Ouch."

"Yeah. New Orleans was hard. Chicago was worse."

"Where'd you scar up from that one?"

"Hands," I said. "Hands and soul."

"Ah. Were you fighting against the . . . the one inside you?"

"No," I said. "That was before I knew she was there. We were on the same team back then."

"And are you now?" he asked.

"Am I what?"

"On the same team."

I started to answer, then stopped. The wind was hissing and gusting outside. Cold radiated from the window behind me, just enough of a chill to make the room's warmth seem cozy. I knew it was listening, wondering what I would say. I wondered too.

"We are. For now," I said. "I don't really know much about her. I mean, Black Sun. Black Sun's daughter. Voice of the Desert. But I don't know what that means. Chapin tells me she's young, so I guess I know that. But how old is old, and how long has she been riding shotgun on my life? Who am I without her? That's why I came here. To find that out."

"I thought you came here to get rid of it."

I thought about that.

"You're right. I did."

"But that changed," Alexander said, and let his head fall back against the pillow.

"I guess so."

"Chapin shouldn't have accepted you," Alexander said with a sigh. "No offense meant, but this was a bad idea from the start. The old man screwed up."

Ozzie whined, her leg twitching as she chased dream rabbits. The television next door switched to the deep, authoritative voice of a news announcer. On the bed, Alexander folded his hands over his chest. The urge to defend myself was like an itch. What was wrong with me? Why shouldn't Chapin have taken me on? But I knew. I'd come out of fear and desperation, but I didn't believe the things Chapin and Alexander—and Ex—did. I had once, or almost did, anyway. But I'd come looking for a cure to a disease. What they had on offer was re-demption from evil. The two looked the same if you squinted, but I was starting to think they were really pretty different.

"Why do you think he took the case, then?" I asked. "My keen fashion sense?"

"Xavier," Alexander said. "He couldn't refuse him. They've got too much history."

"You mean the girl who killed herself. Isabel."

"I guess so. I mean, that was all before my time. I know it was a massive clusterfuck— Sorry. Language. I know it was a huge mess. When that one went south, everyone blamed themselves and each other. There was a visit by the bishop. Chapin had to go to Rome for a while. I don't know what happened while he was out there. But Xavier was gone, and I don't think anyone really got over it. Chapin still won't talk about it."

"But you know?"

"We're priests," Alexander said with a laugh. "Petty ecclesiastical gossip is what we *do*."

"So what went wrong? I mean, I know Ex was sleeping with her, and that she killed herself while he was around. But why didn't the exorcism work?"

Alexander's eyes opened, and he looked over at me. His beard really was awful, but if he'd shaved it off, he'd have looked about twelve. No way to win.

"She wasn't possessed," he said. "She was a paranoid schizophrenic. There was never anything they could have done for her. Carsey says that her delusions were easy to confuse with the real thing, and Xavier pushed for accepting her case. Apparently he has a kind of thing about saving women he's attracted to."

I laughed and I groaned.

"Oh," I said. "He *really* does."

"So Chapin ran her through the rites, and

afterward, when it was clear they hadn't done anything useful . . . she didn't take it well."

"Understatement."

"Yeah."

"So," I said, "Ex felt like he'd failed God because he broke his chastity vow. Chapin felt guilty because he hadn't protected Ex and he hadn't helped the girl. Had even hurt her, maybe. Wow. Yeah. Clusterfuck. And so here I am, with a real live, no-question-about-it rider. And so I get to be the big chance to go back and do everything right. Everyone gets redeemed."

"Chapin and Xavier do," Alexander said. "That's not exactly everyone."

"What did the others think?"

"I don't know, really. By the time they were really putting it on the front burner, I was pretty much out of it, remember?"

That was right. It hadn't actually been a week since Ex and I had walked up to the blue doors at San Esteban. And probably not an hour after that before the wind demon had gotten free. My whole time with Alexander before this had been those few minutes before Chapin had come out of their ongoing rite and Carsey and Alexander had gone in.

My fingers started tapping against the armrest. I shifted in my seat, my bruised rib aching but not screaming with pain. I put myself in the past. How exactly had it gone? Father Chapin had come out.

Alexander and Carsey had gone in. And the wind demon had broken free. Something was shifting in the back of my mind.

"How much do you remember about the wind demon getting loose?" I asked.

"Not lots," Alexander said. "We were doing the long form. It's very effective, but it's also a real pain. Chapin always says that running a marathon's easier. You have to trade off. No one person has the strength to go through that form of the rite alone. But we'd traded off a dozen times before. We're good at working in shifts. Only when Carsey and I got in, it was loose. We tried to get it back under control, but it didn't go too well. And then . . ."

He gestured to his chest. And then it had tried to kill him, only I'd come in. And the Black Sun inside me had saved me and them and—in particular—Ex. As a reward, we'd beaten her until she broke and tried to rip her apart. We, meaning Chapin and Ex and the others, but mostly meaning me. It hadn't seemed like a shitty thing to do at the time.

Ozzie sighed in her sleep. She seemed pleased. Caught her dream rabbit, maybe.

"Has Carsey ever had a rider?" I asked.

"I don't think so," Alexander said. "I mean, that happens sometimes. Occupational hazard. Carsey's problem is women."

"Really?"

"Every couple of years, he goes off for a few days,

comes back, and gets stuck with weeks of penance. He always seems to feel really bad about it. And from what I hear, he's getting better at holding out against it."

"Carsey, though? Really? I pegged him for gay."

"Oh no," Alexander said. His voice was getting weaker. "Effeminate, sure, but he's about as heterosexual as a celibate gets. Tamblen's gay. Miguel gets drunk sometimes and blasphemes. Tomás used to gamble, but he went to some kind of heavy-duty rehab for it and he seems good now. Chapin struggles against wrath. A lot. We're human. We're flawed. We do the best we can."

"What about you?" I asked, and he chuckled.

"I think maybe there isn't a God," he said.

The pause lasted for hours.

"You're shitting me," I said. "You're an atheist?"

"No. I'm a believer who suffers doubt."

"But you're in a hotel room with *for sure* one rider, and waiting for at least one more. By yourself. No backup. And, no offense, but you're still kind of messed up. That's a lot of faith for someone without much faith."

He shrugged.

"If I'd been more sure of myself, I might not have come. I've always wanted my own Nineveh," he said. And then: "You know, if it's okay, I think I need to sleep a little."

"You bet," I said. "I'll keep watch."

"Thank you," he said, then pulled the covers around him in a rough cocoon and closed his eyes. Ten minutes later, he was snoring. The heater clicked on, followed shortly after by the smell of burning dust. I wished I had my laptop. It wasn't even midnight. The other rider might not come before morning, but if it did, I wanted to be awake for it. Fatigue plucked at me, my body trying to convince me that maybe just shutting my eyes for a minute wouldn't be such a bad idea. I went to the bathroom and washed my face and hands in cold water. I paced the five steps between the closet and the door. I fought to stay alert.

Somewhere out there, Ex was looking for me. Part of it was that he cared about me, but somewhere along the line, I'd come to mean something else to him. I'd become a symbol. Maybe it had happened in Chicago. Maybe all the way back in Denver. I was his chance to make things right with the girl he'd failed. And now I'd vanished. As far as he knew, I was totally controlled by my rider and I'd started picking off Chapin's priests. I wondered how hard it would be for him, thinking that his second chance was slipping away. Only I kind of knew. I thought about calling him, telling him everything was going to be all right. It wouldn't have helped, though.

The weeks we'd spent together, just the two of us, started to seem different now. At the time, I'd been so scared and so frightened. And guilty. And he'd been there to make all the decisions, call all the shots. It was classic, really. He needed a damsel in distress. I needed a knight in shining armor. Our pathologies fit together like a hand in a glove. The only surprise was that we hadn't ended up in bed together, and even that had been a near thing. I wondered if it would have been different if he hadn't slept with Isabel. Being head-shy about her could have been the thing that kept us one step back from the edge. If he'd slipped into my bed back at that condo in the ski valley—

Except if he hadn't slept with Isabel, *everything* would be different. He wouldn't have left Chapin's cabal in the first place. He wouldn't have met Eric or been there to lend a hand when I first got in trouble. He would never have been part of my little constructed family. And without him, I wouldn't have gotten out of Chicago at all.

The guy next door turned off his television. I heard the water running in the bathroom next door. A bath or a shower or shaving. That anonymous intimacy felt strange. I could put my hand against the wall and know that two, maybe three feet away, someone was going through the private motions of their night, just as if I weren't there. The wind rattled the door, and Ozzie stretched, yawned, and went back to sleep. Alexander's breath was deep and regular, and there was a little color coming back to his cheeks. I picked up my phone—almost midnight—and checked my e-mail. Three pieces of spam and a Pink Martini fan newsletter I'd signed up for last year and never unsubscribed from. The temptation to call someone—anyone—was almost overpowering. If not Ex, then Chogyi Jake. Or Aubrey. Or Kim. My little brother, Curtis. My old boyfriend from college whom I didn't even want to talk to. Some other human voice.

I'd had three families, really. My real one first: mother, father, Curtis, and Jay, and with them all my friends and enemies at church and school. Then college, and the intimate little circle around my boyfriend and his compatriots. And then the one I'd inherited from Eric. They didn't overlap. No one from ASU had ever met my brothers. Aubrey and Ex and Chogyi Jake didn't know anyone from those earlier parts of my life. There were conversations I'd never be able to have, because the people who could have carried the other half were scattered to the wind. My older brother was going to get married, and I'd never met the girl. My younger brother was going to graduate from high school soon, and then God only knew what he'd do. My friends from college had stopped talking to me even before I'd left. And now Aubrey was gone, back to Kim. And, not putting too fine a point on it, I was gone too.

"Hey," I said softly. "You there?"

Alexander didn't react. Ozzie lifted her muzzle,

sighed, and tucked her head down again. My rider didn't do anything, but that didn't mean she wasn't listening. When I spoke again, it was barely above a whisper.

"When I was maybe five, the church kindergarten had this classroom pet, and whoever had the most gold stars at the end of the day got to feed him. Were you with me back then? Do you remember that?"

I sat down in the chair again. The wind had calmed a little. The neighbor's shower was done. My rider's voice sounded tired, but also amused. Like she was remembering the same things I was.

"Twinkle, the guinea pig,"

"Yeah," I said. "That was his name."

I leaned back in the chair. She didn't say anything else. I couldn't really feel her, there in my own body with me. Or maybe I was just so used to her being there that it was indistinguishable from normal. The idea that she'd always been there was comforting. I pulled up the phone's web browser and read some celebrity gossip, downloaded a cheap pattern-matching game, and tried not to sleep. Every now and then, I'd hear a car pass by, tires humming against the blacktop. I wondered where Midian was, and if he'd gone through the centuries without friends or companions. It sounded like a terrible and lonesome existence, but maybe that came with being the kind of thing he was. Maybe it was like killing people. It just didn't bother him.

Ozzie's head came up sharply. Her ears were canted forward, her wet eyes alert and focused on the door. She growled low and serious. I hadn't heard anything. No cars had driven up. No footsteps on the wood outside. I rose up silently and put my hand on Alexander's shoulder. His eyes opened and I nodded toward the front. He sat up, the bed creaking under him.

The knock on the door was so soft and tentative, it would have been easy to sleep through. Ozzie looked from me to the door and back, anxious but quiet. I patted her back.

"Who's there?" I said.

"Jayné?" a young girl's voice said.

"Dolores, is that—"

The door burst in, the frame splintering as pure animal force pushed lock and bolt out of the wood. The stink of sewer filled my nostrils as the enemy rushed into the room, pulling the dark behind it.

chapter eighteen

There was no mistaking who they were. Or, more to the point, who they had been. I recognized Dolores's wide face. Her older sister, Soledad, still had the unmistakable resemblance of family despite the changes the rider had made to both of them. Their eyes were the perfect black of spent motor oil, and their skin was the same soft brown I'd seen in San Esteban, only covered now with a greenish film like something you'd find on lunch meat left in the back of a refrigerator for years. Dolores wore a dark velvet dress and white leggings soaked with sewage that also clung to her body. Big sister Soledad had blue jeans and a black T-shirt that were just as filthy. Dolores's open mouth overflowed with a huge black tongue, and green-brown rivulets drained from her nostrils. Something like a black fog swirled behind and around them, particles of raw darkness pressing against the light. The stink was overwhelming and familiar.

Behind me, I heard Alexander cry out, but I didn't look back. Dolores—smaller by thirty or forty pounds—leaped in toward me. Her thin arms spread before her, her fingers spread in claws. Behind her, Soledad shrieked and lifted a fire axe over her head, ready to cleave my skull. And then I wasn't driving. Dolores slashed at my belly as the axe blade came down. I felt the cold pain of claws against my skin, but my body turned away, letting the axe fall past my side and pull the larger girl off balance. My right hand closed in a fist, swinging hard toward Dolores's thin chest, but the girl dodged. She moved with a jerking speed, like she was stop-motion animation that had forced its way into real life. Soledad leaped onto the dresser, holding her axe in both hands. My body started to turn toward her, but Dolores's claws dug at my thigh, commanding my attention.

The girl I'd saved a few days before grinned at me and spat. Her teeth were a stained yellow, and the voice that spilled obscenities from her lips was rough and guttural. My body shifted to the right, bringing up my left knee and kicking hard at her belly. She shifted, taking the worst of it as a glancing blow to the ribs, but I still thought I felt something give way under my heel and she stumbled back onto the chair.

I'm sorry, I thought toward the little girl.

She was eight. In a sane world, her biggest problem would be memorizing her times tables.

My hip swung around, my weight following it. When I brought my elbow down, she slipped away. The chair disintegrated under my blow. Somewhere nearby, Ozzie was barking in a frenzy. Something behind me cracked like a baseball bat hitting a home run, but I couldn't even look back to see what it was. Dolores's hand was on my shoulder, the grip colder than snow and stronger than a vise. I heard my voice cry out in pain, felt myself stumble, and then she was up on my shoulders, thighs squeezing my neck and arms wrapped around me. I was blind, and my throat felt like it was about to collapse.

Something in my larynx crackled—cartilage starting to give—and I tried to cough, but no air would go in or out. I started to panic, but my rider spread my stance, bending at the knee like a sumo wrestler, and then bent forward hard from the waist. Dolores spun down through the air, crashing through the front window. Her grip on my throat eased, and I sucked in foul air. I almost retched, but at least I was breathing. My flattened hands forced their way between the possessed girl's legs and my own throat, and we strained against each other. Bones creaked like trees in a high wind, but millimeter by millimeter, she lost ground until all at once, she jumped away.

"Betrayer!" Dolores cried in her loathsome voice, the thick tongue slurring the words. "Meat-fucker! You turn against your own kind for them, and you will suffer the price."

"Oh, whatever," my rider said, then twisted and sunk a balled fist deep into the child's solar plexus. I felt the heat of her will in the blow, and the thing inside Dolores grunted, stumbling back. My head turned. The black fog put the whole room in twilight, lights that had burned gold now struggling to a dirty orange. Alexander was on his hands and knees, the older sister standing above him, axe raised above her head like an executioner. Ozzie had her teeth set in the girl's right calf, pulling at it and growling. The axe arced down as Alexander rolled to the side. The axe rebounded off the floor with a grinding sound. The rip in the carpet bled black.

Ozzie jumped back, barked, and lunged again, taking a fresh grip on Soledad's leg. With a shout of rage, it turned its head, taking aim at the dog.

"Stop," my rider said. Or I did. It was getting hard to tell the difference. The force of our combined will was like an explosion. The thing riding Dolores's sister turned toward me. Cold pressed out from it. A black, snake-long tongue slid out from be-tween the girl's lips, lolling down almost to her belly. Foul saliva dripped in ropes toward the floor.

"The Desert has no hold over us," it hissed. "We stand with the Father Ba'al."

"I don't see Father Ba'al here," my rider said. Soledad's blackened eyes flickered once, looking be-hind me, and my body shifted, bending at the knee and swinging back an arm to meet Dolores in mid-leap. I caught her like a baseball, and my arms lifted the little girl over my head. From my distant place behind my eyes, I could feel her writhing, the slick feeling of her skin against my palms. The smell was nauseating. But even when the dark tongue draped down, smearing filth across my cheek, the Black Sun didn't flinch. Alexander sat up, scooting on his ass until his back touched the wall. His eyes were wide, his face flour-dusted pale.

"I am the Black Sun's daughter. These people are under my protection," my rider said. The voice was like mine, but deeper. More certain. "The dog's under my protection too, so don't fuck with her."

"Your protection means nothing," Soledad said. Above me, Dolores was whimpering. Her thrashing was growing wilder. "We came to end you, and we will."

"You came to kill Jayné Heller," my rider said. "And you came because she tricked you. She was the bait in this mousetrap, and I am the hammer."

Ozzie, backing up from the older sister, growled. Her bared teeth were worn and yellowed, but the old dog's expression promised murder. Soledad looked back at her, then at me, then at Alexander rising slowly to his feet. Above me, Dolores began to wail. The older sister whirled, extending the axe so smoothly it seemed like part of her arm. My body had to move back to avoid the blade, and Soledad sprinted for the door.

"Don't leave me!" Dolores cried, but she was already gone. The unnatural darkness lessened a degree. The smell of filth became a little less overpowering. Alexander limped to the doorway.

"Let it go," my rider said, struggling to hold the thrashing child above me. "You can find it later if you need to. We have what we came for."

"We can't stay here," Alexander said. He was winded. Gasping for breath. If he doesn't pull it together, I thought, we're going to have to take him straight back to the hospital. "The noise. The police. They'll come."

"They might," my rider said. "But they aren't here yet and she is."

My body turned a half step, shifted to the right, and slammed my burden down on the bed. The force of it broke the frame. The mattress tilted in toward the wall, headboard rattling. My hand was around the girl's throat, and it felt like I was holding ice. The other rider's tongue licked out, slathering my face with outhouse slime.

"Take its name," my rider said.

Alexander stood beside the bed and lifted a thin silver cross. Behind him, Ozzie sat back, scratching her shoulder with a rear paw. When Alexander spoke, his voice was shaking.

"I come in the name of Christ, and in His holy name I command you, beast. Reveal your name!"

The thing in Dolores said something obscene and arched its back, trying to break free. The white sheet beside Dolores's head was smeared yellow-green.

"In the name of God, I command you! Reveal your name!"

Alexander's will batted against me like a moth blundering into a window. I heard footsteps coming behind us, but my body wasn't my own. I couldn't turn my head to look. Dolores shouted again, her voice deep as a gravel pit, her words sexual and delighted in their perversion. Jesus, I thought, there's a kid in the room.

"Reveal your—"

"What the *hell* is going on in here?" a man's voice said. My head turned toward the door. A Hispanic man in his middle sixties stood in the shattered frame. His white hair was wild from the pillow. When he caught sight of the thing writhing on the bed, his mouth went tight and thin. He looked from it to me to Alexander and back again.

"We have it under control," Alexander said. "I'm a priest."

"Okay, padre," the old man said. "You need a shotgun? I got a shotgun."

"No, it's all right," Alexander said. "We've got it covered. Thanks, though."

The old man nodded, crossed himself, and stepped back into the night. A woman's voice called out, and the old man said something in a calm, certain tone.

"There are times I love New Mexico," Alexander said, and then turned his attention back to the girl. "In the name of Christ, the Lord, reveal your *name*!"

"I don't answer to your God." Dolores leered. "You and your—"

My rider's will rose up from the base of my spine, gathered in my throat, and pushed down my arm. When it reached my hand, the thing in Dolores shrieked. Ozzie, at my side, barked twice and looked up at me, wagging. She seemed to be having a good enough time.

"Reveal your name!" Alexander said, pressing the thin silver cross forward. I felt my rider trying to gather her power for another strike, and I tried to add my own qi to hers. I had a momentary sense of gratitude, and then we bore down on the girl again.

"Akaname!" it screamed. "I am Akaname of the tribe of Akaname of the legion of Akaname."

"How did you get in this girl?" my rider asked, but Alexander shook his head.

"Don't talk to it. Talking to it gives it power," he said. And then, lifting his voice in a ragged shout: "In the name of Christ the Redeemer, I command you to leave this child."

His will was stronger this time, but I could see the cross trembling in his hands. I'd been on the other end of this rite, and I had the sense of what it would take. He didn't have it in him. He was too weak, too injured, too tired. The thing inside of me hadn't had it particularly easier. Between the fight with the wind demon and my own near exorcism, I didn't know how much juice she had left in her. Like it was reading my mind, the Akaname smiled. Dolores's lips were black, and the dark tongue lolled out of her open mouth.

"I will not," the Akaname said. "She is mine. Forever, she is mine. Shi-neh!"

"We have to do this together," my rider said, looking up at Alexander through locks of my hair. "Will you let me help you?"

I saw him hesitate like a video holding a frame a little too long. It was asking him to cooperate with the kind of beast he'd dedicated his life to fighting against. The betrayal would be small. He just had to make common cause with a rider for a few minutes, just this once. The advantages were unmistakable. Going forward with the rite without joining his will to ours might kill him and exhaust us without ever freeing Dolores. And still, if he'd said no, I would have understood. Chapin would have refused.

"All right," he said.

My free hand took his. Still locked in my own head, I felt an echo of him: the bone-deep weariness and the excitement. He had surrendered himself to this ceremony like a swimmer heading out to sea without keeping the reserves to come back. The Akaname writhed, trying to sit up or slide out from my rider's grasp. The shattered bed creaked and dropped another couple of inches as another support gave way. Tendrils of shadow swirled in the air around us like living smoke.

Alexander took a deep breath, nodded. He was ready. I threw all my own will behind the force rising in my body. Alexander's eyes were closed, his lips moving in silent prayer, and I felt him beside me. The Black Sun, Sonnenrad, the Voice of the Desert, swirled around us. For a moment, the motel room was gone, and we crouched in a vast, empty plain. Something like a sun but not radiated something that wasn't heat. The vastness flickered, and we were back in our little room with the chintzy wallpaper and the ruined bed and the stench. But when Alexander spoke, his voice had a weight and authority I hadn't known he lacked until just then. The words seemed as solid as mountains, and implacable as the sea.

"In the name of God, I command thee, demon. *Go.*"

The sensation of the rider leaving her body was eerie. My hand was pressed hard against Dolores's chest, fingers digging in to keep a grip despite the slime. As Alexander's last word resonated, echoing in a space larger than the room we were in, I felt an icy mist rise between my fingers. It bit at the skin between my fingers, burning like acid, and then dissipated. The scent of the raw sewage boiled up, and I felt more than heard Alexander gagging as he sank down to his knees. His breath was heavy and ragged, like a man who'd just run a race. And then the enemy was gone. The room grew brighter as the unnatural darkness fled, and I had my hand on a little girl instead of a demon.

Her eyes were just brown again, but shocked and empty. Her gaze shifted for a few seconds, disoriented and lost, before fixing on me. And I was driving. My body was once again my own. I stepped back, and her skin made a wet squelching sound. Dolores started to say something, and then her face became a mask of disgust. She rolled to her side and vomited. I stroked her hair while Alexander rose slowly to his feet and stumbled to the bathroom. I heard the water running in the sink, and by the time Dolores had control over her guts again, he was back, a wet white towel steaming in his hand. Dolores sat up, her arms held out from her body, trying not to touch herself.

"Oh *God*," she said.

"I know," Alexander said, handing her the towel. "It's okay, though. It's over."

I stepped into the bathroom, grabbed a hand towel, and started scraping the layer of muck off of my body. Ozzie followed me, wagging and smiling. We might smell like Roto-Rooter's worst night, but we'd won, and she knew it. The version of me in the mirror looked like something from a cheap horror film where they were skimping on the effects. My hair fell over my face. Even after a brisk toweling, my skin looked shiny and slick. My face was pale and my eyes bloodshot.

I smiled and my reflection smiled back.

"Nice work," I said, my voice hoarse.

I heard Alexander and Dolores talking in the front room, but I had the tap on. Their words were lost in the rush of water and the singing of pipes, but the tones of their voices were unmistakable. Alexander thoughtful, gentle, consoling. Dolores frightened and lost, not even crying. The matter-of-fact calm that comes between the blow and the pain. Traumatized. It was over for her now, except that it wasn't. A year from now, five years, ten. It didn't matter. There would still be a part of her here. If not in this room, then in this time when her body was not her own, when she'd been soiled to the soul. When she'd watched the same thing happen to her sister and been powerless to stop it.

What had happened to her wasn't the kind of thing you got over. Whatever girl she had been before the wind demon took her was gone. Whatever girl she might have been if Chapin and his exorcists hadn't handed her over to the Akaname was gone too. In my memory, I heard Midian Clark. *Being a victim gets to be a habit. You stay there too long, you get comfortable. Gets to where a victim is who you are.*

Was that Dolores now? Would she be one of those people who invited trouble by being afraid of it? Was she going to expect evil to jump out of every shadow, and if she did meet it with fear, would that even be a wrong call?

I wondered what I could do or say to her that would make sense. If there was a way to tell a little girl that everything was going to be all right when we both knew it wouldn't, I didn't know what it was. I turned off the tap, lowered my face into the warm water, let my hair float around me. When I rose up, cleaner but not clean, Dolores was crying. Not sobs, but a low keening more exhaustion than sorrow. Alexander's voice was insistent and soft and a little desperate. Whatever the words were, I knew what they meant. Please be okay, little girl.

I took a deep breath. All right, then. I couldn't make anything better. I couldn't undo anything that had happened. But I could offer an example. Here's what a brave face looks like. Do this.

I stepped back out into the room, Ozzie close at my side. Dolores looked up at me. She'd seen me before, but now I saw her recognition.

"Hey, kid," I said with a grin that I meant more than I'd expected to. "We have *got* to stop meeting like this, right?"

chapter nineteen

I wrapped ten hundred-dollar bills in a sheet of paper with the word *Sorry* written on it and shoved it under the office door before we left. My hip ached, my breath was white, and the coating of filth and slime made the night air even colder. I felt like I'd dragged myself through a thousand yards of sewer pipe. Even though no one else had come out to investigate, the darkness felt like it was watching me. Somewhere out there, the rider inside Dolores's sister still knew it was in danger. If anything, it would be more desperate now, and I didn't have a clue what kind of backup it could call on. So the next move was get the hell gone.

The SUV was idling, exhaust pluming out the tailpipe like a permanent exhalation. Alexander had taken the passenger's seat, leaving Ozzie and Dolores in the back. The dog was looking happily into the night, the girl less so, but at least she'd stopped crying. I slid in behind the wheel, buckled in, and flipped on the lights. If you didn't know to look, the door to our thoroughly ruined motel room just seemed a little scuffed above the knob, the dent where the riders kicked it in showing as nothing more than a little discoloration. They were going to have to change the carpet to get the stink out. As I shifted to reverse, I promised to send them more money. A thousand bucks wasn't going to cover the damage we'd done.

The roads were bad—ice and snow and other drivers who seemed dismissive of the dangers of ice and snow—but I'd been bouncing back and forth between Taos and Questa so much, it was becoming familiar. Probably if I came back in the summer, I'd have been lost, but in the black hours before dawn, I was recognizing individual snowdrifts. The heater roared, blowing its artificial desert wind against my cheek and ankles and drowning out the pop tunes on the radio. In the backsplash of the headlights, Alexander's expression was sober.

"It's ski season. We're never going to find a place to stay," Alexander said.

"I've already got a room," I said. "It's kind of craptastic, but it has a shower."

He looked over at me.

"You have a hotel room already rented?"

"Key card's in the glove box," I said.

"Well," he said. "Nice work."

"Makes me wish I'd planned it," I said.

When we got there, we trudged up the stairs in single file. Me and then Ozzie and then Dolores and then Alexander, like ants. Even Ozzie was looking tired, her head hanging at an angle and her tongue lolling pinkly from her mouth. I gave Dolores first bath rights. She handed out her soiled clothes. The slime and filth had begun to dry, flaking off the cloth. I took the plastic liner out of the wastebasket and put her things there. When she came out wrapped in towels, I took the next turn. First Midian's cigarettes, now the Akaname's stench. I washed my hair twice, scrubbed my skin with a washcloth until it hurt a little, and I still caught a whiff of sewer when I got out. I felt much better, but I wasn't sure I'd ever really feel clean. I had one more complete outfit from my lawyer, so I put that on and threw my ruined clothes in the plastic liner with Dolores's.

When I stepped out of the bathroom, Dolores was sitting on the edge of the bed wrapped in her towel, Alexander on the floor beside her. They were watching a morning show on TV. The anchor-woman was smiling at an old Korean woman and talking animatedly about a new movie she'd directed. They were both wearing Santa hats and the network logo was worked with computer-generated holly leaves. Ozzie, curled in a perfect circle with her nose tucked under her tail, snored gently beside them. Outside, the first blue of the coming dawn lit the windows.

"There enough hot water left for me?" Alexander asked.

"Better be," I said. "You smell like ass."

Dolores chuckled. She looked exhausted. I wondered what her mother was going to think, waking up with one or both of her daughters missing. If I were the Akaname, I'd say Dolores had been taken by a crazy Anglo woman named Jayné who'd been staying at the Sangre de Cristo. I imagined myself explaining to the FBI that it wasn't really kidnapping, because if I'd let her go home, the demons would have gotten back into her. Until I heard differently, I'd have to assume there was an Amber alert out for all of us. It always surprised me how much fighting against spiritual parasites could look like crime.

Alexander dragged himself to the bathroom and handed out his clothes. I stuffed all of it into the plastic liner, tied the top, and put it outside the room's door. The sun was almost up, thin clouds glowing rose and gold in the immense blue New Mexican sky. I took the Do Not Disturb sign and hung it on the knob. Dolores was lying on her side now, her eyes glassy and empty. The show broke to a commercial for allergy medicine, and I turned off the TV.

"Get some sleep, okay?" I said. Dolores nodded and closed her eyes. There was an extra blanket in the closet, and I draped it over her. When I knocked on the bathroom door, it took a few seconds for Alexander to answer.

"Yes?"

"I'm going to hit Wal-Mart for some fresh clothes. You stay here and guard the kid, okay?"

"Okay."

"Don't let anyone in."

"I'm a Catholic priest in a hotel room with an underage girl and no clothes," he said. "So yeah, I think I'll try to keep a low profile."

"Funny," I said.

"Here all week. Tip your waitress."

I unhooked the cable that ran from the telephone to the wall and shoved it in my pocket before I left. I didn't think Alexander would call Chapin while I was gone, but I wasn't a hundred percent sure. And it wasn't a risk I had to take.

I got back two hours later with a sweater and two pairs of slacks, one of which would probably fit

Alexander, pink sweats with a pattern of hearts and snowflakes for Dolores, a pair of jeans and a blouse for me, and socks and underwear for the masses. Alexander was in bed, still wrapped in his towel. The wind spirit's wound looked fresh and pink and painful. Dolores was sleeping where I'd left her, above the bedspread and under the spare blanket, curled up like a comma. Ozzie looked up at me hopefully.

"Oh. Sorry. I didn't think about dog food. I'm kind of new at the whole pet thing," I said, and she sighed and put her head back down.

I put the shopping bags down by the door and went to the far side of the bed. I lay down with my clothes on, fitting onto eight inches of mattress that the other two had left me. For a moment, I wondered if this was what it felt like having a family. A man, a woman, a child, all curled up in a bed that was a little too small, all with their own thoughts and dreams and nightmares. I tried to imagine my own mother and father on a vacation someplace when I'd been a little kid, or with my big brother, who was about to have a kid of his own. I couldn't picture it. It wasn't that it seemed wrong or funny or improbable. It was just that when I tried to put them here where I was, my mind went blank. Part of that was the trickling exhaustion that came from a sleepless, anxious night, but part of it was something else. Part of it was not knowing anymore exactly who I missed when I missed my family. My mind wandered to the other people who belonged with me: Aubrey, Chogyi Jake, Ex. Maybe them. I could almost imagine them.

I didn't realize I'd closed my eyes until it had already happened. I left them that way, thinking I'd just rest for a couple of minutes and then go find some breakfast for us all, and woke up with the others a little bit after noon.

"YOU'RE *SURE* she came back wrong?" Alexander asked. "Is it possible that she was okay when we did the rite, but then the other demon was there waiting when it was over?"

Dolores took a bite of her hamburger. She'd gone for a weird Hawaiian thing with barbecue sauce and pineapple that smelled great. She chewed and shook her head. Her frown was entirely made of eyebrows.

"No," she said. "And anyway, that isn't what it did with me, *remember*?"

"I hate to do the dog-pile thing," I said, sweeping a french fry through my ketchup. "But that's my experience too. The Akaname attack was going on at the same time as the exorcism."

The restaurant was a few blocks off the main drag. The decor was prepackaged plastic in reds and yellows, but the food was good. We'd taken a booth near the back so that we could talk with something like privacy. The decision to get out of the hotel room and track down food had been easier than I'd expected. When I'd brought up the possibility that the police might very well be looking for us, Alexander pointed out that kidnappers usually didn't hang out in restaurants with their captives, and that by staying in the room and never coming out, we'd actually be acting more like criminals. And then Dolores had calmly threatened to throw a screaming fit if she didn't get to go out.

The more she talked, the more she impressed me. It wasn't just that she'd been through two demonic possessions in the last few days and was now hanging out with two grown-ups she barely knew. There was a calm about her, and a maturity, that only broke on our way out of the apartment when Ozzie was apparently startled by her own fart. Dolores collapsed with laughter. And in fairness, it was kind of funny.

"I just don't see how that's possible," Alexander said. "You were on consecrated ground—"

"When Soledad came back, it was already in her," Dolores said. "She sat right there with your boss and it was inside her."

"But are we sure that it was there during the rite? If the timing—"

Dolores put down her burger and lifted her eyebrows. It was an expression of challenge and disbelief that came straight off daytime TV, and not the good shows. I wanted to laugh, but I also wanted the conversation to keep moving forward. I tried to imagine what Chogyi Jake would have said if he'd been there.

"So, Alexander," I said. "I'm hearing you say that you have a hard time believing that the Akaname attacked when Dolores and I say it did."

"I am," he said. "All of the protections it would have had to go through. And the Mark of St. Francis. You were wearing that, Jayné. And we know it was working because it stopped the Black Sun from taking control. It wasn't ineffective."

"But my report and Dolores's don't convince you," I said. "Why is that?"

Alexander opened his mouth, closed it, looked down.

"This isn't easy to say."

"Do your best," Dolores said gently. Without saying a word, she'd seen what I was doing and started taking her cues from me. Seriously smart kid.

"Don't take this the wrong way, but Dolores has been through a lot. Sometimes when a person has been through the kinds of things she has, their impressions and memories can be a little scrambled. Disoriented. And you've still got a rider on board, so your report has to be treated with an extra level of scrutiny too. Not that—"

"You have one in you right now?" Dolores said, her eyes going wide.

"Yeah," I said. "But it's not like the ones you had. The thing that's in me has been there for a really long time, and we've got a truce going."

"Is it an angel?" she asked.

"I don't think so, honey," I said. "It's just what I've got to work with. Alexander, I understand we don't have enough evidence here to totally convince you. But can you at least see that we need to investigate?"

"Yes," he said. "I mean, of course there's a problem. If these things have been targeting the people we've helped, it's absolutely our responsibility to go back and check on people. It's just that I don't see how a rider could be in one of the priests."

The front door of the restaurant opened and a middle-aged woman ushered in two boys. She looked tired. Outside, an old man with a cane was trying to negotiate a sidewalk of melting snow.

I understood Alexander's problem. He was an expert. Chapin and Ex and Tomás and Tamblen. All of them were experts on exactly this kind of thing, and that was the one thing that brought them all together. To say that they'd been tricked, that a rider had slipped through their defenses without being seen, meant rethinking everything that group meant. And, just like all of them, Alexander had given up a lot in order to be who and what he was. Dolores crossed her arms, scowling. All she saw was a grown-up who thought she didn't know what she was certain of. There was a rage building in her that would explode if Alexander didn't flex a little. I understood that too.

"Okay, look," he said. "We can get all the information, go to Chapin, and—"

"Unless it's Chapin," I said. "Then we really can't."

At the front, the two boys were shouting each other down over something. Their mother stood at the counter, ordering slowly and carefully so that she could be heard over the pandemonium. I took another fry and a sip of my Coke. The salt and the sweet made a great combination.

"Who, then?" Alexander said. "That same logic goes for anyone. What if it's Carsey? What if it's Miguel?"

"What if it's Carsey *and* Miguel?" Dolores asked.

"I came to you because I knew you hadn't been there when the thing tried to get into me," I said. "But I knew I was taking a risk. We can't assume it's just in one person. Everyone in your group is suspect. And that aside, I'm pretty sure if I waltz into the joint in San Esteban, Chapin's first impulse would be to throw me in the cellar."

"It probably would," Alexander said, then spread his hands. "So what's your plan? If you don't want me to take this to Chapin, where do we go? Father Amorth in Rome? The Pope? You wanted me to come witness what had happened to

Dolores and Soledad. Who am I supposed to bear witness *to*?"

"Ex," I said.

THE PLAN wasn't a masterpiece of elegance, but I figured it didn't need to be. I was pretty sure if I called Chogyi Jake, he'd be willing to broker a meeting. But Ex would be tempted to use it to spring a trap, and Chapin would insist on it. If I warned them I was coming, they'd have the opportunity to do something stupid. So I'd just show up, and I'd show up where Chapin wasn't, and that meant the little condo.

We got there in the early afternoon. The day was bright, but the sun was hidden behind mountains and pines. Traffic on the thin road to the ski valley was thick and slow, and when I finally turned off, aiming for the dirt hill that I'd run down a few days before, it felt a little like coming home. Someone had shoveled enough dirt and sand on top of the ice and snow to give the cars traction. The black sports car was parked at the hilltop. I pulled in behind it and killed the engine. At the condo just down from mine, a girl was struggling out to a minivan on a pair of crutches. Her left leg was encased in a bright pink brace.

"Is there a problem?" Alexander asked.

It had seemed easy, coming up. It had seemed

obvious. Sure, the last time I'd been around Ex, he'd chained me to a ring in the cellar. When he saw me, all he saw was the rider. And Chogyi Jake? I'd almost gotten him killed in Chicago, but worse than that, I'd ditched him. For weeks, I'd excluded and lied to him. Even now, Ex was the one who'd called him first when things went south. My friends were in there, and now that I was here, I had the unshakable fear that they wouldn't be my friends anymore.

But I couldn't drive away. I couldn't even just sit there in the SUV while it cooled down to freezing. The plan was still the plan, and it was still obvious. It was just hard.

"No problem," I said. "Let's get this done."

I got out of the car and held the door open while Ozzie scrambled up from the backseat to go out the same door I had. Alexander got Dolores. I wished I'd bought her warmer shoes. The door of the condo was closed, but I could hear their voices through it. Ex sounded tired and grumpy. I made out the words *can't* and *no matter what*. Chogyi Jake sounded as calm as he always did. He could have been offering to sacrifice his own life or asking if there was any curry left. I put my hand on the doorknob, pulled back and started to knock, then went back to my first impulse. It was my condo, after all.

They were in the main room. Chogyi Jake was sitting on the couch. As I stepped into the little kitchen, Ex stopped pacing and stood frozen in front of the fireplace, looking up at me. The dark circles under his eyes and the pale, waxy look of his skin told me how little he'd slept, how hard he'd pushed trying to find me. Trying to save me. Seeing the damage he'd done to himself for my sake, I could only wish he hadn't.

Alexander, behind me, cleared his throat.

"Hey, guys," I said, sounding nervous even to myself. "So. What did I miss?"

chapter Twenty

I'd forgotten how strong Chogyi Jake was, and how he smelled like sandalwood incense and Dr. Bronner's soap. I leaned into the embrace and closed my eyes. His arms were solid, and his forehead—pressed against mine—was warm. I'd expected him to feel fragile, as if nearly getting kicked to death in Chicago would have made him partly insubstantial. I didn't even know I'd assumed it until being wrong surprised me. Tears welled up in my closed eyes, and something deep and warm bloomed behind my rib cage.

"I was worried," he said so softly that even

Alexander standing two feet behind me wouldn't have heard the words.

"I know," I said. "Sorry."

Another hand touched my shoulder, and I turned. Ex bundled me into his arms without quite getting me away from Chogyi Jake, so that we wound up in a comfortable group, each of us hanging on to the others. The tension and fear I'd felt on the way in evaporated, and I had the powerful physical memory of being six years old at an amusement park with my parents.

None of us stepped back first. The moment just came that the reunion was over, and we were ourselves again. I introduced Chogyi Jake to Alexander and Dolores, and we all went to sit around the fireplace. When I retold what I'd done, I glossed over the part about Midian being there. I called my lawyer and went to ground for about a day.

When I got to the part about tracking down Dolores and Alexander, I went into a lot more detail. The whole story took less time to get through than I expected. Chogyi Jake sat forward, listening carefully. I'd forgotten how powerful it could be to have someone paying attention that intensely. Ex leaned on the back of the couch, his arms folded. The lines around his mouth were deep, and his eyes didn't show anything. He seemed angry, but as Alexander and Dolores chimed in, confirming everything I said, I started thinking it was more pointed at himself than at me.

I brought us up to the present—driving up to the condo, finding them here—then stopped and spread my hands. There you have it. Chogyi Jake laced his fingers over one knee, tilted his head in thought, and frowned.

"How does the dog fit in?" he asked.

Ozzie, stretched out beside the fire, snored.

"She's mine," I said. "I got a dog. Her name's Ozzie."

"Does she have a rider in her?" Ex said. "Someone that got displaced into the dog's body, like Aaron back in Denver?"

"Nope," I said.

"You just got a dog."

"Yeah."

The pause lasted about three heartbeats. Ex shrugged.

"All right," he said.

"We should call Father Chapin," Chogyi Jake said. "There's no reason for him to re-create the ceremonial space for the St. Anthony's Cross."

"Good point," Ex said.

"St. Anthony's Cross?" I asked as Ex went up the stairs, dialing his cell phone as he went.

"Father Chapin and the others were working under the assumption that the rider had taken control of you," Chogyi Jake said. "It seems that tracking you using magic is still as difficult as it ever was, but they felt they should try. The St.

Anthony's Cross is a ritual for divining a person's location."

"If they couldn't find me, why would they be setting it up again?"

"They were going to find Alexander."

"Oh," I said. "Yeah, that would work, wouldn't it?"

"It was the hope. The concern was finding him before you killed him."

"Before I . . . Yeah, wow. Ex and I just had two completely different days, didn't we?"

Upstairs, Ex started talking. The ceiling creaked as he walked in the room over our heads. His voice was soft, and I heard relief in it. Dolores raised her hand.

"Where's the bathroom?" she asked.

"Up the stairs, and turn right," I said. "You can't miss it."

"The rider was . . . I mean the one that . . ." Alexander said, then stopped, pointed at me, and started again. "The rider in *her* appeared to be very passive. As far as I could see, it only really took control when Jayné was in immediate physical danger. When the crisis passed, it seemed to give her entirely free rein."

Dolores padded up the stairs. Ex went quiet, listening, I assumed, to something on the phone.

"Unlike the Akaname," Chogyi Jake said. "I have to say, I'm surprised to find those here."

"Wait," I said. "You know about them? I mean, you know what they are?"

"Filth-lickers," Chogyi Jake said. "They're common in Japan and China, but I've never heard of one in the Americas."

"So they're a whole bunch of different riders that are all related?" I said. "It's not just one big demon taking control of a bunch of bodies at once."

"No," Chogyi Jake said. "It's not a *haugsvarmr*. They've very minor riders. Not mindless, but not strong or smart. Any of them could infect someone who was already vulnerable. They survive at all by being hard to detect and spreading quickly."

"Like the cockroaches of the rider ecology."

"More field mice, but yes," Chogyi Jake said.

"They seemed like pretty strong field mice to me," I said.

"Yes. It's interesting that your rider was able to cast out the wind demon without a great deal of effort but then struggled with the Akaname," Chogyi Jake said.

"You think these are some kind of superstrength version? Cockroaches on steroids?"

"I was thinking more that the rider in you may be injured. As I understand, the exorcism was very nearly complete when you stopped it. I'd be surprised if it came through unharmed."

The idea brought a stab of guilt.

"You spend much time in the East?" Alexander asked, changing the subject.

"I spent two years traveling there when I was

younger," Chogyi Jake said. "I needed to break off connections with a group of people I'd been close to, and it seemed like a good opportunity for that."

"Alexander?" Ex called. "Father Chapin would like a word."

Alex stood up, wincing, and walked slowly up the stairs. I almost told Ex to bring the phone down; Alexander's wounds were still bothering him, and making him climb stairs at almost nine thousand feet above sea level seemed rude. But Chapin probably wanted to talk with him someplace I couldn't hear them, which was probably why Ex went upstairs too. That, and maybe to give me and Chogyi Jake a minute.

With someone else, I might have gone for pleasantries.

"How bad was it?" I asked.

Chogyi Jake's smile was a constant in my world, but I'd learned to read its subtle variations. He looked down now, and the amusement in the corners of his eyes sharpened.

"Bad. I don't think he's slept since you left. And Father Chapin . . . wasn't pleased that Ex called me."

"Why not?"

"I'm not Catholic," Chogyi Jake said. "Father Chapin has sacrificed a great deal to the path he's chosen. I knew that about him from Ex's stories. One of the tenets of his tradition is that all other traditions are wrong. No one has said it, but I think that by including me, Ex might have been seen as disloyal."

"But you know me," I said. "If anyone would be able to track me down, it'd be you two. I mean, if I *had* been taken over by abstract evil, I'd totally want you on the case."

"And I appreciate that," he said with a laugh. Upstairs, the toilet flushed and the pipes that fed the sink whined. The fake gas fire kicked on behind me. "Father Chapin is an uncompromising man. What he believes, he believes wholly, and any deviation is an opportunity for the diabolic to corrupt him."

"Yeah. Well. Sorry about that."

"No. I admire him, in a way. There's a purity to him that's . . ."

"Freaky?"

"I was going to say *remarkable*, but *freaky* works. And he's an important man in Ex's life."

"Yeah, it kind of had that brought-home-to-meet-the-family feeling sometimes," I said.

Ozzie sighed, stretched, and struggled to her feet. I put out my hand, and she came to me, ready to have her ears scratched. I chewed on my lip for a second. Dolores was going to be done washing her hands, and she'd come back down. Ex and Alexander wouldn't be talking to Chapin forever. If I wanted to clear the air, this was my chance.

"So hey," I said. "Talking about how Ex called you in and all that? Yeah, I think I maybe owe you an apology. I've been keeping you kind of at arm's length these last few weeks."

"You have," he said. From anyone else, it would have felt like an accusation. From him, it was just agreeing that the sky was blue. I was grateful he hadn't tried to make light of it, say that I hadn't been, and that if I had, it didn't matter.

"I was doing kind of a rebound thing with Ex," I said. "I mean, there was also the thing where I'm possessed. And what happened in Chicago. And Aubrey. It all got mixed together. I never thought it right out loud, if you know what I mean, but if you'd been here, you'd have put it in perspective. And I kind of didn't want perspective. I wanted to make the mistake and not think about how it was a bad idea."

"Are you certain that it is?" Chogyi Jake asked. "A bad idea, I mean."

"Which part?"

"Do you love Ex?"

Ozzie chuffed impatiently and pushed her head against my palm to get me petting her again. I started to speak, stopped, tried again.

"I love my brothers. I love my mom. And I love Aubrey and you. I don't think there are two times in my life I've used the word *love* and meant exactly the same thing by it. No matter what I say about Ex, it's going to mean something different."

"I think that's a powerful insight," Chogyi Jake said.

"You're just not going to give me anything, are you?" I said, grinning. "You're just going to listen to whatever I say and make me think through all of it for myself."

"Yes," he said, his grin answering mine.

"I missed the hell out of you."

Dolores came down the stairs wiping her hands on her shirt, then came over to sit next to me. I watched her open and close her hand, the fingers uncurling slowly as a blooming flower and then folding back to a fist.

"Feels nice, doesn't it?" I said.

"What does?" she asked.

"Being in control of your own body again. Not having something else calling all the shots."

Her expression was hard, but she nodded. Between the wind demon and the Akaname, she hadn't been in control of her own flesh much in a long time. I wondered if being young made that harder or if children were built to have other people making decisions for them in a way that softened the blow. Probably that was wishful thinking on my part. *Please be okay, little girl.*

When I'd been her age, my little brother had still been in diapers and my older just in middle school. It had been the first time I'd gone to school without a sibling there with me, and I'd known that another one was coming up behind me. There had been a freedom to that. A sense—however small, however brief—that I was my own person and not just a part of the larger unit that was my family.

I wondered about her sister, Soledad. She was firmly in the middle of her adolescence, when girls were building who they were independent of their families. To be ridden then, to have those first green shoots of autonomy and independence crushed flat, might be worse. I wondered if she'd gone home to her mother and Dolores's yet, and what the rider said. It wasn't hard for me to imagine myself in her place, trapped and powerless while the rider drove me out into the night and I strained to go back for my sister . . .

"What about you?" Dolores said. "Are you you, or are you it?"

"I'm me," I said. "The one inside me doesn't take over very much, and then not for very long."

"Why not?"

"Because she's a little kid like you," I said. "She's a really strong little kid, but she's young. I get the feeling she's been young for a pretty long time."

"She isn't like the ones I had," Dolores said. "The ones I had sucked."

"Yeah. They really did."

"I like yours," she said, making the pronouncement. The official Dolores seal of approval.

Clumping feet announced the end of the cell phone call to Chapin. Ex and Alexander came down together. They both looked exhausted. As they walked down the stairs, their footsteps fell slowly out of sync.

"Chapin wants us back at San Esteban," Ex said.

"I'm shocked," I deadpanned. "We're not going, though. Right?"

Alexander sat on the couch's armrest and leaned forward, catching his breath. His skin was getting grayer, and the angle he held his shoulders at was changing. Even though I was pretty sure he wouldn't go, I was tempted to take him back to the hospital. Ex leaned against the counter between the little living room and the kitchen, his arms crossed. The two priests exchanged a glance.

"What exactly we should do next is open to debate," Ex said. "If we're certain that the group has been compromised, going back there is problematic. But I don't see how we walk away either. Whether they are coming from inside the group or not, we've clearly got an infestation."

"And there's the reason you came in the first place," Alexander said. "I don't mean to be rude, but we haven't addressed that yet."

"Nothing's happening with the Black Sun until the rest of this is sorted out," I said. "Not open to debate. You're telling me Chapin's not convinced he's got a cuckoo in the nest?"

Ex shook his head. The gas fire behind me turned off with a tiny pop.

"It's a hard argument to make," he said. "Akaname

can be subtle when they want to. They have to be, because they're so weak. But how likely is it that a rider could live in a society of men dedicated to destroying riders and never be noticed?"

"Seems pretty damn likely to me," I said. "Who'd look there? And, not to put too fine a point on it, how would you know? If my rite had gone through, at the end of it, I'd have been sitting at the table just like Dolores's family did, and saying how much better I felt and how grateful I was. And if I seemed a little off, it would have been because I'd just been through this huge thing, so of course I'd be a little forgetful or irritable or whatever. How would you know?"

"They've been doing this for years," Ex said. "At some point somebody would have noticed."

"Yeah, and that would be me," I said. "*I* noticed."

In the silence, Ozzie lay down. Dolores slipped off her shoes and scratched the old dog's back with her toes.

"If one of the priests is ritually impure," Alexander said, "they might have been open. I know Tamblen fights against his nature, but—"

"Please," I said. "He's just gay. He's not ritually impure."

"Homosexuality is a sin," Alexander said. "I'm not saying Tamblen is a bad man, only that—"

"Everyone's unclean," I said. "*You* told me that. You were the one who went through everybody's problems. Your doubt, and Carsey's lust, and Tomás's gambling. If we're looking for who's pure, I'm pretty sure everyone looks bad. But you're not possessed. Ex isn't. It's not about purity."

"I think," Ex said, "we need to consider this from Chapin's perspective. What if the Akaname isn't in one of the priests? It could still be waiting nearby for a steady supply of vulnerable people."

"That's not what *happened*," Dolores said. Her voice had enough exasperation for both of us. "It tried to get in when the other one was in there too. It went on at the same time."

"Then it could have been anyone," Ex said. "Miguel or Chapin or Tamblen. Any of us who were there."

"No," I said. "Not for Dolores."

"What?"

"Everyone was there for mine because we were doing the short form. They'd been working on Dolores for days, and thought they'd be doing it for days more," I said, then turned to the girl. "When the wind thing got loose, it was because the other one was trying to get in. That's when it happened?"

Apparently eye rolling starts sometime well before the eighth birthday. "That's what I *said*."

"But Chapin was talking to us, Ex," I said. "He was right there in the room with us when it happened. So it can't have been him."

Ex's scowl almost covered the relief. It didn't

completely let Chapin off the hook, but it sure made things look better. Alexander cleared his throat. His eyes were narrow.

"Carsey and I were going in to relieve Chapin and Tomás," he said. "If we're all still willing to assume I'm not being ridden—"

"We are," I said. "At least I am."

"—then that means Carsey or Tomás."

"St. Francis," I said.

They looked at me. I wasn't sure quite what I'd meant. I wasn't even a hundred percent positive I was the one who'd said it. But something was shifting in the back of my mind.

"The Mark of St. Francis," I said. "I was wearing it and it stopped the Black Sun. But it didn't stop the Akaname. So if the group's compromised, then maybe the Mark was broken. Maybe whoever made the medallion left a hole the Akaname could get through."

Alexander shook his head.

"That would take a level of control and power that—"

"That you couldn't do without a rider," I said. "But that's the point, right? Even small fry like the Akaname are better with magic than people are. So if someone who knew the rituals had a rider, he could maybe do things that he couldn't have by himself. The Black Sun helped you cast the Akaname out of Dolores, Alexander. You couldn't have done that alone."

"If I'd had time—"

"You didn't have time," Ex said. "She has a point. Even if a normal man couldn't make a sabotaged Mark, someone with a rider might. And Tomás made the Mark."

"Ex," I said. "You said he was kind of before and after for you. He went away for his final vows and then came back. Do you remember where he went?"

"Japan," Ex said. "A mission in Japan. Where Akaname are more common. And if he had been possessed by something while he was there and had it cast out, it wouldn't have been that hard to conceal. He was already part of the group. Chapin wouldn't have any reason to examine him again when he came back."

We sat in silence for a moment, but I felt like crowing. My heart was a great big bubbling fountain of I've-got-you-now.

"Well, okay, then," I said. "I think we've got a hypothesis."

chapter Twenty-one

If I'd tried to, I couldn't have pointed to the change that came in that moment. I only knew that it had happened. It wasn't just that Alexander and Ex stopped arguing against the rider-in-priest's-clothing idea. It was also something in the way they looked at me, the way they held themselves. When I was a kid, my older brother, Jay, had shown me how to get iron filings out of the sand in the school sandbox. He'd had a sheet of white paper with a bunch of black dirt on it until he put a magnet under it, and then like magic, everything lined up. It was like that now. The case against the angel-voiced Tomás came together and now we were all pointing in the same direction.

Almost.

Chogyi Jake's smile was as pleased and enigmatic as ever. Alexander leaned back on the couch, whistling low. Even Dolores seemed pleased that we'd figured it out. Only Ex looked like he was braced for a blow. He met my eyes and looked away. The pain would probably have been invisible to someone who didn't know him as well as I did.

"Hey," I said to him. "Can I borrow you for a minute? You guys talk amongst yourselves."

I stepped out the back door. Snow covered the hot tub's deck. The air bit, and the calling of crows was like the announcement of a funeral. Ex closed the door behind us, the latch clicking into place. In the sunlight, he looked even paler. His white-blond ponytail was loose. His eyes were bloodshot, and he still moved stiffly when he twisted. I wondered how the wounds on his back were doing.

"Hey," I said.

He nodded.

"I think one of us owes the other an apology," I said, "but I'm not sure how it goes."

"Don't worry about it."

"You know that stuff I said about how much I appreciate everything you did for me?"

Ex leaned against the wall, his arms crossed.

"I do."

"I meant all of it."

"I know you did," he said.

"We only had the information that we had," I said. "There were two ways to read it. I went one way and you went the other. I was right, but it wasn't like you could have known that. We made our judgments and we acted on them."

"Nothing else we could have done," Ex agreed.

"We're cool, then?"

"Of course we are. Why wouldn't we be?"

I pushed my hair back from my eyes. Above us, a thousand icicles glittered and shone like tiny transparent teeth.

"Maybe because you chained me up in a cellar, and you were going to feed me to a shit demon. Or how about because I beat you unconscious and spent days running while you worried yourself sleepless. It seems like someone here ought to have some hard feelings about something."

He shrugged.

"For what it's worth, I'm sorry I was wrong about there being a second rider," he said. "Anything else?"

Are you angry with me? I almost asked. But he'd say he wasn't, either way. And that wasn't really what I meant.

It was just a few days before that he'd lain on the couch wearing a blanket and told me in a soft voice about falling from grace with God. I'd hesitated at this cracked-open door to see him sleep, and he'd promised that if my feet were too bruised, he would carry me. I wanted to know if we were still those people. The long nights of distracting me when I woke up screaming, the mornings of making coffee for me quietly enough that I didn't wake up. They'd been hellish, and every single time, he'd risen to the occasion. I didn't know how I'd have made it through without him. He'd never tried to use my bad nights to make a pass. He'd never been anything less than great, crisis after crisis after crisis. There was an intimacy in it that I hadn't totally recognized until now. And now I was afraid it was gone.

I wanted to know if the man who'd protected me when I was broken was able to forgive me for saving myself without him. I wanted to know what was behind the poker face. I wanted him to kiss me just so I'd know that he wanted to.

"Seriously," Ex said. "Is there something you want to say? It's cold out here."

"No," I said past the thickness in my throat. "I just wanted to make sure we were good."

"We are," he said shortly.

"Okay," I said, and he opened the door again and walked inside. It took me a second before I was ready to follow him.

Alexander was standing at the kitchen counter, Ozzie sitting at his knee with her long, pink tongue lolling out. Dolores's arms were folded, her face a mask of disapproval. Chogyi Jake leaned against the back of the couch, his brow furrowed in thought.

"Do we have any alternatives?" Chogyi Jake asked.

"Alternatives to what?" Ex demanded.

"We're having a tactical discussion," Chogyi Jake said.

"I'm not going to stay behind," Alexander said. "For one thing, I'm the best evidence you have that the attack in Questa happened. You can't take Jayné in by herself and expect Chapin to believe her."

"Okay, roll this back," I said. "Why do we want Alexander to stay behind?"

"Someone has to take care of Dolores," Alexander said, waving toward her.

Dolores's scowl deepened.

Truth was, I'd been thinking we'd take her with us. Until that moment, I hadn't seen how bad an idea that was. She was a third grader, thin from growing too fast and still marked by the sores and cuts from the first time we'd met. The chances weren't good that the thing inside Tomás was going to sit back and take this lightly. We were walking into a trial where she'd be a good witness, but we were also walking into the near certainty of violence.

Of course I couldn't take a kid into a fight. Especially not one who'd already been traumatized three or four different ways within the last week. I pushed away my sense of confusion and loss around Ex and focused on the girl. As if she could feel the weight of my consideration, she looked up at me.

The first time my mother had left me at home by myself, I'd been fourteen. She'd been going to the grocery store because we were out of milk. I'd been watching TV. It had taken her twenty minutes, but for that time, I'd been alone in the house for the first time in my life. I could still remember the exhilarating sense of power and fear. Dolores was six years younger than that, and we weren't going on a quick errand. We were going to a confrontation whose outcome we couldn't know.

I imagined leaving her here on her own, and I couldn't see doing it. And I couldn't take her with us into the teeth of danger. We could leave Alexander behind with her, in which case I wouldn't have any witnesses besides myself. I could leave Ex behind, except that in a million years, he still wouldn't agree to being ditched. I could ask Chogyi Jake to babysit, but he was the only one who'd come in from outside. He'd be able to see things in the tight-knit group of Chapin's cabal that no one else could. Besides which, I didn't want to leave any allies behind. We could take her home, except the Akaname would be waiting there, wearing her sister's skin and waiting to retake Dolores's. And, to round out the problem set, just having Dolores with us might count as kidnapping and child abduction, and for all I knew, the FBI could be looking for her.

The room had gone quiet, everyone waiting for me to speak.

"How long do we have before we're supposed to see Chapin?" I asked.

"We can wait as long as we want," Ex said. "But the longer it takes, the more the Akaname can prepare. It probably didn't know that we're aware of it, until Ex told Chapin that we had Dolores back, but now it's got to be feeling jumpy. And since the one in Dolores's sister escaped, it's also possible that it's gotten a more explicit warning. Or will soon."

"So the longer we take, the more time the enemy has to prepare," I said.

"Or escape," Ex said. I had a momentary sense of Ex feeling pleased to see me struggling with the dilemma, but that was just me being paranoid.

I wondered if my lawyer had any friends or contacts in Taos willing to be an accessory to child abduction. I wondered how I'd ask the question even if I did call her. I hated this. No matter which way I looked at it, there was a problem. If it had just been fighting the rider in Chapin's group, I'd have known what to do. If it had just been keeping Dolores safe, I could have come up with something, even if it was something incredibly illegal. Doing both seemed impossible, and they both had to be done.

"I'm open for suggestions here," I said low

enough that my rider would know I was talking to her. I waited a few seconds, but I didn't get an answer. Either she wasn't listening or she was stuck too. I knelt at Dolores's side, putting my eyes even with hers.

"Hey," I said. "You have anything you want to have happen, because the options are looking pretty bad to me."

"I want to go with *you*," she said.

"I'm going someplace dangerous," I said.

"I don't care," she almost shouted. There were tears in her eyes. She turned away from me. "I want to go home."

"We can do that," I said. "But your sister might be there. And she's still got the demon inside of her."

Dolores was quiet for a moment.

"I don't want to go home," she said.

"Jayné," Chogyi Jake said. The two syllables of my name were all it took to carry a truckload of meaning. *She's a kid, so stop asking her to take responsibility* and *This decision has to be yours* and *I'm sorry.* I hung my head.

She had been through so much that she hadn't deserved. I wanted to give her her own voice in whatever happened next. I wanted her to have power, or at least to feel like she did. That giving her that was also another burden on her shoulders seemed profoundly unfair. The kid needed someplace safe and someone to watch out for her, and she also needed to stand up on her own. I didn't know how to get that for myself, much less for her.

"Okay," I said as much to myself as to anyone. "Dolores? Sweetie? I need you to be a big girl right now, okay?"

She turned back to look at me. Her eyes were wet, tears streaking down her cheeks. She looked about as unlike a big girl as humanly possible. She didn't have her family. Didn't even have her own clothes. I'd saved her from riders twice when everyone else around her had failed or betrayed her, and now I was going to abandon her. The thought rested uncomfortably in my gut. I nodded to her and smiled, hoping it would get her to smile back at me.

"I'm going to go try to stop the thing that's been doing these things to you and your sister. And I need you to stay here and take care of Ozzie while I do it."

The dog's ears shifted forward at her name, and she started wagging her thick tail. Dolores sniffed wetly, looking from me to the dog. She knew it was bullshit. I'd have left Ozzie alone or even curled up in the back of the SUV a hundred times before I left a little girl by herself.

"What am I supposed to do?" Dolores asked in a small voice.

"You just stay here with Ozzie. There's a TV upstairs and I've got some snack food in the car. If the dog needs to go out, let her out. When she wants in, let her in. There's some dog food for her. And I can help you find a bowl for that and her water before I go."

"What if she goes out and she never comes back?" Dolores asked, and I knew from the high, rough voice that we weren't just talking about the dog anymore.

"She'll come back. It might take some time, but she will come back," I said. "And I will too. Your job is to hang out here for the night and be safe. Knowing that you're okay is what's going to let me do the things I need to do next, okay? Can you do this for me?"

Dolores hesitated, then nodded. She wasn't looking at me. I leaned close, kissing the top of her head.

"Thank you," I said.

Twenty minutes later, the rest of us were piling in the SUV. I had my laptop and the leather backpack I used as a purse. Chogyi Jake had meditated in the master bedroom, focusing his qi and calming his mind. If you had to pick whether Alexander or Ex looked worse, it would have been a hard call. Next door, three snowboards were leaning against the little fence, and four guys about my age were shouting at each other about how to get a grill started. They sounded drunk. I ignored them, climbing up behind the wheel. Chogyi Jake took shotgun, looking back at the lights shining in the condo's windows as the sun began its winter descent among the high peaks in the west. All around us, the pines had gone from green to black. I started the engine and paused.

From the time I'd arrived at Denver International Airport, just shy of my twenty-third birthday, until Chicago, I'd driven only when I was alone. Aubrey was our default driver before he left, and Ex had taken over in the weeks since. Now I was sitting behind the wheel, and it felt as natural and obvious as something I'd done every day. I had the feeling it meant something. I hoped it was something more than *If this all goes south, it'll be my fault.*

"Will she be all right by herself?" Chogyi Jake asked.

I followed his gaze. The condo was dark, already in shadow despite the blue still showing in the sky and the glorious gold and pink cloud lace of the coming sunset. It was like a Magritte painting made real. One of the upper windows began to flicker the television's blue.

"I don't know," I said. "Probably."

"I can stay," he said. "Take care of her."

"For how long?" I asked. "Her home won't be safe unless we win this. So unless you're thinking you'd like to flee the country and raise her yourself, you're better off coming with us and making sure we win. There are kids her age and younger all across the world who are dealing with worse than having a place to themselves for a night."

"It just feels wrong," he said.

"Really does," I agreed, then slid the SUV into drive and headed down from the mountain.

NIGHT FELL as I drove. The twisting little road down from the ski valley was thick with skiers heading down from their day on the slopes. The music on the radio was all "Winter Wonderland" and "Rockin' Around the Christmas Tree," every jolly note and unseen smile like a parody meant to make the evening feel more threatening. Once, near the last cliff on the road, a fallen boulder squatted in the middle of the lane, and I had to swerve around it. The snow and ice made everything slow and dangerous.

In the backseat, Alexander's eyes were closed, but he wasn't sleeping. His hand was pressed to the wound in his chest. I shifted the rearview mirror to catch a glimpse of Ex. He was brooding at the darkness. He'd tightened his ponytail, until the skin at his temples looked stretched back. It reminded me of war paint and smiley-face stickers on combat helmets. The ritual preparation for violence.

This was everything for Ex. His past with Father Chapin and his failure with Isabel and his redemptive drive to care for me. By slipping into Tomás, the Akaname had managed to threaten all of it at once. I couldn't imagine what it would feel like to have everything in your life come to a single point like that.

An event where it could all be won or all be lost. For a moment, I was in Chicago again, in the basement, driving nails into the coffin while an innocent man screamed inside it. The sick dread and fear flowed into me with the memory, and also Ex's voice reciting in Latin. Performing the last rites over the man I was killing in part to save the man's soul, and in part to be there with me during the worst of it. Making sure I didn't go through it alone.

"It'll be all right," I said to myself, and then in an almost perfect imitation of me, my rider took my throat and spoke. No one listening would have noticed the transition.

"One way or another."

I didn't know what she meant, but a chill climbed up my spine that didn't have anything to do with the teeth of winter all around us. I looked back to the road, reached up to shift the mirror away from Ex and closer to where it was supposed to be, and headed for San Esteban for the last time.

chapter Twenty-two

By the time we got there, the town was a study in black and white. The last traces of sunset faded as I watched, leaving black sky with a billion stars and a sliver of moon haunting the horizon. Snow caught every ray of light from moon or star, glowing blue. The black-barked trees were like cuts in the world with the darkness behind everything showing through. The few bits of light and color—the yellow of a lit window, the single red eye of a truck's unbroken taillight—only served to make everything else seem bleaker. Ansel Adams meets H. P. Lovecraft.

I parked almost exactly where we'd been the first

time. When I killed the engine, the only sounds were the whisper of the breeze blowing snow against the SUV, the ticking of the engine cooling, and the commentary of the crows. I pushed the door open and stepped down into the road. The building looked dead, the blue double doors made darker.

"Okay," I said. "Alexander? How're you doing there? You all right?"

"I'm fine," he said. I didn't know what I'd have done differently if he'd said he wasn't.

"Ex?"

"Ready," he said.

I was stalling. An electric knot of anxiety was spinning in my rib cage, and my shoulders and neck felt tight enough to snap. I willed myself to stay calm, but my body wasn't having any of it. I felt vaguely nauseated and edge-of-my-seat excited and a little hungry. And I needed to pee.

"Let's get this over with, shall we?" I asked, and started up the snow-slicked walk before anyone could answer. The three men's footsteps behind me were reassuring and unsettling at the same time. I had to walk carefully to keep from slipping. When I got to the doors, it felt like I'd come from a long, long way away. Maybe I had. I knocked bare knuckles against the wood three times. It was hardly a breath before the door swung open and light spilled out around us. Father Chapin stood in the doorway. He'd changed into an outfit with the familiar black-and-white clerical collar. His close-cropped hair was combed back. His eyes were merciless as glass.

We stood there for a moment, the priest bathed in light, and me and my cadre on the edge of darkness.

"I am surprised that you've come back," Chapin said.

"Unfinished business," I said. "You mind if we come in? Little chilly out here."

He hesitated, then stepped back, letting us pass within.

The others were in the ceremonial room where the exorcisms had taken place. I could almost see myself there in the soiled white shift, covered in sweat and my own vomit. Everyone there had seen me like that, battered, vulnerable, exposed. Everyone except Chogyi Jake, and he was the one I would have minded least if he had. Carsey and Tamblen were sitting at the table where Dolores and her family had met with the priests after the wind demon's defeat. Miguel and Tomás stood at the double doors that led out to the courtyard, their arms behind them. Everyone was in black tonight. The air itself felt charged, like there had been ceremonies and incantations prepared for us. Probably they had been.

Behind me, Ex, Chogyi Jake, and Alexander stopped. The division was unmistakable, and Chapin had engineered it as cleverly as a stage set. His guys with him, mine with me. Chapin turned, leaning against the table.

"Alexander," Chapin said. "I'm pleased to see you. We were worried."

"I'm much better," Alexander said. "Not that there's no room for improvement."

His attempt at lightening the mood lay on the floor. Chapin's smile was sharp and cold.

"Come, my boy. Let me look at you."

Like a pawn pushed down the chessboard, Alexander stepped from my side of the room to Chapin's. This was all being done to belittle me, to show that Chapin and his cabal had the power, and I didn't. I felt my jaw slide forward a few millimeters. Chapin clapped his hands on Alexander's shoulders.

"I'm glad to see you," Chapin said. "We were concerned."

"I'm sorry about that," Alexander said. "When she came to me, I thought it would be better to go with her."

"Brave, but foolish," Chapin said. "But it does not matter now. All is well that ends well, yes?"

"Didn't know we were ended," I said. My voice was stronger than I'd meant it to be, but the anxiety in my gut was shifting rapidly toward pissed. Tamblen and Carsey exchanged a look.

"Yes," Chapin said, turning his attention to me again. "Xavier has told me of this astonishing news. A hidden devil in the heart of the Church. It is not the first time such a subterfuge has been used to divert our attention from the true matter at hand. What you suggest is, of course, impossible."

"Father Chapin," Alexander said. "It's not. I was there. The two sisters were both possessed, and the spirits in them came to attack Jayné."

"Perhaps," Chapin said, "and perhaps not. Ask yourself: Is it more likely that we have had a devil in our midst for all this time and with no sign, or that the devil's work is subtle and his agents legion? Alexander, I will agree that these poor girls have suffered again at Satan's hands. But can you tell me what evidence you have that the new assault on them came from us?"

"The girl said so," Alexander said. Chapin's gaze was fixed on me, and Alexander looked at the other, his hands out as if in appeal. "Dolores said that it happened during the exorcism."

"And yet when she left here, she was not possessed," Chapin said.

"No," Alexander said, "but that was because Jayné . . . I mean the rider inside of Jayné—"

Chapin raised his hand.

"Xavier," he said. "Will you come to me, please."

Don't, I thought, but Ex was already walking briskly across the room. Behind me, Chogyi Jake stepped closer, closing ranks with me. Ex stood in front of Chapin like a schoolboy in front of the principal.

"You brought this woman among us," Chapin said. "You asked our aid. When she escaped, you were as dedicated as any of us to her recovery. What is your opinion of this accusation?"

Ex was silent for a long moment. When he spoke, his voice was shaking with an emotion I couldn't identify. Anger or fear or sorrow.

"We know the cost of making assumptions," he said. "Jayné came here in good faith the first time, and now she's come back. She took Alexander, and I don't see any evidence that he was hurt or corrupted. I think we have to take her accusations seriously."

"Do you?" Chapin said. "You think it plausible that I am the victim of the devil's cunning. You have brought a woman to me who is now using the aid we have offered her to tear apart the trust and camaraderie that we rely upon. Are you certain that you are not the one who is wrong? Ah?"

"I'm not certain," Ex said "It's possible the Black Sun put the whole thing together from the start to undermine you and this group. I don't think that's what happened, but no, I can't be sure."

The sense of betrayal, of loss, was like getting punched in the gut. The air actually went out of me.

"Ex," I said, and Chogyi Jake put his hand on my shoulder.

"I am a little confused by all this, though," Ex said, waving at the room. "This is something we can test. Akaname are subtle, but they're not perfect. Now that we know what to look for, it won't be that hard to figure out whether it's true or not."

Chapin folded his arms. His face was flushing red.

"You would do her bidding, then?" Chapin said. "Take the weeks or months it would require to cleanse us all and in the meantime let the devil rule the countryside?"

"Won't take weeks," Ex said. "We can get this done in ten minutes."

Ex drew a small velvet box from his pocket. For a second, I pictured him going down on one knee in front of Chapin. Ex opened the box and casually withdrew something wrapped in a bit of white cloth. I looked over my shoulder, but Chogyi Jake shook his head. He didn't know what Ex was up to either.

"I have the Mark of Taiqing," Ex said. "I got it a few years back when I was tracking a noppera-bo. I didn't wind up using it then. So . . ."

He held up a bright silver disk. Chapin shook his head sadly.

"There is no holy magic save that which is given us by Christ," Chapin said.

"It won't do anything more than identify the presence of a bakemono. It's folk work, but it will do for what we need now. If nothing comes from it, then we can stop screwing around with it."

Chapin shook his head in disgust, but held out

his arm, as if daring Ex to touch the little silver disk to his skin. Ex shook his head.

"Not you, Father," he said. "Just Tomás."

All eyes turned to Tomás. His thick shoulders, his well-worn face, the brown of his eyes. After the oil-black eyes and filthy tongues of the Akaname that had possessed Dolores and Soledad, the pistol in his hand seemed weirdly prosaic.

"Umm," Carsey said. "Tomás, my dear, you seem to be pointing a gun at us?"

"My old friends," Tomás said, his voice rough and sweet as salt and honey. "You will step aside. Now."

Chapin's expression was disappointment and disdain.

"I will not let you leave, demon," he said. "I have been humbled enough for one day. In the name of God, and of his Son and the Holy—"

Tomás raised the gun almost casually. The report was louder than I'd expected. Father Chapin doubled over, clutching at his belly as the rest of us jumped into motion. I ran toward Tomás as Miguel threw himself onto the shooting arm, dragging the gun down. The second shot dug a hole in the brick floor. Ex and Tamblen got to the rider a half second before I did.

"The gun! Get the gun!" Carsey shouted from someplace behind me as I plowed into Tomás like a linebacker trying to knock down a fence. I felt the bones creaking in my shoulder, and the rider

stumbled back, the four of us weighing it down.
And then the Black Sun took over, and I dropped to
my knees. Ex had Tomás's gun hand now, helping
Miguel push it down. Tamblen was behind Tomás,
wrapping him in a bear hug. From where I knelt,
my fists went out in a flurry of straight punches
to Tomás's groin, ending with a furious uppercut.
Something under my knuckle went soft in a way
that felt painful even to me. Tomás staggered, his
mouth gaping open and his eyes closed like a cari-
cature of agony. I shifted back, rose to my feet, and
sank my right heel just below his rib cage. The gun
went off again, but my gaze didn't leave the rider.
When his eyes opened again, they were a perfect
black.

With a roar, the Akaname lifted its arms, toss-
ing Ex and Miguel backward to the floor. The
stench of sewage rolled through the room in a
nauseating wave. Tamblen, behind the thing, had
his arms around its neck. Faster than a snake, the
black tongue flickered out of Tomás, wiping across
Tamblen's lips and forcing its way into his mouth.
He fell back gagging, and the rider lifted its arm
toward me.

It still had the gun.

"I forbid this," my voice said without me.

"You forbid me nothing," Tomás said, his voice
lisping, slushy around the inhuman tongue.

I felt something behind me, soft and warm, like

someone had turned on a heat lamp. Like knowing someone from the sound of his cough or a single footstep, I recognized Chogyi Jake's gathering will. The rider's dark eyes flickered away from me. It was all the chance we needed.

I kicked hard, the front of my foot hitting squarely on the butt of the gun. The pistol went off again, the bullet hissing past my ear, but the rider lost its grip. The gun spun through the air, landing with a clatter by the far wall. Dark blood poured from Tomás's hand, and his index finger bent at an improbable angle. The rider howled in pain, the raw power of the sound staggering us. In my peripheral vision, I saw Chapin trying to sit up, Carsey at his side.

The Akaname was becoming less human with every second. Slime bubbled out of Tomás's skin. His hands and face lengthened, his mouth pressing out from his face and growing round as an O. Its tongue whipped out faster than I could dodge, wrapping around my ankle and pulling. There was no way to stay standing, so I didn't try, dropping to the ground instead and rolling away.

"In the name of Christ, I bind you! In the name of God, I bind you!"

The voice was Ex's, but the power in it felt strange. I looked over for a quarter second. At the side of the room Ex was kneeling, Miguel and Tamblen at his sides, their heads bowed, their hands in his. The force in his words was the three of them, joining together. The Akaname turned toward them, and I kicked the back of its knee, staggering it.

"In the name of the Father and the Son and the Holy Spirit, I bind you, demon! You have no power here."

The words carried their collected will like hammers falling on an anvil. I'd felt something like it before: the relentless, punishing assault of the rite of exorcism. It wasn't the most powerful magic I'd seen. Calling upon God to help didn't seem to give them any more power than three disciplined, trained, practiced minds joined together might give.

It was plenty enough for my purposes. I rolled up to my feet, using the torque to drive my elbow up into the bottom of its jaw. I felt the jawbones come together hard as pincers, and the three feet of reeking, corrupt tongue fell to the floor, writhing. The rider pressed both hands to its mouth, black, clotted blood gouting between its fingers. I willed myself to attack again, to beat its skull concave and end it, but my body wasn't my own. Instead, my hands lifted the severed tongue. It shifted against my palms, pulsing and alive. It was about the texture of liver, but rougher. I held it over my head.

"I am Sonnenrad, who you denied. I am the Voice of the Desert. I am the Black Sun and the Black Sun's daughter!"

What Chapin and his men had gnawed and

beaten and pried to get came out now like a flood. I felt its will burning, rising up from the base of my spine, through my belly, my heart, my throat, and I screamed it out. For a flickering moment, we weren't in the snowbound sanctuary but the desert. My desert. The tongue in my hands tugged and whipped itself in the heat and dryness and vastness.

When I spoke again, I could feel the words tearing at my throat like I was screaming them, but they sounded barely louder than a whisper.

"In my own name and the name of my mother, I bind you. You are ended. Go."

My will detonated, the wave front running out in all directions, as I stood at the center, the Akaname's tongue lifeless and dry as ash in my hands. A profound silence took the room as I lowered my hands. Tomás lay on the brick floor, curled in a fetal position. Blood poured out of his mouth. His eyes were glazed and empty, but he was breathing. Chogyi Jake came to my side, his hand on my shoulder.

"I'm fine," I said as I turned and almost fell to the floor. "Okay. I'm not."

Carsey helped Chapin to sit on the table. There was blood sheeting down the old priest's belly and leg. Wide red streaks marked his face and neck. But the tough old bastard was smiling.

"Well done," he said. "Oh, well done, well done."

I leaned forward, resting on my elbows. I couldn't catch my breath.

"That was a good day, I'd hate to see your bad ones," I said. "Ex!"

"I'm right here," Ex said. He was maybe six inches to my right and I hadn't seen him. I was distantly aware of the others moving in the room. Tamblen walked by. He was weeping, but he still looked bored. Something about the shape of his face, I guessed. Chapin's blood smelled hot and coppery, and I realized the stink of the Akaname was gone. Also, I'd been going to say something, but I couldn't think what it had been. I let my head sink down for a second, resting my forehead on the table between my wrists.

Beating the wind demon hadn't done this to me. To us. I wondered how much damage the exorcism had done to my rider, and how—if—she would ever recover.

"Mark of Taiqing?" I said. "Where'd that come from?"

"Actually, it was just a quarter," Ex said. "Figured the bluff was worth trying."

"We're going to get the car ready," Carsey said as he stroked Father Chapin's hair. "Tamblen can drive and I'll apply pressure. We'll have you to the medics before you can finish doing penance."

"No," Chapin said. "We cannot leave. Our work is not done. It must be bound. We cannot leave the beast free."

"It's more than bound," I said. "Seriously, we kicked its ass."

Chapin looked at me, and then grasped at his wounded gut, hissing in pain. His face was pale as paper, but he shook his head.

"We do not take sides in the wars of Hell," he said. "We do not have alliances against the will of God."

"He's delirious," Miguel said. He had a massive bruise forming on his cheek. It actually looked kind of good on him. Rakish.

"He isn't," Carsey said grimly.

"I *will not* leave while the beast is free," Chapin said, his jaw tight. His eyes were bright and fierce. They bored into me like a message I was supposed to understand but didn't.

And then I did.

"Wait a minute," I said. "You mean *me*?"

chapter Twenty-three

The room went silent. I fought to clear my mind, but the effort of the battle made clarity hard. Miguel and Carsey stood on the opposite side of the table. Ex stood to my right, Chogyi Jake to my left. Father Chapin lay on the table between us. Alexander and Tamblen had almost lifted the blasted shell of Tomás up to a sitting position. Carsey and Miguel looked at me, the relief and exhaustion and fear on their faces shifting. They looked hardened. Resigned. They looked like sailors who'd just figured out that the calm wasn't the end of the storm but the eye of the hurricane. I figured I probably did too.

"There is a demon inside of her," Chapin said. "It is the reason that you brought her here, Xavier."

"You have *got* to be kidding," I said. "Did you just miss the part where you've had a ringer in your group for . . . I don't know. Years? Or that I just got rid of it?"

Chapin's lips went tight and he shook his head.

"I have many failures," he said. "Many, many failures. I will not be turned from my calling. The beast is here. It is within you, Miss Jayné. You have done us all a great service, and I will not leave you in the claws of Hell."

I stepped back from the table, my legs still unsteady. Chapin tried to sit up. Blood poured out of his wounded side.

"Don't be frightened," Chapin said. "We will save you. Even if we are saving you from yourself."

"Well," Carsey said. "This is less convenient than I'd hoped."

"Has to be done," Tamblen said from behind me. I turned toward him as wide, strong arms wrapped around me, lifting me off the floor. I kicked back, but it was only my own strength. Even when I hit something soft, the only response I got was a grunt. The grip didn't go slack.

"No," Ex said. "Stop. This is a mistake."

"There can be no mistake, Xavier," Chapin said. "Nor any room for compromise. It is through exceptions and weakness of will that Satan wins the world, and so—"

Chapin winced, clutching at his wound.

"Put me down," I shrieked, twisting my weight. Tamblen turned, and someone—Miguel—grabbed my ankles. Lifted in the air, I turned toward Ex.

Over the years I had known him, I'd seen him in a hundred different moods. I had seen him in the depths of rage and joyous, exhausted past the point of illness and sleeping with the sunlight in his hair. I had felt the passion and guilt and longing that he kept bottled up in his soul, and I had wondered what he was thinking when he closed himself off from me. For less than a second—less than a heartbeat—as I screamed and twisted and fought against Tamblen's arms, I saw Ex, and the desolation in his eyes was unfamiliar and terrible. I thought, *This is what a nightmare looks like,* and the gun went off again.

Chogyi Jake lowered his doubled fists until the barrel was aimed unmistakably at Tamblen's heart. His smile was the same one he always wore.

"I'm going to ask you to put her down now," Chogyi Jake said. "Next time, I will not ask."

I stopped struggling. Tamblen shifted my weight but kept me on his shoulder.

"You don't understand," the big man said.

"You won't be the first man I've killed," Chogyi Jake said.

He won't? I thought, and Ex stepped between them, his hands held out. Where he stood, Tamblen couldn't reach the door to the courtyard without pushing him aside, and Chogyi Jake couldn't shoot Tamblen without the bullet passing through him.

"All right, we're just going to calm down now," Ex said. "No one's getting shot. I mean Father Chapin is, but no one else."

"I know you love these men," Chogyi Jake said. The gun hadn't shifted an inch. "But they are zealots, and—"

"Just don't shoot them," Ex said. "Just wait."

Chapin coughed and swung his legs off the table. He tried to stand; he cried out in pain. Miguel put an arm around him.

"Chewy," Miguel said. "Please. We don't have much time. He's losing blood."

Ex swallowed, nodded to himself, and turned to face Father Chapin. My old friend looked about six years old, lost and determined and frightened to the bone. He licked his lips and I tried to turn so that Tamblen's shoulder wasn't digging into my liver.

"Father Chapin," Ex said. "I know Jayné. I trust her, and after tonight, I think she deserves your trust too. She wasn't wrong. She was the one who found the taint in our society, and she stopped it. She wants to be free of this thing. She only made common cause with it when we forced her to. Us. Ask her to renounce it. She'll come back again just like before."

Chapin's eyes narrowed. He looked at Tamblen

and nodded. The big man lowered me to my feet.

"Is this true?" the old priest asked. The blood on his cheek was dry and dark and flaking. "Do you renounce the Black Sun, and will you swear to me on peril of your soul that you will return here and complete the rites that you began?"

I took a breath. It was what I'd come here for. It was the reason I'd been running like hell since Chicago. One of the reasons, anyway. I thought of the hours I'd spent waiting for my body to move without my willing it, watching for evidence that I wasn't in control of my own flesh. It had been terrible. All I had to do now was say that I still felt the way I had then.

But I didn't. I'd made my truce with her, and she hadn't betrayed me. There weren't all that many people I could say that for.

"No," I said. "No, I won't renounce her."

Ex's cry of despair broke my heart a little. He sank to his knees, his eyes closed. I thought he might be crying. It was all spinning out of control now. All of the people he wanted to keep safe were destroying themselves and each other, and all his efforts to protect us were falling through his fingers like sand. I stepped forward and put my hand on his shoulder. He was shaking.

"I'm sorry," I said. "I really am."

"Father Chapin? I think you're making a mistake."

Everyone turned toward Alexander. He was stroking his terrible little goatee thoughtfully.

"You think . . . what?" Chapin's voice was a rasp. "A Princess of Hell stands before us in the flesh of this poor sinner who came to us for aid. Tomás's corruption was terrible, and the price we will pay for it will beggar us, but there is this thing still before us that we *can do right*."

Alexander pressed his fingertips to his lips, scowling.

"No," he said. "If she wants our help, I'll do whatever I can to help her because I think she has a good soul. But if she doesn't want it, we can't force it on her. She's not even a Christian, Father."

"Meaning what?"

"Meaning you shouldn't have accepted her in the first place," he said. "She's only here because you and Xavier killed that girl years ago, and somehow she's supposed to make up for it."

"Well, there's an uncomfortable perspective," Carsey said. "So we should just open the door and usher her out into the world? With what she is?"

"We will not!" Chapin shouted. "We will not free the devil! What I have done wrong, I will answer for, but I will not sin again. I refuse to. I will die here if I must, but I will not leave while she is free!"

There were flecks of foam at the corners of his mouth and tears poured down his cheeks. Tomás was still on the floor, his eyes empty. A shell. He didn't even turn to see what the commotion was about. I knew that some riders did more than lurk in the back of a mind. Some kicked the original owner out, taking the body whole. If the Akaname were like hermit crabs, taking over the bodies that other riders had already opened up, that meant Tomás had been ridden before, and maybe that first rider had killed his soul years before. Maybe he was only qliphoth now, an empty shell without self or rider. And even if there was something of the man left in the body, he was broken in ways that wouldn't ever be made whole.

And then I knew what they reminded me of. They had been parasitized. Tomás had been the one with the actual beast in it, but they had all been used. Tamblen and Carsey, Miguel and Chapin. All these men dedicated their lives to freeing people from possession, and instead they'd become an engine for spreading riders. Tracking down the Akaname they had spread would be the work of years, if it could even be done. Right now in front of me, Chapin was doing anything he could to distract himself from the grief bearing down on him. And grief, I knew, made people crazy.

Chapin really was going to let himself die.

"Jayné," Ex said. "I need a favor."

"You want to lock me up," I said.

"Just long enough to get him to the hospital. So that he can know you're safe."

"Is that what you call it?"

"Please," Ex said. "I need to save him. At least let me try."

I looked over at Chogyi Jake. The gun in his hand hadn't moved. I had the distinct impression that if I'd said so, he'd have shot everyone in the room who tried to keep me from walking out. It wasn't what I'd expected of him, but the fact that he was there—that the choice was there—made choosing possible.

Ex stepped closer, leaning in. His voice was low and fast, and his hands fluttered in front of him as he spoke, like little sparrows trying to take wing.

"If you don't want the rite of exorcism, I'll make sure you don't have it. Just let me put you down there for now. I promise I'll free you again later."

"I'm sorry. It's not my call," I said. And then: "Hey. We've got a situation here. You want to chime in?"

Always before, the rider had come suddenly or not at all. My hand might move on its own, or I might say something I hadn't known I was going to say. Or else she just took the wheel, and I was a passenger. This time, it felt like she was welling up around me, pulling herself up to control my body through an act of will. Like running things was hard for her. Like it was a chore.

Ex saw the change. His face went pale and he

started to step back, then caught himself. Behind him, Carsey's eyes went wide. I couldn't see the others.

"You've got no reason to trust me," Ex said.

My rider swallowed carefully, like my throat was sore.

"Will you help me?" Ex asked.

The pause lasted years.

"Yes, I will," she said. "Take me to your prison."

Ex sagged with relief. I heard Carsey and Miguel moving behind me. Tamblen put a hand on my shoulder and the rider shrugged it off.

"Don't touch me," she said, and then I was in control again. I turned to look up at Tamblen's face. "Yeah, I can walk it."

OUTSIDE, THE cold was bitter. Ex and Chogyi Jake and I walked through the snow together, Tamblen and Alexander following just behind. It wasn't eight o'clock yet, and it felt like midnight. Overhead, the crows were wheeling in great, excited flocks, calling to one another. Moonlight silvered the black wings. The smell of snow had the taint of fumes; it was like standing beside a gasoline pump. I stopped and looked up at the stars. Chogyi Jake was at my side.

"They're beautiful," I said.

"They are," he agreed.

"Can you go make sure Dolores is all right?"

"I'd be happy to."

"And thanks for offering to shoot Tamblen."

Tamblen cleared his throat and looked pained.

"You're welcome," Chogyi Jake said.

It took a few seconds to knock the ice off the cellar door. I walked down the rough concrete stairs, ducking under the doorway that led to my prison. The ring waited for me, and the chains. I sat down, my legs crossed, and held out my wrists for the manacles. The others watched while Ex squatted beside me and carefully, gently fastened the metal around me. There were spells and cantrips worked into them, and I could feel my skin trying to pull away from the contact. He closed the locks, the bolts making a final-sounding steel trill as they shot home.

"How are we feeling about the space heater?" I asked.

"I'll see what I can find," Ex said. "Thank you for this. I owe you."

"Not me. I'm just backing her play."

"Well," he said, and then left the word hanging there in the cool air. They turned to walk away, Ex going first, with Tamblen and Alexander following him. Before Chogyi Jake could leave, I called out to him.

"Hey!"

He stopped, looking back over his shoulder. I

could see the others had paused on their way up the stairs.

"Yes?"

"You're going to need the car key."

"An excellent point," he said, coming back to me. I dug in my pocket as best I could with my restraints, then handed him the fob with the key on it.

"Make sure Ozzie gets fed too, okay?"

"I'll be back," he said.

"I'll be fine."

I watched them walk away, listened to the cellar door close, and settled back to wait the long hours—maybe the whole night—before they came back for me. For me, and for the rider in my flesh. I thought about the choice it had made, surrendering to Ex and the others. And on what? The strength of Ex's promise. It was an act of faith I couldn't help admiring. I wasn't sure I'd have taken the risk. I lay back, the chains hissing against the concrete, and hoped he'd remember the space heater. Or at least a couple of good blankets.

The summer before I turned five, my mother put me in church day care. Five days a week from eight thirty until noon, I played and fought and laughed and cried in the basement rooms under the church. One of my most vivid memories of childhood was pelting through the great maze of rooms, running until I was out of breath, screaming with delight. At fifteen, I went back as a volunteer, and the rooms I'd known as a girl were gone. Instead, there were three relatively dingy boxes in a straight line, one after the other, that had clearly been designed for storage. Some carpet had been put in, and the walls painted in nursery colors. That was all, and what was more, that was all that had ever been.

The prison was the same. I'd been here a few days ago, bound by the same manacles to the same floor-set ring, and even though it looked the same, smelled the same, felt the same, it barely had any relationship to the place I'd been. It was hard to believe I'd changed all that much until I started thinking about exactly what had happened.

If I went back now to that little church pre-school, I wondered what it would look like. The artifact of an alien planet, most likely. How could it not when the places I'd actually been seemed to change so much, and in so little time?

It wasn't quite a sound that made me sit back up, my heart racing. It was deep and powerful, like the stroke of a church bell or a gigantic gong. If there had been any noise at all, it would have been deafening. Instead, my heart was doing double time over something I couldn't even describe. I tried yelling, to see if anyone would hear, and it wasn't more than three minutes before the cellar door scraped open and Ex came down. He didn't have a space heater, and his lips were pressed tight.

"What's the matter?" I asked.

"Small change of plan," he said.

"There was something. I heard . . . well, not heard. But something happened, right?"

"Yeah," he said. "The sanctuary is warded against spiritual and magical attack. Even against physical, a little bit."

"Okay. And that plays in how?"

He knelt beside me, pulled the keys out of his pocket, and started unlocking my manacles.

"Well, I figure in the last five or six years, Chapin and the others have probably performed a hundred, maybe a hundred and fifty exorcisms."

"Ballpark," I said.

"Ballpark."

The chains fell off. I'd been incarcerated for less than twenty minutes. Ex nodded toward the stairs, and when he stood I followed, rubbing at my wrists.

"They're here," he said.

I stepped back out into the night. The cawing of crows was thicker now, loud enough it was hard to talk over. The courtyard stank of smoke and gasoline, and a line of fire marked the edge of the building. There were shapes silhouetted by the flames. Men and women. Children. One of them raised a club over her head.

No. Not a club. A fire axe.

The voice that boomed out toward me could

have come through a bullhorn, except it didn't have the tinny, electrical reverberation. The words were deep and wet and they carried over the crows and the flame and the pounding of my heart.

"I'm the hammer now, bitch!" Soledad yelled.

"Oh," I said. And then: "Spiffy."

chapter Twenty-four

I should have seen it coming. The situation might have changed, but the logic of it hadn't. I'd gone to Questa and threatened the riders. They'd come after me. Now, in San Esteban, I'd exposed the rider that had spawned them all. They'd had the same choice as before—fight or flee—and they'd made the same decision.

They'd come to fight. The wards and protections might keep them at bay for a little while. They might not.

We were all in the kitchen now, sitting in a circle made by the chairs and the couch. Someone had pulled the back cushions off the couch to make a kind of bed for Chapin, and Carsey knelt beside him and pressed a bloody towel against his wounds. They hadn't been able to get him out to the car. The shell of Tomás leaned against the wall, eyes fixed and empty. The rooms were just as bright as they had been before, the religious art gracing the walls was the same mixture of uplifting and horrific, but the air had changed. Everything was pressurized, thick, dangerous. I'd been under siege before, and I recognized the feeling.

"How long have we got before they break through?" I asked.

"An hour," Miguel said. The bruise on his cheek was darkening nicely. "Not more. Maybe less. They've already tried to set fire to the place."

"They know it's made from mud and stucco, right?"

"Pour enough gasoline on it," he said with a shrug, "and you can burn water."

"Cheerful thought," Tamblen said.

The not-sound ran through me again. Another attack turned aside by the weakening wards and protections built into the sanctuary. It would keep stopping the riders until it didn't. Chogyi Jake stood, walked to the doorway, and peered into the next room like he was checking to see if he'd left the lights on. The pistol was in his hand again.

"Okay," I said. "So if we keep Carsey on

nursing duty, that gives us six folks on our side. Seven, counting the Black Sun. They've got a hundred or so riders, just one of which almost kicked our collective ass less than an hour ago."

"Yes," Ex said.

"And we're totally surrounded, right?"

"Right."

"Also, there's an eight-year-old girl who will eventually be delivered back to her family and taken by demons again if we can't get out of here," Alexander said.

I pressed my palms against my eyes until little globs of color appeared. Chapin's ragged breath was the loudest sound, but just below it there was something else. Inhuman voices lifted together.

"We could call the police?" Carsey said.

"No offense," I said, "but I don't think a bunch of dead cops is going to help. Do we know anybody with a helicopter less than an hour from here?"

"Creative thought, but I don't even think the medevac from Albuquerque could get here in an hour," Miguel said.

"We're on our own, then," I said. I thought about it for a few seconds, trying it from every angle I could think of. "We're not going to make it."

"No," Ex said. "We aren't. But if we do it right, a few of us might get out in the chaos. I think we should take the fight to the riders. Concentrate all our effort in one place, and then sneak as many people as we can out the other side."

He was right, but the weight of implication behind the plan was vicious. The wounded—Tomás and Chapin—would have to be abandoned. For the distraction to be effective, most of us would have to be part of it, meaning most of us were about to die. Including me, because I had the Black Sun's daughter living inside me, and if there was a distraction, she'd have to be part of it.

I didn't want to die. The primitive monkey part of my brain was screaming and bouncing around the inside of my skull just to remind me how much I didn't want to die. But if that wasn't an option, at least I didn't want to die for nothing. And that was all the choice I had left. I felt like a balloon with its string cut, spinning up into the sky.

"Well," I said.

"Yeah," Ex replied. Meaning he'd thought all the same things I had and come to the same conclusions. "There's a kind of beauty in heroic last stands."

"Remember the Alamo," I said.

"I thought we lost that one," Carsey said. "Didn't we lose that one?"

"Depends what you mean by *we*," Miguel said. "My family's Mexican."

The gallows humor was as comforting as anything could have been. It didn't quiet my fear, but it made it easier to ignore. Another wave of not-quite-sound. This one felt closer, more threatening. Time was running out.

"Who makes a break for it?" I asked.

"Alexander and Miguel," Tamblen said.

"They're hurt but not incapacitated," Carsey said. "They'll be the least use in a fight and still have a decent chance of getting away. And, more to the point, Alexander's young enough that he'll have more years spinning fantastic tales of our glory. If Tamblen went over the fence, he'd tell it all in three sentences and a shrug."

Tamblen grinned. "True," he said.

For a moment, I saw it. Just a glimpse. For a moment, here in death's waiting room, I knew how these men had been a family. The shared jokes and the shared secrets, the sorrow and the dedication and the willingness to die together. It made them beautiful, and for the moment I was part of it. I rose first.

"Well," I said. "If we're going to do this, we'd better get going. Hate to be late for the party."

Ex stood up too, and Chogyi Jake stopped pacing to come stand by me. I felt Aubrey's absence just then, and I was more grateful than I could express that he wasn't there. A weird kind of peace settled over me. I wondered if it was from my own mind, or if my rider was letting her feelings be known. I couldn't tell the difference.

"We should go out the main doors," Carsey said, still pressing the bloody cloth to Chapin's side. Chapin looked like a man made of wax, less realistic than some of the crucified saviors on the walls. "It's the widest entrance. And there's a window on the north side wide enough for the runners to squeeze out."

"Do we try to press out into them or open the doors and fall back, try to get them to follow us inside the sanctuary?" I asked.

"Stop!"

For a moment, I couldn't tell who'd spoken. Then Chapin opened his eyes. I was amazed that he was conscious, but he turned his head toward me, pointing with two bloody fingers.

"You . . . submit to me, to my will . . ."

I had to laugh.

"Seriously? I'm about to go sacrifice my life to save a couple of your boys, and we're still on how I'm the beast and evil?"

He shook his head. His face was white. Even his lips had lost all color.

"You mistake me, Miss Jayné," he said. "There is another way, but I cannot do this. You must submit yourself to my will. I will guide you. I will guide the *both* of you."

Slowly, I walked to him. Three steps had never seemed like such a long way. He tried to smile, his bared teeth hardly paler than the gums they sat in. He'd bled white, but he held on to consciousness through brute force of will. All around us, the others had gone silent.

"I'm listening," I said.

"I am an old man. I have many, many years of finding the thin places between the demon and its prey. I have freed many, many people."

"That didn't work out all that well," I said.

"Be quiet! Listen!" His shout was only a change in the shape of his mouth. It didn't have more power than a whisper. "With only the human will given us by God, I have defeated the lords and presidents of Hell. With the power of a few brave souls, I have conquered demons. To do so much with so little can only be accomplished with great knowledge. Much practice. With the power that lives within you and the craft of the life behind me, these little evils can be broken. Even though they number in the hundreds."

He wanted to work together. An hour ago, he'd been willing to risk his own death to keep me in chains, and now he wanted something closer than an alliance. The desperation burned off him, or if not desperation, certainty.

"Can he do that?" Carsey asked of no one in particular.

I knelt beside the dying man. Pride flickered in his eyes. Pride and defiance and fear. The non-sound washed over us again and left the smell of sewage behind it. Something physical crashed far down at the end of the building, followed by the sound of voices raised in anger.

"Jayné?" Chogyi Jake said. "Whatever we do, we need to do it very, very soon."

"You still think she's evil," I said.

Chapin's throat worked, half swallow, half spasm.

"It is," he said.

"And you'd still work with us?"

His smile was built from regret. His eyes were seeing something else now, something only he remembered.

"I will save my little boys," he said. "If the price is damnation, I pay it. Take me."

Tears poured down Carsey's cheeks. His eyes locked on mine, and he shook his head in refusal. Glass broke, a window shattering and the shards dancing on brick. Then a second shattering, and the unmistakable roaring of fire.

"Give him here," I said. Carsey closed his eyes, bent down, and together we scooped the old man into my arms. Chapin's head turned toward me, nestling between my shoulder and my neck like a sleeping child's. His breath was soft against my skin. When I stood, I had more than my own strength.

"Go," I said. "All of you. Now. I don't know if we can do this, but even if we fail, I will give you the best distraction you've ever seen."

"I'm coming with you," Ex said. Chogyi Jake didn't speak, but his smile was enough to tell me he was being polite. He would be two steps behind me whichever way I walked. White smoke was trickling in from the rooms west of us, the fire burning between us and the blue doors at the front. I hefted Chapin and walked toward the flames.

We ran through the rooms as the images of Hell split and curled; real fire consumed them. Christ burned on cross after cross as we passed them. I felt Chapin's heartbeat and the patterns of his shallow breath, and the answering pulse of the rider rising up inside me. An eerie serenity came over me. I heard Ex and Chogyi Jake coughing, but the smoke and heat didn't bother me. I had a sense of peace that had nothing to do with the conflagration. My rider welled up around me again, and I slipped back behind my eyes, curling up in the space that was my own, but as I did, I tried to pull Chapin's soft, fluttering breath with me, to keep my connection with him and the three of us together. The roaring of the fire and the riotous anger of the attackers were quieter than his gentle breath, like they'd had the volume turned down almost to nothing.

I had worked group rituals before. I had felt the different personalities of the people involved touching one another, supporting one another, making the group stronger than the whole. This was nothing like that. We were something else, something new. I breathed in Chapin's breaths, and my footsteps changed. I sank into my knees and hip, the power of the stride riding lower. I walked the way a man walked, and I saw the world with a vision that belonged to the closed eyes resting against me. We weren't priest or possessed or spirit, but we also were. It felt as natural as falling.

In the spreading fire before me, two bodies seemed to condense out of the smoke. A young man and an old woman sprinting toward me, hands spread wide and black tongues whipping through the searing air. Still carrying Chapin across my forearm, I waved one encumbered hand. The motion was simple and graceful, and the will it directed was cold and hard as a chisel. I felt it strike a fault line too subtle to see at the place where soul and demon met, and I felt my enemies shatter. The black tongues vanished. Man and woman stumbled, fell screaming, and Ex and Chogyi Jake hunched forward to grab them and haul them away from the flames. Five more were waiting at the broken blue doors. I could feel Chapin's joy in slipping forward, ahead even of our bodies, and popping the riders off their victims like crushing ticks between his thumbnails. The Akaname shrieked, falling back into the abstract space of the Pleroma.

I stepped into the doorway, and they were waiting for me. The crows whirled through the sky, drawn by the battle and fleeing from it. The snow glowed blue from the moon and red from the flames, and on it, rank upon rank of rider stood, with rifles and blades, baseball bats and demonic, whipping tongues. I turned my head to where Ex and Chogyi Jake were crouched behind the doorway, their heads low to keep from breathing the smoke. Seven others were with them. People who had been my enemy moments before, and now were my charges. The innocents I had spent my life protecting.

"Stay here," I said, and my own voice seemed distant, drowned, not entirely my own.

I stepped out into the mob. Their foul voices rose up together, their combined will hitting me like a hard wind. A rifle cracked, and I shifted my weight, letting the bullet slip by me like a bee in a meadow. An aluminum baseball bat already stained with someone's blood swung toward Chapin's head, and I turned just enough that it ruffled his close-cropped hair as it passed. A boy in a pale sheepskin coat ran for me, knife in hand, and I bent one knee, twisted, and slid away out of his reach.

They tried to stop me with the raw press of bodies, the riders using the flesh they'd stolen to limit my movement. I danced through the assault, untouchable, like I was walking between raindrops, and my threefold will reached out to devastate my enemies. I could see our power swirling around me like a white aurora, shifting with Chapin's attention, striking with my rider's strength. I felt their cries of horror and despair. I watched the lolling, evil flesh of their filthy tongues boil away into smoke. The black eyes faded to blue and brown and white. And with every one, I felt the old warrior bare his teeth in triumph.

Dolores's sister, Soledad, appeared amid the crowd, her mouth a square gape of rage. The red steel axe swung toward me and the old man in my arms. Freeing her took no more than a breath. She and Dolores had almost beaten me in the hotel, days or weeks or years before, and now breaking her bonds was just one note in a symphony. It was the grace and knowledge of a lifetime translated into a few moments of transcendence. Our dance was the final product of Father Chapin's life lit from within until, together, we glowed brighter than the sun, violence without the violence. I never hit anyone, never felt the bones give way under my foot or fist, only reached out with our combined will where Chapin showed us, and they fell before us like mown grass.

And then it was over. I stood in the winter night, my enemies sent broken back to Hell. The ground was littered with the confused, stumbling people from whom the unclean spirits had fled. The sky was a mosaic of crows and floating embers and stars.

The three of us looked around, suffused with the combined sense of profound satisfaction and desolating regret.

The work of a lifetime, now finished.

I fell back into the world like I was waking from a dream. There were voices all around me, crying and shouting. Someone to my right was retching violently, and the sanctuary was in flames, the heat radiating out into the darkness. Fire spat out from a half dozen shattered windows, and men still coated with nauseating greenish slime were throwing handfuls of snow into the flames. As if that could stop it.

Ex touched my shoulder, and I turned. There was blood at the corner of his mouth and soot streaked his face and hair. He was grinning.

"Are you okay?" he shouted.

"I think so," I said. "Where is everyone? Are they okay?"

"I don't know. Chogyi Jake's over there. The others went toward the back like you told them. I think they made it out, but I'm not sure. I'll go check for stragglers."

"Don't go alone," I said. "We cleaned these out, but there may be more Akaname out there. I may have missed some."

The fire lit half his face in the warmth of red and gold, and the moon shone white-blue on the other. He shook his head.

"You didn't," he said. Before I could say anything else, he leaned in, kissed me on the lips, and then turned and marched off into the night. The fatigue was sudden and absolute. My arms ached. My legs burned from the muscles out. Slowly, gently, I put Father Chapin down in the snow. His eyes opened, tiny glittering slits between the lids.

"Not bad for an old, gutshot guy," I said, and his lips widened a millimeter.

He opened his mouth, trying to speak, but I could no more hear him than I could turn dim the moonlight. I shifted forward on my knees, leaning into him until his breath warmed my earlobe.

"I am sorry, Miss Jayné," he whispered, "that I could not save you."

It was the last thing he said.

chapter Twenty-five

Chapin's funeral filled the cathedral in Santa Fe. Men and women, white haired and weak with age to babies still in strollers. It seemed like a lot of people knew one another. On the way in, there had been lots of quiet conversations and long-held hand clasping. I sat in the back in a pew beside three old men who pointedly didn't look at me and Chogyi Jake. Every now and then, I caught sight of the back of Ex's head far ahead of us. Near the altar. Miguel sat to his left, Carsey to his right. Carsey was getting a little bald spot. I hadn't noticed that before.

At the pulpit, the archbishop said the Mass. I

followed along as best I could. It had been a long time since I'd gone to church, and when I had, it had all been in English. Here, it was all *Requiem aeternam dona eis, Dominae*. On the one hand, it seemed like it didn't have anything to do with Chapin as a man. On the other hand, it was what he'd dedicated his life to. What he'd died for.

The requiem began, the notes of the organ rising toward heaven. I felt like an impostor. I folded my hands in my lap and waited. Somewhere nearby, a man was sobbing uncontrollably. I didn't know who. When the time came to go forward for communion, the three men shuffled past me with sour expressions on their faces. The urge to go up to the front and take the body and the blood tugged at me, but I couldn't. I imagined Ex trying to retake his vows, unable to say the words because he couldn't mean them. I was there. I got it.

When the recessional finally came, Chogyi Jake and I stood out on the steps. The sun was warm, even in the winter air. The snow had melted off everywhere except the deepest shadows where it still lurked, dark and light at the same time. The other attendees streamed out past us, heading left toward the parking lots or the plaza. Ex appeared at my side. In the three days since he'd kissed me as the sanctuary burned, he hadn't touched me, and he didn't touch me now.

"I'm going to need a few minutes," he said.

Looking back through the doors into the beautiful darkness of the cathedral, I could see Alexander, Carsey, and Miguel talking together. Tamblen sat in a pew beside them, his head still bowed in prayer. They were all that remained of Ex's previous family. Alexander looked up, his gaze meeting mine. He lifted a hand, and I waved back.

"As long as you want," I said. "There's no rush."

He walked back in with his shoulders stiff. The gouges on his back hadn't healed yet. My bruised rib still ached sometimes when I breathed in too deeply. My feet hurt a lot, but they'd pretty much stopped bleeding. From all I'd heard, rebuilding the sanctuary was dicey, and there were still a couple of dozen Chapin's group had "saved" in the last few years who hadn't been part of the attack. I guessed tracking down the remaining filth-lickers trumped fixing the architecture, but it wasn't my call to make.

I watched the cars go by, one after another, going about the business of the world. Most of the people on the street didn't know or care what had happened in San Esteban. I envied them that.

"How are you feeling?" Chogyi Jake asked.

"Tired," I said. "Weirdly lonesome. Undercaffeinated."

"Lonesome?"

"Yeah. Can't explain that," I said. "But I do."

"Do you miss Aubrey?"

"Sure," I said. "Are he and Kim . . . Are they happy, do you think?"

"Yes. They're happy. And they're sad. Confused, grateful, hurt, angry. They're all those things, and will be, I think, for a while before they find a place of relative calm."

"Do you think they'll make it?"

"I don't know."

"What about you?" I asked. "Are you still angry that I ditched you in Chicago?"

I smiled when I said it. I wanted it to be a joke.

"Yes," he said gently. "I am. But the anger comes from being hurt. When the one fades, the other will."

"I know it doesn't help, but I'm really sorry."

"No," he said. "That helps."

I looked back. Ex and Miguel were walking away from us. Miguel had an arm over Ex's shoulder, like they were brothers or lovers. Intimates. I knew how I would have felt if Chogyi Jake or Ex or even Aubrey had given me the runaround for weeks. Months. I'd have been a lot less Zen about it.

"Forgive me?" I said.

"Yes," Chogyi Jake said.

Four men came out of the cathedral. Two I didn't recognize, one was the archbishop, and the last was Tamblen. He nodded at me as they passed. A truck drove by playing music loud enough to shake the air. Charming.

"Jayné!"

Dolores ran up, throwing her arms around me and grinning. She looked so bright and delighted, I had to smile back. Funeral black couldn't keep her down. The marks of what she'd been through were invisible. She'd lost her body twice now to beings of terrible power. No matter how much she looked like a child, no matter how bright her eyes were, she and I both knew that her life had been touched by fire. There would always be a scar.

And we both knew it was true for me too.

"Hey, kid," I said. "You're looking better."

"I get to go back to school after Christmas," she said, bouncing on her toes. I wondered if I'd ever been that happy at the idea of going to class. Probably, but I didn't remember it. "Where's Ozzie?"

"Back at the ranch," I said. "Holding things down. How's Soledad doing?"

Dolores wrinkled her nose.

"She's a little fragile," she said. Her inflection was so adult, I was sure she'd been hearing her mother and grandmother saying it.

"Well, be a little patient with her. She had a hard time."

"I had a hard time too," she said, frowning.

"We all did."

The new voice was sharp as a cracking stick.

"Dolores, come *here*."

The three women stood at the curb below us. The

oldest one stared up at me with something that bordered on hatred. The youngest—Soledad—wouldn't look at me. Dolores hesitated for half a breath, then gave me a fast hug.

"I love you," she said, then turned and bounded down to her family. Her grandmother's eyes fixed on me as she crossed herself and spat over her shoulder. Her grip on the little girl's arm was steely as they walked away.

"Well, that seemed uncalled-for," Chogyi Jake said.

"Yeah, well," I said. "I didn't really keep my situation a secret from Dolores, and they've got a thing about people with riders living in them. Got to say it's honestly come by."

"I suppose so. And you?"

"And me what?"

"How do you feel about people with riders?"

I squinted up at the sun. The only thing it radiated was heat and light. The question hung in the air for a few seconds. A sparrow sped by us, its dust-brown wings fluttering.

"You know," I said, "I think there's a coffee shop down there on the left. Buy you a cup?"

"All right."

THE BLACK Sun.

Once I had the laptop in range of a real wireless connection, I found encyclopedias' worth of information. It was central to the Nazi occultism. In some traditions, it was the burnt-out antisun that heralded regeneration, in others it was the actual physical ball of burning gas that seemed to rise in the east and set in the west every day, called "black" because it was made from matter and was therefore spiritually impure. The Black Sun was the symbol of Left-Hand path groups like the Temple of Set, or it was a name for Jesus. It was Blavatsky's Invisible Sun around which the universe revolves, it was a cult of Finnish serial killers in the 1960s, it was the most powerful crime syndicate in the *Star Wars* universe.

When we went into Santa Fe, I downloaded everything I could find. Back at the ranch, I sat on the couch and read until my eyes hurt. Chogyi Jake and Ex were in full research mode with me, and the dinner conversation was equal parts theosophy and alchemy and whether we had enough coffee beans for the morning. After four days, I felt like I knew less than when I'd started.

I kept waiting for *her* to reach out and point me in the right direction. Pick out a particular document or point my finger at a sentence or a symbol that would draw a line through the rest of it. She was as quiet as the dead. I knew she was in there, but I didn't know what shape she was in. My half exorcism and the battles that had followed from it had hurt her. Weakened her. I could still see the desert of my dreams scorched. Maybe it was something that a young rider shrugged off like a bruise. Maybe we'd broken her in some fundamental way. I didn't know, and she wasn't telling me.

Still, I was pretty sure that if someone jumped me, she'd be there. And she had to know I'd had the chance to renounce her and I'd chosen not to. I didn't know what was living inside of me, but she'd revealed herself in the first fight against the wind demon in order to save Ex. And she'd let herself be chained in order to convince Chapin to go to the hospital. And she'd stood by me when nobody else in the world had. Until I had evidence to the contrary, I figured the truce was still on.

My nightmares didn't stop, but they slowed down a little. Chogyi Jake's presence got me back to meditating once a day. Or every other day. More than I had been, anyway. It seemed to help, though there were times I could still smell the dirt and cyclopropane. Hear the screaming. Sometimes it was just the fear.

Ex didn't talk about Chapin or the other men in the group. It was almost like none of it had happened, except that I caught glimpses every now and then—when he was starting to nod off to sleep by the fireplace, when he was trying to figure out the connector on the satellite dish I had installed, when he thought no one was watching. I saw the pain and the loneliness that echoed against my own, but if I tried to approach him, he changed the subject. He didn't touch me even to see how the wounds on my feet were healing, and he didn't ask me to wash out his wounds. He slept with his bedroom door firmly shut. I wasn't sure if I was relieved or disappointed.

Maybe there was room for both.

The closest we came to calling the question was a week before Christmas. It was half past four in the afternoon, and the sun was about to set. The clouds to the west were glorious and gaudy—pink and gold and scarlet and blue, like someone had slipped some kind of mild hallucinogen in the world's drink. Chogyi Jake was in the kitchen chopping vegetables for stir-fry and singing along with the carols on the radio. He had a surprisingly good voice. Ex and I were in the back den, and I was trying to coax a little more bandwidth out of my cellular card. He was reading something called *The Nightside of Eden* with an expression somewhere between amusement and disgust.

"Got anything?" he asked.

"A strong urge to leave Santa Fe," I said.

"This isn't Santa Fe," he said, and pointed out toward the horizon. "Those lights way over there? That's Santa Fe. We're lost in the desert."

The phrase caught me. Lost in the desert. It was like the words meant something I used to know.

"Well, a strong urge to leave, anyway," I said. "Spend the winter in Australia or something. Somewhere warm. With some sunlight."

"Where *are* we going?"

He wasn't asking about geography. From the time I'd figured out I wasn't alone in my skin, we'd had a purpose. Just the two of us. We were going to scratch it out, get me back to myself. Make me safe. Now that I'd stepped back from that, Ex didn't know what the agenda was. Before *that*, we'd been bouncing around the world like a pinball cataloging the things that Eric had left me. Did we really go back to plan A now? Picking a place on the list, and rushing into it, hoping that somewhere, he'd left me the clue that made it all make sense. That told me why putting me where I was made the world the way he'd wanted it.

"I'm working on that," I said.

"Let me know what you come up with," he said.

We went quiet for a moment.

"You know," I said, "there was something we were going to talk about."

He looked up from his book. His eyebrows were quizzical. Chogyi Jake segued from "O Come All Ye Faithful" to "Feliz Navidad." Ozzie trotted into the room, wagged twice, sighed, and trotted back out. I looked down at my laptop, blushing, and then back up.

"Back at the condo," I said. "At the ski valley. You

said that when this was over, there was another conversation we needed to have."

His face was smooth and calm, giving nothing away.

"There is," he said. My heart picked up speed a little. I felt like I was going down a long hill in a go-cart whose brakes I didn't trust. I lifted my chin.

"Well?"

"It isn't over."

And of course he was right. It wasn't. A few minutes later, he went into the kitchen to help with the rice and left me alone with my semifunctional laptop and my thoughts. I did need to decide what to do. It had been easy before, when I'd believed Eric was one of the good guys. I lost my innocence in Chicago, and since then I'd put up a campaign of lies and misdirection against Chogyi Jake, hung out with Midian Clark despite the fact that he was actively killing people, abducted an eight-year-old girl and left her unsupervised in a place where her family couldn't find her. And none of them particularly bothered me. I knew the worst thing I'd ever done, and beside it none of these minor sins seemed to matter much.

But probably they did.

My life had been picked up in the whirlpool he'd left when Eric died, and I'd been spun around ever since. Me and the little family I'd made for myself. And as much as I'd learned, and as much as I knew now that I hadn't before, I still felt like I was listening to someone speaking in a different language.

I couldn't go back to the cataloging project. We'd done that for months, and all I'd gotten from it were lists and notes and a sense that I would never get my homework done before my paper was due. And I'd chosen not to cast out the rider in my skin. Not yet, at least. Not until I knew how she'd gotten there and how Eric's plan involved us both. It didn't seem to leave me with much. All of Eric's notes and letters were like reminders for himself, as if all he ever needed to do was jog his memory. There was nothing anywhere to tell me what the greater plan was. Nothing for me.

And, what was more, nobody knew him. Eric Heller had been a chameleon, changing to show whomever he was with what he wanted them to see. He hadn't had friends, he'd had playing pieces. I'd been one of them. His promoted pawn.

Giving up on the Internet connection, I pulled up the local copy of our organizational wiki and clicked through to the listing of properties. Cairo. Westport. Toronto. Page after page after page. And at any one, there might be a folder with my name on it that laid out everything I wanted to know. Or else that file might not exist. I was flying blind, and I couldn't do that. Not anymore.

I needed to find the mother lode of raw information. I needed to know all the things that Eric hadn't bothered writing down. And, reading over the list of all the cities and nations we hadn't even been to once yet, I knew I was looking in the wrong place. The answer I needed wasn't on the list, because whatever ambition or need or plan had driven Eric, he hadn't owned it. If anything, it had owned him. Just the way it owned me.

I had to go where the answers were. Where the history was. I had to find the people who'd loved Eric. Or hated him. The ones who knew.

Before I could change my mind, I took my new cell phone out of my backpack. It had two bars, which was a lot better than the old one had managed. I keyed in the phone number from memory and waited while it rang.

Some moments go on for longer than the actual time that they take. The time between the click of someone picking up a handset and the first soft opening of lips as she prepares to speak can take years. Maybe a lifetime.

"Hello? Who's there, please?"

Her voice was as clear as if she were sitting next to me. There was Christmas music in the background, her "It Came upon the Midnight Clear" clashing with Chogyi Jake's jazzy "Santa, Baby" from the kitchen. I closed my eyes, and I must have let out some little sigh, some tiny sound small enough that it was below my own awareness but still enough for her to recognize.

"Jayné? Is that you?"

I closed my eyes. If this was a mistake, it was the mistake I was making. I cleared my throat. When I spoke, I tried to sound bright and confident and undamaged. The last one was the hardest.

"Hi, Mom."